C000254944

THE *Walk*

EMMA MARNS

CRANTHORPE
MILLNER
PUBLISHERS

Copyright © Emma Marns (2023)

The right of Emma Marns to be identified as author of this work has been asserted by them in accordance with section 77 and 78 of the Copyright, Designs and Patents Act 1988.

All rights reserved. No part of this publication may be reproduced, stored in a retrieval system, or transmitted in any form or by any means, electronic, mechanical, photocopying, recording, or otherwise, without the prior permission of the publishers.

Any person who commits any unauthorised act in relation to this publication may be liable to criminal prosecution and civil claims for damages.

This book is a work of fiction. Names, characters, places and incidents are either products of the author's imagination or are used fictitiously. Any resemblance to actual events or locales or persons, living or dead, is entirely coincidental.

First published by Cranthorpe Millner Publishers (2023)

ISBN 978-1-80378-140-2 (Paperback)

www.cranthorpemillner.com

Cranthorpe Millner Publishers

For my mother

Dear Jacqui,
Great to meet you!
Ed.Mary

This book is dedicated to the thousands of women and children who disappeared behind the gates of Bessborough and institutions like it across the world, and to those who did emerge, but were never the same.

PROLOGUE

It was almost the very height of the Irish summer, so it was a gleaming and warm day when Maire finally returned to Bessborough. She remembered how much she used to love Cork, years ago, when she was a child. Just the sound of the word used to make her skin prickle with anticipation and joy. Maire used to love the summer too. But not now. Not anymore.

Today she walked the uneven pavement she'd seen just once before, and not well as it had been dark then. She watched her shadow march ignorantly ahead, feeling desperately that she was approaching the worst place on earth with no obvious alternative. But at least, Maire knew, that this was the last time she would ever come here. She didn't really want to take this in, bank it in her mind for drawing up again later. She never wanted to think about this again and she assumed Ailbe would feel the same once they finally saw each other. The sun was starting to burn the back of her neck – the ponytail had been a mistake. She used to love Cork. She didn't want to remember this.

All was ruined now.

Maire shivered; despite the sun, she felt cold run to her bones as she approached the gates. Her fingers trembled as they gripped the handle of her suitcase. She didn't have a suitcase last time and she now felt like it was an extra, awkward part of her.

Goosebumps spread over her body as she recognised those unbearable gates from before – towering and unfriendly, attached to great stone pillars. Maire closed her eyes and hoped they'd disappear. She thought of the last time she had seen them, through hurried torchlight in the darkness, clinking and creaking like the gates to a horrifying castle with all manner of demons within. Opening her eyes, she squinted through the iron filigree to the driveway beyond, a long and sweeping avenue. On a beautiful day like today, it looked like it could have been pleasant – there were trees, well-groomed gardens, and roses even. She couldn't see anything that resembled a building, or house, even in the furthest distance. Bessborough, whatever people chose to describe it as, was extremely well hidden.

She creaked open the gates – no padlock this time – and started up the pathway. She walked what would have been Ailbe's very route; she passed the trees; she passed a small lake; she passed the rose bushes. Ailbe must have been terrified. Actually, no, Maire thought, as she pressed on without looking around for fear of slowing down. That wasn't right at all. Ailbe was never frightened of anything. But what she must have been thinking… Maire couldn't imagine. She herself had been so lucky, so incredibly lucky, and she'd never forget that. Ailbe wasn't as fortunate as Maire was – not then, and not ever. She hoped there wouldn't be a scene – in and out, back at these gates with Ailbe in tow in just a few minutes. In a few more minutes, they'd be together again. Maire sped up.

The silence and the beauty of the place made her feel inexplicably sick, even just the sight of the pretty roses – but Maire assumed, whatever Ailbe had endured here, she had been brave. Ailbe was always brave.

So Maire was going to be brave now.

PART ONE
1979–1980

CHAPTER ONE

The day after Ruth's fifth miscarriage, her husband suggested a holiday. The last time they had been to the Aran Islands was about five years before, and, before that, the whole family had clubbed together for a little jaunt to Mallorca for her and Donal's honeymoon – a wedding gift – but those were the only holidays they had taken in all their time together. Her sister Bridget invited them every year on her annual trips to Liverpool and Bray and Waterford, but they'd always refused. Bridget seemed happy enough on her own, and Ruth had always worried about making advance plans. Not that it had made any difference to them in the end.

She thought about the ones she had lost. She'd never known if they'd been sons or daughters, of course; it was always much too early for that. Just great blobs of blood, excruciating stomach cramps and so many tears. Another dream gone, just like that. The first would be seven by now, in a stiff school uniform and taking Holy Communion for the first time. The next one about five, she supposed, learning to read and wanting everything its big brother or sister had, wanting to do everything they were doing. Then, two, a week apart; one went in the supermarket one morning and the other by the duck pond at St Stephen's Green. She hadn't known it was twins until the second one went as well. They'd be toddling, babbling and having accidents, calling her Mammy. And this little one now, well. Not even a heartbeat yet.

The doctors just shrugged at her and said they were sorry; that these things just happen. Donal never blamed her; he was good like that. He patted her knee each time and said 'Oh

5

God. Poor Ruth. Poor Ruthie girl', as though it was happening to a different Ruth, somewhere else in the world. He filled the teapot and kissed her cheek. He didn't like to talk about it.

Ruth and Bridget's other siblings had managed to keep the family going; their eldest brother John had a wee boy almost thirty years ago now. Three older brothers had reproduced in fours and fives with their wives. They were perfect Catholic families, the pride of the parish. Ruth and Bridget had chosen to stick together all their barren years, coming home to their neighbouring houses after yet another baptism, yet another wedding, giggling in Bridget's kitchen about the hats and the dresses and inevitable drunken dramas. Bridget became a nurse and jollied about the place, never marrying or seeming to want to. Ruth married Donal and sat. in her house with her ghost children.

Ruth had written to her brother John in Donegal to tell him of their most recent tragedy. Since she and Donal had married almost fifteen years ago, she'd gradually stopped informing the wider family about the losses. It had taken seven years to get pregnant at all; everyone had been waiting with bated breath for the news that they would eventually start a family, like everyone else had dutifully done, and when they finally did, they had spent the most joyful three hours of Ruth's life, making phone calls. When the tragedy happened, there followed the worst three hours of Donal's life, making the phone calls all over again. Although the period of infertility was over, she felt that the losses were worse than the constant absence they knew before. She couldn't bring herself to tell everyone that she'd somehow killed the baby yet again.

Nevertheless, she always wrote to John, as they had been close over the years despite their difference in age of almost twenty years. John had been the only father figure the sisters had known; their own father had died shortly after Bridget's birth. John's children served as an in-between generation, not quite old enough to be their contemporaries, but close enough that words like 'niece' and 'nephew' made Ruth feel old. John would fill in the others on her behalf, and when she saw them again at Christmas in a few months' time, no one would mention it. They'd just smile at her, fetch her a drink, and say very little, if anything at all.

Ruth knew that this loss would be her last one. She couldn't really believe that pregnancy at forty-one was even an option; but there it had been. Just for a little while, anyway. There would be no more hopeful times – not that falling pregnant ever filled Ruth with hope anymore. It was always just a dread, a plea, a panic-filled prayer, until the inevitable happened all over again. Women she saw now who had babies were young and pretty, and had perms, and wheeled their babies along the street in pushchairs to nursery school. They sat in the trendy coffee shops that had started popping up all over Dublin, chatting about TV programmes Ruth didn't watch. She wasn't like them. There had to be at least ten years between her and the oldest one of them. She felt so very tired now.

CHAPTER TWO

The two girls sat in the back of the car as it rattled through the darkness. Their driver was a stranger, and their destination was unknown to them. The girls knew, though, that they were further from home now than they had ever been before, and the darkness was such that any fragment of the outside was invisible. More so, they'd probably never be going back to where they'd come from. But truly, that was the least of their concerns. Their crimes – the crimes that had led them to this – were worse than murder.

Maire was seated behind the driver. It had been a long time since she'd been in a car; her family hadn't had one for a while. She remembered, though, being a small child in the back of the car behind her father, the driver, wondering how he knew what to do and marvelling at the dance his hands and arms made. It made her feel safe. Now, her cheeks were burning, her eyes were stinging, and she had bitten all her nails, which bled and hurt. She had cried silently for the first hour or so, and now she couldn't cry anymore. She felt empty. Usually when she was distressed, she liked to pray, but she didn't think she'd bother with that just now. Surely, He wouldn't even be listening anymore, after what she had done.

Maire looked over at Ailbe, seated next to her. It wasn't Ailbe's fault, although Maire knew her own family would blame Ailbe for this entirely. Ailbe was just… one of those girls, from one of those sorts of families, who everyone talked about and everyone dismissed almost straight away as absolutely no good. No one was ever surprised when bad things happened to them; in fact, they rather seemed like they deserved it.

Bad things like this.

Everyone would blame Ailbe for what had happened to them both, but Maire knew she was the least at fault out of the two of them. She knew the story. She knew how it had all happened.

Ailbe didn't look upset. She never looked upset. Her black eye was darkening with each passing minute and it made Maire feel queasy to watch the bruise grow and Ailbe's previously pale flesh swell, but she couldn't help it. She'd seen Ailbe bruised and hurt before, of course, but this time it looked so much worse. Ailbe had limped to the car like a wounded dog. She was wearing a coat too big for her that she had presumably stolen from somewhere to cover up more injuries that she didn't want Maire to see. She'd smiled at Maire weakly when she'd arrived at their meeting place after dark, and she put on a brave face for her, but it was obvious that it had hurt to do so. Ailbe hadn't been able to hide it for long enough, apparently. They had found her out and beaten her senseless, before sending her out alone into the darkness.

Maire had taken a decidedly different approach – she'd confessed to her parents and sisters in a letter, left them the last of her wages in an envelope, packed a small overnight bag with a couple of things and bolted away with her heart in her mouth while her family were out visiting their elderly neighbours. Maire couldn't come this time, she'd said, because she had to work – but pass on her best, of course, and she'd see them soon. The family had celebrated her birthday just a week before. She had felt so horribly, desperately guilty as she ate the birthday cake her mother had made especially for her, and listened to their prayers about how she was a treasure in their family. Ailbe never had that, but Maire had – and now she had thrown it all away. And for what? She still didn't know. She still didn't know if it had all been worth it. She hadn't been riddled with the horrendous vomiting like Ailbe had, and she was a few weeks behind her, so it had been easier for her to hide it from her own sweet and unsuspecting family. No one knew Maire's secret except Ailbe, and the father.

It had happened in their village just once before as far as Maire and Ailbe knew. Mary Mulligan had three daughters and it was her youngest one, Alma. She was fifteen when Maire and Ailbe were twelve or thirteen. They knew her from school; she smoked almost constantly and wore big, hooped earrings and never came to Mass. Alma and her sisters didn't look, or dress, like anyone else they knew. One rainy Tuesday morning Alma was missing from school; there were rumours that she'd got herself in trouble and she hadn't been seen since. Mary Mulligan refused to discuss her daughter's mysterious disappearance, and eventually started telling people that she had only ever had two daughters, not three. Alma's whole existence just scrubbed from their memories almost overnight – Maire sometimes wondered if Alma had ever even existed at all, or if she alone had imagined her. Maire wondered if her own mother would do that as well.

It had happened to Ailbe first. Her parents had taken her cousin in, reluctantly and out of familial duty, because his drinking had become so severe that his own mother could no longer stand the beatings and the poverty. His mother was Ailbe's aunt, and being sisters, she and Ailbe's mother were very much alike. Ailbe's mother didn't care much for the beatings and the poverty either. When she was drunk herself, she sometimes told Ailbe that her father wasn't really her father. Ailbe didn't know whether to believe her, and anyway, she didn't really care. Her father was a monster and a criminal and the whole village knew that. The whole village always knew everything, sooner or later. No one would employ Ailbe. No one would speak to her. They'd all been cheated by her family one way or another and, in their minds, the apple didn't fall far from the tree. They all said that Ailbe was serious trouble, and headed for terrible things, and nothing anyone could ever do was going to save her from that. So they did nothing, to save themselves the trouble.

Maire had sobbed, feeling sick when Ailbe had told her about it. Ailbe hadn't been completely sure but she knew that he'd done something to her that felt painful, agonising really. Ailbe had shouted and shouted for her mother for help but she hadn't come. Ailbe had tried to fight but she was half asleep to start with, and he was so much bigger than her. She was bruised a lot and bleeding a bit. But she was all right, she had insisted to Maire. She was all right. She'd been all right for a whole six weeks before she realised the bleeding had stopped and never come back. If Maire's boyfriend hadn't been a doctor who knew people, God only knew where Ailbe would be now.

She for one was grateful that the car had come, wherever it was they were going.

Outside the car was nothing but constant and unrelenting darkness; the roads weren't lit where they lived. The one long road out of the village didn't meet a junction for quite some distance and, when it did, there was a tiny wooden sign that indicated right towards Cork city or left, all routes north to

Dublin. They went right. Ailbe flashed Maire a fragile, apologetic smile but didn't say anything. If they weren't going to Dublin, it meant he wouldn't see Maire. He'd seemed keen on her of course, to start with; he'd arranged the car and its ultimate destination – whatever it was – for Ailbe quickly and with no issue. When Maire wrote to him to say the things he'd used hadn't worked (Ailbe had got them on the quiet – they were illegal here and almost impossible to come by) and that she also needed the car, his letters and phone calls had completely stopped. Ailbe would never say that she'd told her so, even though she had. Maire didn't smile back and started to cry again.

Less than four months ago, she and Ailbe had been simple, unassuming girls. They had been best friends since they were tiny children; they'd seen each other almost every day of their lives from the day they'd first met to this very moment. They had always been so different – Ailbe, with her dark hair and sallow eyes, Maire with her boisterous curls, bright smile and loving family. Maire's family didn't approve of the friendship – how could they? – but it had endured regardless. Now, Maire thought, it wasn't just Ailbe that her family would hate and turn their backs on.

As it turned out, they were *both* in serious trouble and headed for terrible things.

*

Maire had told Ailbe she was madly in love with the doctor after spending just five minutes with him that week. Ailbe had laughed, of course.

"He's old enough to be your da!" she scoffed. She was

12

sitting cross-legged on Maire's bed one Sunday after Mass. She was only allowed round because Maire's parents were out, in their capacity as church volunteers, delivering communion to the housebound. Ailbe slopped some of her tea over the side of the mug onto the bedsheets as she laughed.

"He is not!" Maire retorted. "He's just... a grown-up. We're not exactly overrun with those around here. And he's twenty-nine; that's only ten years. And he's so *handsome*." Maire had sighed, leaning her head back and staring out the window. "Don't you think he's so handsome?"

"I've literally never seen him, Maire. And ten years ago you were nine."

"He's doing the visits down here once a month for a while. He's from *Dublin*," Maire added, feeling even more a grown-up herself just from mentioning such a place.

"Ooh, the cosmopolis," Ailbe said. "A city lad then? God, what must he think of us?" She laughed.

Maire smiled weakly back. She didn't like to think about that.

"And what did the two of you talk about, anyway? For the thirty seconds that's led you to this" – she gestured dramatically towards Maire with her hand – "hysteria?" She smiled as she said it, altogether not remotely convinced, but she did enjoy the rare occasions when Maire was happy.

"Well, he was in the queue in front of me at the post office, so, not much." She sighed. "He trod on my foot, apologised; I said it wasn't a bother and..." Maire had drifted off again.

"And?"

"Well, he said if he'd hurt me, he was the visiting parish doctor and was going to be here until tomorrow so he could

13

fix it!" Maire giggled.

Ailbe forced a smile and swallowed a huff of derision. This would end poorly – she could feel it, and anyway, Ailbe was getting a bit tired of all the gazing and sighing; she wasn't romantic like Maire. She really felt quite strongly, in fact, that *no one* should be romantic like Maire – it was so desperately annoying.

"So that was it?"

"That was it," Maire said, looking unhappily down at her hands. "We just sort of stared at each other and then he was called up to the counter."

"Love at first sight?" Ailbe said, dryly.

"Absolutely."

"Huh. Probably married."

"He is not!" Maire said with triumph. "No ring. I checked."

"Oh well, he can't be then."

Maire raised her eyebrows at Ailbe in frustration. Ailbe wasn't looking. She was picking determinedly at a scab on her knuckles. There'd been an altercation again, recently – Maire didn't like to ask, but as usual it seemed Ailbe had given as good as she'd got.

"I suppose unless I catch something awful between now and tomorrow morning, I won't see him until next month. And, even then, I'd have to catch something awful to see him, and I'll be looking terrible. Oh, Lord."

"Oh well, love's lost and all that," said Ailbe, drinking the last of her tea and setting the mug on the floor. "Come on, yer lovelorn, I'll walk with you. It's getting late."

Maire had been working at Brannigan's, the village's only pub, since she left school. She hadn't dared say the word

14

'university' with things as tight as they were at home, and anyway, she'd imagined that she probably wouldn't fare that well away from home. She'd never been alone before. Since birth she'd shared a bedroom – first, with her parents, and then with her sisters – and she still did now. It wasn't that she wasn't clever enough though, so that was a shame. Last year she missed out on a scholarship to university by one point, and it had broken her heart beyond words. But the family needed her income, and she didn't like to let them down.

Maire had loved going to school. She couldn't think of a single subject she hadn't enjoyed to some degree, and she had done well in all of them. To her peers, education had seemed an unfortunate formality – the inconvenient trickling away of time doing tedious homework in itchy stockings and horrifying shin-length skirts until they could go and rejoin their farming families full-time. But to Maire it had meant much more. She loved books, absolutely treasured them, and was fascinated by almost everything they contained. Maire happily sat with her younger sisters and helped them with homework, encouraging them to draw and write stories in their spare time, and aspire to things – anything they could think and dream of, she wanted it for all of them. She had tried the same with Ailbe, but she hadn't been cooperative at all. Ailbe hadn't been to school for years.

So it wasn't that Maire disliked the work in the pub, not at all. It was easy, and people were usually nice to her. Their other girl was prettier than Maire but had to use a calculator and a notepad for everything. Maire didn't; that was her one pride. Besides, Ailbe was always there at the end of the bar, making one pint of Guinness last a couple of hours, keeping Maire company and making her smile. She had just rather hoped for more by this point, that was all.

"You're not going home then," Maire had said to Ailbe after a few hours during one shift, as only the most fiercely loyal regulars remained shadowed in corners. The evenings were still light; the sky out of the window was slightly orange and pink as darkness settled. It was going to be a stiflingly hot summer. Maire had cleaned every glass, dusted every surface and was now resting her chin in her hand across the bar. She pinched her arm to keep herself awake.

"Ideally not," yawned Ailbe, draining the rest of her glass and peering into it with one eye closed. "My ma's horrible nephew is staying with us. Cathy's thrown him out again after he gave her a black eye. He'll be blind drunk with my da by now. Abigail!" she bellowed to the kitchen behind Maire. "Can I stay upstairs?"

The rarely booked room above the pub was often Ailbe's solace; Abigail knew what Ailbe went home to every day because she'd gone home to the same when she was Ailbe's age. She said nothing about it, of course, but let Ailbe use the room for free, in exchange for a couple of hours of pot washing the following day. She hadn't been allowed to employ her formerly – the landlord had been one of Ailbe's father's earliest victims.

"Ah, no," Abigail said. She appeared from the kitchen holding a bowl of stew and dumplings. "There's some doctor up there this week. The Ship overbooked for the weekend because of some wedding, so they sent him here."

Maire stood up with a start and the colour drained from her face as she shot a panicked look at Ailbe. Ailbe burst out laughing.

"Speaking of which, Maire," Abigail said, "run this up to

16

himself will you, with a pint? I'm going for a smoke." She pushed the bowl into Maire's hands and disappeared back to the kitchen.

Maire stood in stunned silence. Ailbe was still laughing.

"Well go on, missus," she sniggered. "Pour the future Mr Maire a nice Guinness there."

Maire still hadn't moved.

"Oh Christ, Ailbe, don't leave me."

"You're a grown woman, Maire," Ailbe laughed. "You'll be grand. To think, you didn't expect to see him for another month!"

Maire was not amused.

"I'll come and see you tomorrow and you can tell me all about it." Ailbe winked.

Maire's heart was in her throat as she knocked on the door. It might be a different doctor. He couldn't be the only doctor in Ireland. When the door opened, she thought her heart would stop.

"Oh," he said, with a half-shaved face and his shirt untucked. "It's you!"

CHAPTER THREE

For most of her life, Bridget had heard over and over again how much she wasn't like Ruth. Everyone in the family had already come before her, setting the pace, as it were, for those that came after. She had been smaller than she ought to have been, blue, and lucky to be alive – that's what she'd been told. Ruth had arrived promptly on her due date, with soft fair hair, lovely green eyes, and a bright smile. She had walked at ten months, toddling herself over to baby Bridget the day after Bridget was born.

John was the eldest, followed by Liam a year later and then Dermot a year and a half after him. Having produced three boys in under four years, their twenty-two-year-old mother Mariah had taken a well-earned break from pregnancy and child-rearing, not having Ruth until almost fifteen years later. Bridget had then been a New Year's Eve surprise; none more surprised than Mariah's husband Seamus, who dropped dead of a heart attack not four months into her life.

Bridget looked nothing like Ruth – not when they were children, and not now. She was chubby and dark-haired and had sucked her thumb for much too long which had made her teeth stick out. Ruth was slim and beautiful with a perfect heart-shaped face. But Bridget stopped being jealous of Ruth's looks when she whizzed through her classes and exams without missing a beat, skipping the first year of secondary school and reluctantly becoming Ruth's classmate.

People started asking then if they were twins, and Ruth

didn't know what to say. Ruth sat and struggled over notebooks and textbooks, in tears as Bridget tried to help her and make her understand. She had never really understood, as much as Bridget had tried, and left school with nothing but relief for the end of her sentence, and bitter memories.

The longest the sisters had ever been separated since Bridget was born was after Bridget went away to Galway to study nursing. She had taken the first job she'd been offered at Richmond Surgical Hospital in Grangegorman to be closer to Ruth when she finished, and she had never moved on. By that time, John had moved to Donegal and their mother had died, leaving the house and everything in it to Bridget. Ruth, for her part, was written out of the will and had married the boy next door.

Bridget loved nursing. When she'd first mentioned that it was what she had wanted to pursue, Mariah laughed at her scornfully and said she wasn't surprised. She said it made sense that Bridget would be still trying to save her father after all this time. Bridget was hurt and always said that was nonsense; she didn't like it when Mariah said it to other people. She didn't even know who he was, after all; he was just a stranger and a stone in the ground. Her career choice was nothing to do with him, but she pursued it ardently.

Despite years of night shifts, long hours and rarely ever a break, Bridget never tired of taking blood samples and using soothing words for her patients, whom she loved as though they were her own family. More than that, she was proud to do it, and it made her happy, day after day and for years on end. She had always been quite sure that a man could never make her that happy; consequently, she had refused to look for one. Nor did she ever feel worse off for having not done so, when people smiled patronisingly and told her 'not to worry', he was 'just around the corner'. Relatives at weddings had finally moved on from telling Bridget she'd be 'next', and Bridget was all the gladder for it. She had her own house. She had her own life. What else could there really be?

She was, however, secretly delighted that Ruth had married Donal. They had been such awkward and yet thrilling teenagers to watch; Donal, having no siblings and no ma at home, seemed to struggle to string a sentence together around Ruth for the first years they knew each other. He used to call shyly for her over their shared garden fence, and they'd play quiet, mysterious games without coming within ten feet of each other. As they'd got older, Mariah had called him a shrimp and said, quite plainly, that Ruth would be wasting her life on a soulless man like that, who hadn't one word to say for himself.

Yet words had been the least of what they had needed to find each other. He was gentle and quiet, perfect for Ruth, as it turned out. Mariah had disliked Ruth's meek personality and made no secret of how she much preferred the company of Bridget instead, who had, in Mariah's words, 'some spirit about her' and 'was closer to herself in mind and matter'. True to form, Ruth had been hurt, but said nothing about it. Ruth and her beloved 'shrimp' had a very basic Wedding Mass without Mariah present; John had given Ruth away in their father's place. He'd promised to do the same for Bridget one day, and she'd laughed him off. The new couple had sandwiches in Finnegan's pub afterwards and then returned peacefully to Donal's childhood home. No one was more thrilled than Donal's father, after the formalities of the day were complete, to have a longed-for daughter in the house at last.

So they had continued like that for the best part of ten years: Donal working in his flooring shop that sold tiles and carpets, Ruth staying at home taking care of Mr Quinn. They were happy. Quietly, contentedly happy, but for the one thing. Mr Quinn lived to witness the first pregnancy and subsequent loss; it was he who had phoned Donal at the shop, held Ruth's hand until Donal arrived home, he who had discreetly mopped the kitchen floor and wept silent tears for his grandchild. He told Ruth that Donal's mother had gone through just the same thing, once, and it'd be all right in the end. Look at Donal! He was a fine man now. He had been her pride and joy. But it hadn't been all right in the end, not at all – thankfully, Ruth had always thought, he just hadn't lived long enough to see himself proved wrong.

CHAPTER FOUR

Maire really believed, when the first signs of what was going to happen had started to appear, that all she would have to do was tell him and she would be safely married by the end of the year. The worst she would have to endure was the occasional raised eyebrow when comparing their first wedding anniversary to the child's birthday. Ailbe had, as gently as she could, told her not to be so incredibly stupid.

"This happens, Maire; they get their fill and then they feck off," she said. "Look at Alma Mulligan, Jesus. He was supposed to be the love of her life, so she said." Ailbe had been holding a despondent Maire in her arms when she said it, as her letters and secret phone calls went unanswered. It hadn't helped all that much.

"But he-he said he loved... he loved—"

"I know, and maybe... I'm sure he does." Ailbe tried to be encouraging for Maire's sake, although she didn't believe it for a second. "Maybe he does. Maybe he's going to be the one driving the car – it's a car, isn't it? Is that what he said? And whisk you away into the sunset. Isn't that where people like yis go?"

Maire had chuckled and sniffed. "The sunset, yes, that's the one."

"Sunset it is. Don't worry. He's probably just panicking. He's going to be a da; he wouldn't have expected that. Men panic. It's all right."

"Hmm." Maire had chewed at her nails. "But what about you?"

"Oh, what about me?" she said. "Wherever it is, I'm sure

I'll survive. If it's not him, at least we'll be together."

"We'll be together," Maire repeated, cheerfully. "Always."

"Always. Now. Tell me what he said again. Maybe it's not as bad as you think."

*

The car was stopping. Maire's heart felt like it would explode. The driver got out and walked around the car, opening the door on Ailbe's side. In the distance was a dim torchlight, approaching quickly. That and the headlights illuminated towering iron gates that were padlocked shut.

"Right, girls," the driver said, with an awkward stiffness like he was checking them in for a school trip. "Which one of you is Ailbe?"

Maire realised then that he had a Cork accent, like her grandfather had once had. He'd be so ashamed if he could see Maire now, and the thought made her burn inside. Ailbe was sliding obediently out of the car and Maire followed, out of Ailbe's door instead of her own. She grabbed Ailbe's hand and gripped it.

"I'm Ailbe," she said, without the slightest quiver in her voice. "And this is—"

"Right, Ailbe," the driver interjected. "This is Bessborough. You'll be here for the… duration."

The girls looked at each other. They'd never heard of it. But then, what had they been expecting? They'd gone right towards Cork; Maire had been to Cork before to visit her granda. But she'd never been here; she'd never seen it, never even known it was here – whatever it was. The torchlight had reached them and was now clinking against the padlock, as the enormous gates creaked open.

"Okay…" said Ailbe slowly, "but what about—"

He had already stopped listening. The torch was being held by a stern-looking nun in her fifties, who had approached them and was now hissing and whispering to the driver. They were pointing and gesturing at Ailbe.

"Right, Ailbe, is it?" said the nun, flashing the torch at her. It lit up Ailbe's gaunt face and swollen, battered eye – the nun didn't react. "Your name is Ciara from now on. You can forget your old name for now and, for that matter, your old everything." She glanced coldly at Maire. "There's lots of other girls here like you. We have to do something in the meantime to preserve your…" – she looked Ailbe up and down scornfully – "dignity."

Maire looked at the driver; he was just staring into space, like he'd heard it all a thousand times before. She wondered what her new name was going to be.

"What's left of it, anyway. Well, come on," the nun said, snapping her fingers impatiently.

Ailbe and Maire took a step forward together.

"Ah," she said, pointing at Maire's face with a long, bony finger. "Where do you think you're going?"

The girls looked at each other again. They hadn't spoken a word to one another since they'd left home and, for the first time ever, Ailbe was starting to look nervous.

"Well, I-I'm… as well—" Maire stuttered.

"No, no," the driver interjected. "You're going somewhere else, if you're not Ailbe. Mary?"

"Maire. Where?"

"Best get back in the car there, Maire. This isn't your

stop."

Maire was confused. Did that mean good news? She wasn't sure. She was miles from her mother, in the dark, and she was about to say goodbye to Ailbe for the first time in her life. They were supposed to be together – always. They had promised each other. Suddenly she didn't feel up to it after all. She crumpled and pulled on Ailbe's arm like they were children again.

"No, Ailbe—"

"Girls, say your goodbyes and make it quick."

"Maire, unless this is an abattoir, this is good! What's wrong with you?"

"Ailbe! I can't! I can't go without you!"

"Oh, that's enough!" cried the nun. "We don't have time for this nonsense." She wrapped her sharp fingers around Ailbe's other arm and pulled her abruptly away towards the gates.

The driver linked his arm firmly through Maire's and manoeuvred her determinedly back towards the car. Maire called after Ailbe as she struggled and sobbed.

"You know where I am!" Ailbe called back. "He said it, Bessborough, or whatever. Write to me. You'll be fine."

The light from the torch flashed intermittently over Ailbe's face and Maire saw that she was crying silently. Maire had never, ever seen her cry before.

"You'll be fine," Ailbe stuttered. "Just go, Maire. Have a nice wedding!"

Ailbe turned away from Maire and the driver and tried to shrug off the nun, who grabbed her even more roughly than before and shoved her through the gates, padlocking them behind her as the two of them disappeared into the darkness.

"I'll come back and get you!" Maire screamed into the darkness. "I'll come back!"

She heard nothing but the diminishing sound of crunching shoes on gravel. It didn't take long for even those slight sounds to fade into silence.

"Come on now, miss," the driver mumbled, finally letting go of Maire's arm after the gates were safely locked. He stood in front of her to block her view of the place that had taken her friend and gently but firmly nudged Maire to sit back in the car. "I'm sorry about all that."

Maire sat where Ailbe had, in the warmth of her seat, and put her arm where Ailbe's had been. As the torchlight disappeared further up the lane, the car pulled away, and Maire started to wail – long, noisy sobs that drenched her face. She knew it was undignified, but she really didn't care. Ailbe was gone, and that nun had been horrible. She'd never known nuns to be unkind before. She was afraid. Ailbe could be wrong. So very, very wrong.

"Where..." she sniffed, an hour or so later, when she finally felt like she could speak, "where am I going then?"

The driver didn't answer at first; he let another car out at a junction and fiddled with his headlights. They were on main roads now, lit by tall lamps.

"Well, it's... somewhere a damn sight better than that place," he muttered, not quietly enough.

"What?" Maire's already frail stomach started to sink. "What's wrong with Bessborough? Is Ailbe—"

"Please, miss, I didn't mean anything by that," he said gruffly. "Don't worry. It'll be nice. You'll be fine."

He didn't answer any more of Maire's questions. The car sped on.

To Maire's immense surprise and considerable relief, the car came to a halt outside a particularly ordinary looking house on a very ordinary looking street. It was one o'clock in the morning by now; they'd been told to wait for the car in the dark outside of the village, and by the time they'd been to that Bessborough place – Maire's heart clenched at the thought – and left again, they'd been travelling for several hours.

The driver switched off the engine, got out, and started rolling a cigarette as he walked around to Maire's side and opened the door. She breathed in the cold air that had breezed speedily into the car.

"This is Dublin, miss," he said softly, "and there's nothing to be frightened of."

Dublin. Where he was from. This must be his house. That was why she wasn't going to Bessborough with Ailbe – of course. Ailbe had been right. Maire couldn't get out of the car quick enough as she joined the dots in her mind and broke into a slight smile of relief. She was embarrassed at how much she'd cried and panicked and doubted him. Of course she was going to come to Dublin. The driver smiled back wearily and took her bag out of the car's boot. She had managed to pack a small number of things she'd wanted to keep with her for – as the driver had said a few hours before – 'the duration'. Ailbe hadn't had anything to bring.

She fiddled with the straps on her little bag as the driver knocked on the front door and stepped back. He looked at Maire awkwardly.

"There's nothing to be frightened of," he repeated. Maire watched her breath form clouds in front of her face. Ailbe wouldn't have been frightened.

"I'm not frightened," she said sternly.

The door opened. Maire looked up expectantly.

"Thank you, driver," the lady on the other side of the door whispered, reaching out her hand. They shook hands formally and the driver walked away without looking back at Maire, his shoes crunching on the frosted ground. The woman quickly scanned the dark and silent street over Maire's head, before looking kindly into Maire's disappointed and confused face, mistaking it for fear and exhaustion.

"Come in, quick, out of that cold," she whispered, as she reached and took Maire's bag from her hands. Maire turned back to see that the car, which had taken her so far from her home, and her mother, was already off the drive and disappearing back into the darkness of the street. The lady stood expectantly with the door to her home wide open and Maire's bag in her hand.

Maire stepped in and was relieved to feel the warmth of the indoors around her. She was also relieved to be standing up, she realised, and she stretched out her legs and aching back. The hallway seemed colossal compared to her parents' house; the stairs were carpeted red and a large beige lampshade hung a few inches too low from the ceiling, above Maire's head. The light was too bright after spending so long in the dark. A big side unit to her right was cluttered with photo frames. The pictures aged from black-and-white photographs of men in military uniforms, to recent photos of chubby pink babies. Maire touched her stomach instinctively. She looked for the familiar face she was hoping desperately to see. She didn't see it.

"This is my family," the lady said kindly, noticing Maire's

gaze. "My name is Bridget." She held out her hand to Maire, which Maire shook lightly in silence. "Oh," Bridget faltered. "Um… *is… is ainm dom…*"

"No, no! It wasn't that rural." She smiled at Bridget, surprised to hear herself speak. "My name is Maire."

"Oh, thank goodness." Bridget chuckled to herself and held on to Maire's hand, placing her other over it. "My Irish is dreadful."

"So is mine."

"Aren't we shameful!"

Shameful. Yes, she was. Maire was starting to feel unwell again.

The two women stared at each other for a moment, until Bridget let go of Maire's hand and needlessly patted down her clothes.

"You're safe here with me, Maire."

"I know."

"And I'm sure you have lots of questions," Bridget said.

Maire nodded. Then she yawned widely.

"But perhaps bed first, questions in the morning?" said Bridget, and Maire nodded again. She only really had one question, but she didn't like to ask it. Bridget started up the stairs and beckoned Maire to follow her. "I'll show you your room."

Maire climbed the stairs slowly, wondering if this was his mother. That would make sense; she looked a bit young, maybe, but it wasn't completely inconceivable. She was young, after all. Suddenly it was obvious – he had brought her here to have their baby under the watchful eye of his loving mother, somewhere safe and familiar, because he loved her. They could be married by next weekend. She

29

wished Ailbe was here too – she missed her so much already, and she wanted to tell her that she was okay – but at least she now understood why she was here. She felt the lump of despair rise in her throat again as she pictured Ailbe disappearing into the dark.

"Here we go," Bridget was saying, as she opened a door to a bedroom at the end of the landing. Maire blinked at her. "All yours!"

She peered in and there was a towel and a nightgown folded neatly at the foot of the bed, and a toothbrush and tiny bar of soap in a packet beside them. It was like the room setup at Brannigan's for guests. She felt like she was walking into a hotel.

"I've never had a room to myself before," said Maire, stepping lightly into the room. Bridget turned up the dimmer switch and put Maire's bag down on the small chair by the wardrobe and gestured for her coat.

"I shared a room growing up too," Bridget said. "You'll love having some space to yourself at last, I'm sure."

Maire knew Bridget was trying to be friendly and put her at ease, so she didn't like to say that space to herself was the last thing she wanted. She wanted to be in her room at home with her sisters, or on the moors with Ailbe; in fact, she'd rather be at the pub appeasing their rudest and most violently intoxicated customers than be here, dealing with this. She wished she could be lying with him, feeling warm and safe and happy, even though that was what had started this whole desperate mess.

"I want you to know you are very, very welcome here, Maire," Bridget said. "I'm going to look after you and everything is going to be just fine."

Maire smiled. She did believe her. She seemed earnest and tender, like she'd raised ten children in this house. This must be his mother, or a sister, or something. It just had to be – why else would she be here, instead of at Bessborough with Ailbe? He'd be here in the morning, she was sure, to explain. Bridget had said she was going to look after her – just for tonight? The week? Until they were married? She supposed the particulars didn't matter too much. He'd probably be here himself right now if he wasn't busy with patients – there must have been an emergency in the middle of the night. As likely an explanation as any.

"Thank you," Maire said. "I'll get to bed. Thank you for waiting up to meet me."

"Anything," said Bridget, "anything at all. Sleep well," and she shut the door.

Maire looked around at the first bedroom she'd ever had to herself. She turned the dimmer down, as the light was giving her a headache after hours in the dark. There was a bookcase full of books; she'd always wanted that. She assumed she'd have a lot of time on her hands to read now. She opened the wardrobe doors and found a cluttered mess of dresses, hat boxes and odd shoes. She wondered if Bridget had a husband, snoring away in the next room, or perhaps he worked nights somewhere? Wherever he was, she hoped he'd be as nice as Bridget seemed to be. The thought of sharing a house with a strange man that wasn't her father made her feel nervous.

There was so much she wanted to know, so much she wanted to have explained, but the thought of a comfortable bed in a nice house with a nice lady was as good an outcome as she could have hoped for if he wasn't here to meet her right away. She didn't know what had happened to Alma Mulligan, no one did. All they knew was that she got herself in trouble, didn't come into school one rainy Tuesday in March and was never seen again – if, as Maire had sometimes wondered, she ever existed at all. That was three years ago. Maire realised now she'd probably gone to Bessborough too, or somewhere like it. She wondered how many places like that there were in Ireland – how many Almas, how many Ailbes had disappeared behind their gates. She blinked back tears at the thought of it and a wave of guilt overcame her, thinking of Bridget, this house and a room of her own. She hoped Ailbe had a comfortable bed for the night too. Or just a bed at all; she didn't know how bad it was going to be for her. That nun didn't seem very hospitable, rather thoroughly disgusted with Ailbe. But then, Ailbe was used to that. Surely though, behind those gates, things could only be so much worse.

Maire wasn't going to see Ailbe again for some time; the creeping realisation of that was only just beginning. She hadn't gone longer than a week's holiday without seeing her before. Years ago, when they'd been giggling thirteen-year-olds, they'd made all sorts of plans: that they were going to marry a handsome pair of brothers so they could be proper sisters forever, and they'd have all their babies at the same time and their babies would grow up and be best friends as well. And Ailbe and Maire would be old widowed women, living in the same street, drinking away their widow's pensions and smiling over photographs of their dozens of grandchildren. Ailbe had been very enthusiastic at the idea of having a noisy house full of her own offspring, and Maire had been very surprised by that revelation. Maybe, in the future, they could still have that.

Maybe.

The nightgown was too big and at least ten years old looking at its design; it felt strange to be wearing someone else's nightclothes. But by now Maire was too tired to care. It occurred to her fleetingly that over time it wouldn't be too big anymore; it'd be snug around her chest and tight over her belly. She wanted to sleep well because he was sure to come tomorrow to see her, explain everything, and maybe give her an address for Ailbe – 'Ciara' – that she could write to. She and Fionn hadn't seen each other for almost six weeks; she ached at the thought of him. He hadn't abandoned her. Just panicking, as men do, like Ailbe had said, and busy making these arrangements.

She wondered if her parents and sisters had gone to sleep. She wondered if they'd sat around the kitchen table with mugs full of undrunk tea, not understanding, silently devastated. Or maybe they'd torn her letter up, scratched her face out of the family portrait already, and were lying stony-faced in bed staring at the ceiling, wondering how they could have accidentally raised such a foolish, hateful girl. She hoped they were all right. She hoped, desperately, that they wouldn't really miss her.

Oh, Lord – in the frantic devastation of the evening, she'd forgotten to say the rosary. She crept out of bed and pulled the cross and beads out of her bag. She must say it – God had brought her here to keep her safe; she must have been forgiven. Thank Heavens. She scurried back to bed, feeling the winter cold she hadn't felt quite so strongly before. She wrapped the beads around her hands and gripped them; it was so familiar, like being home again. But that was the point of it, after all. She pulled the blankets over her head and breathed in their strange scent, and before she had reached the end of the Apostle's Creed, she was asleep.

CHAPTER FIVE

Ailbe couldn't work out how she was going to get any sleep for what was left of the night, let alone the remaining however many months she'd have to spend here. Her mattress appeared to be more than twenty years old, on an iron bedstead that probably would have been more comfortable on its own, she surmised. She had a blanket, but it didn't quite reach her feet, and she was freezing to her bones. The dark was such that she could barely see her own hand in front of her face. She wished she'd packed a bag now like Maire did, but there was hardly anything left in the house that her father and her cousin hadn't pawned for drink, and she'd hardly been a person of many possessions in the first place. She imagined her mother would need anything that was still left in any case, now more than ever.

She'd been led to the room she was in by some other poor pregnant girl, lit by candlelight, after the nun she'd met had stomped off into the darkness without a second word once they'd reached the house. At least, she thought it was a house. It was too dark to tell. She'd been given a shapeless white nightgown to change into once she'd made it up all the stairs to the dormitory – she assumed that was the correct word for it – and huddled herself under her blanket.

She didn't want the baby but that wasn't the point. This wasn't how she'd imagined it would all happen. Half her and half that drunken, despicable… she felt no connection to it or the situation at all, but she didn't want a bad ending for it all the same. The cold couldn't do it much good, could it? She had no idea. She had no idea what was good or bad for the little thing she was growing inside her, against her will, but she wanted to do her best. Then, some decent couple would come and get to take away a healthy baby or, at least, a baby. That's what she was doing here; she'd worked that much out so far herself.

The girl in the bed next to hers had been crying since Ailbe had laid down and begun the impossible task of getting comfortable. The other girls seemed to be either ignoring her or were sleeping through it. They breathed softly; some snored and purred like cats. She wasn't sure how many beds there were in this room – six, maybe seven? – and they had passed other rooms on their way to this one.

"Are you all right?" Ailbe whispered to her neighbour. The crying muffled but didn't stop. Ailbe tried to reach out, but the distance between their beds was too far. "Look, it's... it's going to be—"

"Don't bother," came a voice from across the room, not bothering to whisper. "She does this every night."

The crying continued. Ailbe frowned at the ceiling she couldn't see.

CHAPTER SIX

Fionn was panicking. His hands were shaking as he shut his car door and tried to plug in his seatbelt. On the whole, he wasn't a nervous person; it was what made him such a good doctor. But, today, he'd turned up the radio to cover up the sound of his vomiting and, now, he couldn't even attach his own seatbelt without fumbling about like an idiot. The drive from his own house to Aunt Bridget's was approximately twenty minutes, and he couldn't decide whether he wished it was longer or not. He didn't want to do this. He couldn't do this.

Every time he approached a set of traffic lights they changed to green. He really wished they hadn't. He thought about the last time he'd driven there; it was only four weeks ago. He'd delivered news that would alter the course of all their lives. He'd desperately wanted them not to be ashamed of him but, as it turned out, it didn't matter what anyone else thought. He was so ashamed, deeply disgusted with himself, and nothing any of them had said or could say made any of it any better.

*

"Please don't be ashamed of me. I couldn't take it."

Fionn had been sitting on the smaller of the two sofas in Ruth and Donal's front room for quite some time that day before he had admitted why he was there. He didn't make unannounced visits, as a rule. He held a Dublin GAA mug of tea in his hands that had started to go cold; the milk had begun to curdle on the surface and an unpleasant film wrinkled on top of the liquid as he fidgeted. Ruth and Donal sat together on their bigger sofa in silence, holding hands.

"Please," he begged again.

"It's just all rather a shock to us, Fionn," said Donal in a quiet voice, without looking at him.

Fionn hadn't expected him to be the one to speak. Donal's disappointment felt worse somehow than even his own. Ruth had started to cry softly.

"Not that we're not grateful you are thinking of us."

Fionn looked at the clock and realised that only four minutes had passed since he'd said the words: some of the longest minutes of his life. It had all come out in a bit of a rush and a babble, and they had just stared at him, then at each other, and then back to him. At least it wasn't going as badly as when he told his da.

"I think," croaked Ruth, and then cleared her throat. "I think we'll do it. We'll do it."

"Ruthie!" Donal whispered. "Are you sure?"

Ruth nodded adamantly. "Yes, yes, it's the right thing; it's what we've always wanted, and this is our last chance," she said, squeezing both of Donal's hands in her own. "That poor girl. She didn't know. So, she's one of us now." She shot a look at Fionn that was not particularly forgiving.

He was surprised to realise that he had anticipated more resistance about the girl – unmarried mothers were called hussies, tarts, a disgrace. Fallen women. He'd expected to have to leap in and defend her, persuade the family with all his heart to take the misguided young thing into their lives and to find it in themselves to treat her with an ounce of respect. But no – it wasn't her they were disappointed in. It wasn't her they were disgusted by.

Fionn thought about how different it could have been, if he'd waited before getting married five years ago, like his family had said he should. *I've met a girl,* he could be saying today. *A beautiful girl from the country. I'll bring her for Christmas and, next year, we'll get married.* But no. Now that could never happen, and her life would never be the same. It was all his fault. But this way – *this way,* he persuaded himself – he could do one decent thing for her. And the baby.

The baby.

He already had two babies and had delivered a few over the years, when things got complicated and a doctor had to be called for. In a medical emergency, he looked at the babies the way mechanics looked at cars – does it have this in the right place? Is this part working? Is the engine rumbling as it should? What needs fixing and how? He filled in charts and paperwork, checked miniature hips, inserted tiny needles into impossibly tiny veins.

When his boys were born, he forgot he was a doctor and simply looked at them in bewildered awe. Generally, men didn't accompany, but given his position, there seemed no harm… He searched for parts of himself in their faces. This baby could have his whole face for all he knew. He might never know.

Donal put his arms around Ruth and patted her shoulder gently as he spoke about all the things they would need to think and talk about. Ruth would have to stay out of sight for a while, towards the end. So would the girl. Donal would paint the room himself. What should they tell the family? It was up to her, he said. Whatever she wanted. Anything she wanted, as long as she was happy.

This part Fionn felt prepared for. He'd had some very long, sleepless nights lately to think about all this.

"Of course, I'll pay for—" he began.

"You will not," snapped Ruth.

Fionn started. There was an uncomfortable silence.

"You will not," repeated Donal more gently, patting Ruth's hand as she looked down. "Thanks all the same, Fionn. But… if it's ours, it's ours."

It. He wanted to protest, but he could already see it wasn't his place. Fionn couldn't help but feel the warmth of their protectiveness over the child they didn't even know yet. Just like that, they were already parents. In fact, they'd been parents for decades. This was right. He felt better.

He stayed longer to work out a plan. Ruth being Ruth went to get a notepad and a pen from the kitchen drawer and started to make a list. Bridget would have to be told and asked if she would help. She'd be safer there with a nurse on hand, Donal felt, and Ruth decided she couldn't bear to watch her baby grow inside someone else every single day; the jealousy and the pain would unravel her. Next door would be better. They'd pop in and be friendly; they'd show themselves to this girl as the worthy parents they knew they were, so that she knew she was doing the right thing. Bridget would make her at home. Was she likely to resist? Change her mind right at the end? Fionn assured them not. What choice did she have, after all?

"What does Clodagh think of all this?" asked Donal.

Fionn had hoped they wouldn't ask.

"Will she want you seeing the baby – our baby? At Christmas and at Mass and things? It won't be easy for her."

Ruth looked up from her notepad and peered at Fionn with interest. To her shame, she realised she'd barely thought about Fionn's wife Clodagh since he'd first said what he'd done.

Fionn didn't speak. He avoided their gaze.

"Oh my Lord," said Ruth at last. "She doesn't even know yet, does she?"

*

Fionn clicked his indicator off as he turned off the roundabout on to the long avenue that Ruth, Donal and Bridget all lived on. No, she hadn't known then – and she still didn't know now. He just had to see Maire, once, apologise and try to explain that everything he was doing, he was doing for her – and for the child, of course. He didn't expect her to believe him. The last time they'd seen each other, six weeks ago, she'd asked him about marriage. How could he do this?

Reaching the shared driveway to Bridget's and Ruth's houses, he thought about carrying on, driving to the airport and back just to gather himself, have a few more minutes of his current life before it disappeared forever. Give Maire a few more minutes to think her thoughts and believe her joys. Maybe, while he was there, he could do all the branches of his family a favour and get on a plane to somewhere, and never return.

The car was parked without him realising; he'd done it on autopilot. He had no choice now. He'd been here so often, of course, as a boy and as a man. They'd bought champagne for him when he first qualified, and they'd had a big family party in the garden. He'd brought Clodagh along to meet everyone.

He could tell even then that they didn't really approve, but they were polite. Everyone – well, except Bridget – was always so polite.

Bridget had already opened the front door and was standing, expectantly, with a thunderous face. Ruth was immensely docile, Donal also, but Bridget could really frighten him if she wanted to. Some of his old medical school colleagues worked as doctors at Bridget's hospital now, and they remarked, frequently, that she wasn't one to cross. They didn't fancy the thought of Christmas dinner with an aunt like her, one had joked. Then, Fionn had punched his friend in the arm and told him not to be so rude about his family. Now, he couldn't agree more. He swallowed hard. God – Christmas. Imagine.

He locked his car and shuffled to the front door. He felt like a child due for a major telling-off. He tried to remind himself that he was an almost thirty-year-old man and he had no business at all being afraid of Bridget. It didn't work.

Bridget didn't look at him as she gestured to the stairs.

"She's in the spare room," she sighed. "She's decent. Don't drag it out."

His footsteps felt heavy as he climbed the stairs. The spare room was where he and his younger brothers had stayed as children, when Bridget babysat them. He felt despondent. He hadn't seen Maire for weeks, and he'd missed her. He was sure she'd missed him; she always did. She was going to be thrilled to see him. Just this once. Just this last time.

The door was already open and so he peered in to see Maire sitting in the chair by the window, gazing out. He knocked gently on the wooden doorframe. She turned and smiled – a huge smile of relief and joy.

"Oh," she said, her eyes filling up. "It's you."

CHAPTER SEVEN

As soon as Ailbe was awake, the other girls hounded her for information about herself and the outside world in whispered, frantic voices.

"Good God, don't you read the papers," she had said, yawning, and was met with blank faces. They didn't get papers, or letters, or anything. Ailbe – Ciara, she had to remember to tell them she was called – was Bessborough's first new arrival in almost a month.

The girls were always hopeful that someone would arrive from a similar locality to themselves, with local news and knowledge. Something about their own families maybe, or, God forbid, the whereabouts and behaviours of their babies' fathers. Unfortunately, no one had ever heard of Ailbe's village, much less been there themselves. Their accents seemed to cover the length and breadth of the island. Ailbe said she was sorry. They asked her if she knew where she was, and why she was here. They asked her how she got her black eye and the marks on her neck and told her it all looked sore. Ailbe didn't feel like responding to that.

Now there was daylight, Ailbe looked around the room. She had massively misjudged its size in the darkness. There were twenty beds in this room, and she was sure there were other rooms because she could hear movement and voices on the other side of the wall. Each bed looked in a shoddy state, and all the girls wore white ill-fitting nightgowns, identical to each other's and her own.

Ailbe glanced at the bed beside her, and the girl she saw sleeping there looked barely older than a child. Her pillow was still damp from tears and her face was blotchy and swollen. Ailbe could see the dark circles under the girl's eyes from where she stood, even though the girl was still sleeping. She was so tiny that her body actually fit under the meagre blanket, baby bump and all.

"We have to go to Mass, get dressed," one of the girls was saying to Ailbe.

Ailbe groaned internally, nodded outwardly and started towards her neighbour's bed.

"No, don't," the girl whispered. "Give her five more minutes. The poor wee thing is so little; she's always so tired."

Ailbe nodded sympathetically. She was little. Incredibly little.

"Okay," Ailbe whispered, feeling the familiar bile creep up her throat. "Listen… is there somewhere I can… go and get sick, first?"

*

The last person out was always the one to wake Milly; it was the dormitory rule they had created amongst themselves. The girls gradually shifted from small, sleepy groups into military file as they approached the chapel. Ailbe followed without speaking, but she seethed on the inside. She hated Mass. She never went at home; hers was a Catholic household in name only. She smoked outside in the graveyard and waited patiently for Maire, who loved Mass and went diligently three times a week. Ailbe smiled to herself at the thought of Maire. She hoped to God that, wherever she was, she was all right.

45

There was a huge, imposing crucifix outside the chapel and at the front of the alter inside it. Ailbe looked around the chapel and saw the magnitude of the numbers there for the first time – two hundred women, she estimated, maybe more. There were lots of rows of women who didn't look pregnant at all; they were at the front, but they all looked withered and exhausted to some degree. Some of them had stains, patches of wet, on their fronts. Ailbe and the other girls, with all their varying sizes and shapes of pregnancy bumps, were at the back. Ailbe had never seen so many pregnant women all together at once; she found it odd, alien to her. The nuns of the convent sat elsewhere in the chapel, in view of the priest, but so the girls were out of their sight.

"Do we only have to do this on Tuesdays?" Ailbe whispered hopefully to the girl beside her.

She shot a look at Ailbe as though Ailbe had just asked if it would be all right to wash her dirty face in the font.

"*Every* day," the girl hissed back incredulously, and turned away from Ailbe. A priest had hobbled to the alter at the front.

"The Lord be with you," the priest said, as though it were a threat.

Ailbe thought he looked about a hundred years old. *Every day.*

"And with your spirit," the girls and nuns echoed.

"We gather here this morning in the sight of God to repent *the most terrible of sins*; we are *grateful* to those who *care for us* as we reap the consequences of our sin and experience that which is our *earned* suffering…"

CHAPTER EIGHT

Ruth had seen Fionn's car pull up on their drive from her armchair and she watched him disappear into Bridget's house with her heart in her throat. She hadn't slept a wink all night and felt an aching in her soul for the mother upstairs in Bridget's house. She'd never known anyone to get into trouble in this way herself, but she could only imagine the depth of the girl's despair. Fionn was very handsome and successful; she didn't blame the girl for not being able to resist. Of course, *she* had waited, but God knows she knew it happened elsewhere, with other young women and handsome men. But this was, after all, her and Donal's last chance. Their *only* chance: if this meeting went badly, their dreams would be dashed yet again. As much as Fionn had said it was definite, she didn't like the way he seemed to speak for the girl. She didn't like to judge what went on in other people's homes, with other people's children. There was a human being at stake here – two humans, really. Ruth clasped her hands in prayer. *Please God*, she prayed. *Please let her say yes.*

Donal had seen the car too and was determined to distract Ruth. He could barely imagine the turmoil in her heart on this morning of all mornings. He tiptoed into their quiet lounge with a box that he'd clumsily tied a bow around. He coughed.

"What's that?" Ruth asked absent-mindedly.

"I got it for us," said Donal, putting the box into Ruth's lap. "Don't worry. It wasn't expensive. I mean, it was, when it was new, I suppose." He shuffled from one foot to the other.

47

Ruth looked up at him and didn't say anything.

"It's a camera."

Ruth regarded the box with confusion and carefully opened it. She had never held one before; not many people she knew had one of their own. It was enormous and so heavy.

"It's a treat," said Donal. "A little present, you know. After everything. For the holiday," he added, quickly.

Ruth smiled at him and he smiled too, relieved and happy. "We can keep the photos to remind us of our lovely time, just the two of us."

Ruth had learned to wince at his mishaps so slightly that he didn't notice anymore. She stood up and pecked his lips lightly. "Thank you," she said. "It's wonderful." She peered through the tiny window and pressed down on the button. The flash made Donal jump.

"Jesus, Ruthie," he laughed. "Don't go wasting that film on pictures of me now. Save it for the baby."

CHAPTER NINE

Fionn hadn't said much before Maire noticed it, on the fourth finger of his left hand, something she'd never seen before because it had never been there until now. It glinted at her, like it was deliberate. It was tormenting her with its dazzling smile. He was wittering on about her journey, sorry the driver wasn't very chatty but—

"We're not getting married, are we?" she sighed.

Fionn looked down at his feet so he didn't have to see her face as he said, "No. We're not. I'm sorry."

"How long?" she asked in a whisper.

He bit his lip, slowly, then rolled the ring between his fingers like it was stuck. He looked up at Maire quickly, and back down at his feet again.

"Five years," he answered.

Maire grimaced.

"I'm sorry—"

"Does she know?" Maire had found her feet and stood to face him. To her, he now seemed half the height he was when she first met him. She looked up at him but felt she was looking down.

"No," he said. "No, she doesn't know. Yet. I will tell her. I'll have to tell her," he added with a sigh.

Maire remembered what Ailbe used to say about 'all the sighing'. She was right. It was infuriating.

"Oh, you poor sweet thing, yes, you will," Maire snapped.

He looked tragic; his tone was so self-pitying, it exasperated her. What business had he looking so sad now? She felt like the walls of the room were collapsing around her. How could she have been so incredibly stupid – all this damn time? The words were swirling in her brain and making her feel sick. She pictured him in a church. *He has a wife. He has a wife. He had a wedding. He has a wife.*

"What'll happen then? Will she throw you out?" Maire asked, trying not to give away the slightest hint of hope in her voice.

"I don't suppose so," he responded forlornly. "That sort of thing isn't allowed. Especially in our family. Surely you know that, Maire? I—"

"Still, a first baby, it's exciting, isn't it?" she went on. "Perhaps it'll be like you and be a doctor or something. Something useful."

He looked at her and said nothing; he didn't need to. Almost as soon as she heard herself say it, she knew she was wrong. She felt even more stupid now.

"Oh," she said softly, as Fionn's complexion turned greyer. "It's not going to be your first, is it?"

Fionn briefly wondered if he could get away with not telling the truth. And for that matter, if he could get away with not telling Clodagh at all... Ruth was going to tell everyone the baby was hers anyway. Clodagh saw them so rarely. He could lie to Maire again now and say it was his first, that he was so very nervous about the prospect of being a first-time father and didn't have a clue what he was doing. That he couldn't wait to see who the baby looked most like. Except, of course, he wouldn't be the father anyway – so it made little difference, really, whether it resembled him or not.

"No," he said. "I have two. We have two."

We. Maire wanted to bury herself under the covers and

50

pillows on the bed and scream – make him go away. She'd loved this man; he'd loved her. Physically and in every way. Or so she'd thought. So she'd been foolishly led to believe. And here he was – someone else's husband, and father to someone else's children, standing here, sighing and feeling gloomy that he'd have to go to the trouble of telling his wife that he'd been sleeping with a nineteen-year-old all summer. She searched for memories, for clues. What had she missed? Had she really been so blind? Maire had never felt so ashamed. She had felt loved. Now she just felt cheap and filthy, and so incredibly stupid. She thought of her family, the family she had left behind for this.

He'd already paced outside a room, waiting for tiny lungs to screech – and she hadn't known. She, Maire, hadn't known that these three living, breathing people had existed, not just in the gaps of time that Fionn had been back in Dublin between visits when she had missed him so much, but while she was with him too. Those three people didn't know about her either. Her, and the two extra tiny lungs she was growing. He wouldn't be there. Outside the room, waiting for them to screech. He'd never hear it.

"Who was that man, the driver?" Maire asked.

"He's one of the ambulance drivers from my old hospital. He sometimes does… private work."

"Right." Maire sighed heavily and rubbed her eyes. Perhaps she hadn't slept as well as she thought she had. "So," she continued, "you brought me here because…?"

He didn't answer for a while; he had hoped it would be obvious and she would agree with him that this was the best course of action. For all he knew, she was aware what Bessborough was and she'd had time to accept the reality of

51

the situation on the drive up to Dublin. Not to mention that it was terribly kind of him and his family to not put her through all that; to make it happen this way instead. He'd heard the stories of that place. He had colleagues who had tended to some of the victims. Although, of course, he hadn't told her that this was the plan.

"*Because?*"

"I thought that… well, with you on your own…" His mind was spinning. His own thoughts rallied against him. He was making a terrible, terrible mess of this; he flushed with embarrassment. "My Aunt Ruth and Donal, they live next door – they've tried for years, and never been able to have—"

"Give him away?"

The words hung in the air like cobwebs. Fionn didn't like the way those words sounded, although he knew that was true. She called the baby him. She'd only said 'it' before. If only there was a better way to say it, he would.

"You want me to just… give our child *away*," she repeated.

There was a hopelessness in her voice that she'd never felt before, and he felt it too. Fionn just stood there, like a naked mannequin in a shut-up shop window. He felt hollow. Her words: our child. He couldn't explain that he'd have loved a child with her, and a whole life with her after that. He swallowed hard.

"Maire, I don't *want*—"

"You don't want a third baby with a stranger," Maire said, matter-of-factly. "A teenager. That's understandable." She hoped he would feel as ashamed as she did.

"No! No, that's not what I… and you're not—"

"And you've already arranged for parents for our unwanted little bastard, without even asking me. Well, I suppose I should say thank you. *Thank you*."

She waited for him to say something. He looked like he was welling up, furious with her and about to faint all at the same time.

"No, really, thank you, because why would I want to have a child that was half you," she continued.

She regretted it as soon as the words left her lips, but it was too late now. Anger was a sin, but she couldn't help it. She'd never felt like this before; it was like indigestion, but so bad she thought she might die. Her skin was on fire. She'd never been this rude to someone in her whole life. She didn't feel good about it. She noticed that her nails were digging into her palms where she'd clenched her hands so tightly. She hadn't even realised that it hurt.

Fionn had never felt so dreadful. This was going about as badly as he expected, if not worse. His wedding ring suddenly felt too heavy, itchy, like a massive tumour growing uncontrollably on his hand. He had hoped, fervently, that she would understand.

"Maire, I'm so sorry. I did… I did say arrangements had been made. You know we cannot raise this child together—"

"Sure, I know that *now*."

"And you cannot raise… him or her alone."

"Can't I really?" She looked down at his ring. "How come I never… I mean, how come you didn't…" Maire was catching her breath. "Why weren't you wearing your wedding ring before?"

"It was accidental," he said quickly. "I swear. I swear. The first time we met, at the hotel, you remember I was shaving so I'd taken—"

"No, no, the first time we met we were in the post office, and you weren't wearing it then either," Maire said sharply. "I... checked. At the time." She tried to suppress her embarrassment and hoped to God she wasn't blushing. Fionn was, a bit.

"Oh," was all he said. He searched his mind. "Well, I'd had examinations to do in the morning, so I suppose I wasn't wearing it. Then I was shaving so I wasn't wearing it then either."

"And then?" Maire said.

She felt calmer now, but it was the sort of apathy that came with having your soul crushed in a pestle and mortar of disappointment. The waves of realisation had subsided from a tsunami to a gentle crash. It was ridiculous. Her father had never taken his wedding ring off once, from the moment it was placed on his finger. He'd been very proud of it.

Maire sighed, hard. The boat was sinking and she couldn't save it. She was getting a headache.

"And then..." He looked down at the ring and grimaced. He didn't try to hide it. "And then I stopped wearing it because I didn't want you to know. I wanted to be someone else when I was with you. I felt like a totally different... such a happy—"

"Yes, all right, I understand," Maire said. "What is Bessborough, anyway?"

He paused. He'd rehearsed this part. "It's a... home," he said, hesitantly. "For people in her situation. I'm sorry about your friend, but she'll be all right."

"So, it's a convent?"

54

"That's rather an old-fashioned term."

"I would have preferred to stay with Ailbe."

"You wouldn't. I'm sorry. But she really will be all right."

"Well, let's hope so," Maire said darkly, glaring at Fionn with disgust. "How about you just give me a postal address for whatever it is and get out of my room."

The longer he stood immobile and in silence, the more the waves of rage consumed her. He looked tragic, so pathetic, but she – *she* was the tragedy. It wasn't fair. She couldn't understand why he wouldn't just... *go*. Leave. She could hear the blood rushing in her ears and she wanted to cry but not in front of him. He didn't even remember the first time they'd met. The memory of that had sustained Maire for weeks at a time; it was all she'd thought of, all she'd dreamed about. And he'd already forgotten it. She knew the hopelessness of the situation now that there was no wedding. There was nothing else to be done.

For Fionn's part, he'd never been thrown out of a room in his life. He didn't like it at all. But Bridget had told him not to drag it out and he knew he couldn't stay forever – he just wanted a few more seconds with Maire before he left her, presumably, forever. Slowly he reached into his pocket and brought out a piece of paper, neatly folded into a perfect square. He placed it in her now-ridged palm and closed her fingers with his own hand. He wanted to hold on, but she pulled away with a snarl on her face.

"You can try," he said, "but I don't think they pass letters on."

He didn't shut the door behind him when he left.

CHAPTER TEN

After Mass, Ailbe had to go and see the midwife. She was
concerned about this. She'd never seen a doctor or a nurse in
her life, and so had no idea what to expect. It would be
another nun, she assumed, which didn't fill her with
confidence. She didn't want to answer questions about how
she'd become pregnant – she knew it wasn't her fault, no
matter what the priest said. She didn't like priests very much
anyway, and she didn't like this one either. She hadn't
'earned' this suffering, but nevertheless she had expected it –
and so she would bear it, like she always had, and emerge
victorious on the other side. Of that much she was absolutely
certain.

Another girl from her dormitory had shown her the way
to the hospital. It was in a separate building to the main, grim-
looking house where they ate, slept and worked. The hospital
felt cold and she was embarrassed at how her shoes squeaked
on the floor. She heard crying. Babies crying, women crying.
She knocked on a door with a frosted-glass panel. A voice
inside told her to come in.

"Good morning. Ciara, isn't it?" the lady said kindly. She
was like a nun but in a nurse's uniform, with a veil.

Ailbe was relieved. She tried to smile. "That's right."

The midwife glanced at Ailbe's beaten face and said
nothing. Ailbe guessed she wasn't the only one to have ever
arrived here like this. Men are a plague, she thought bitterly.

"Excellent. I am the midwife here. I need to make some
checks, take some notes, and then we can have a quick chat
about what's going to happen while you're here. Try not to

worry."

"I'm not."

The midwife bade her sit on a stool in the middle of the room, and she took Ailbe's date of birth, measured her blood pressure, and gave her a small cup to urinate in. She felt around her growing bump, pressed and measured. She asked Ailbe to stand on the scales.

"Hmm," the midwife said. "You could do with weighing a bit more yourself."

Ailbe wasn't sure she could do much about that. She told the midwife how she'd been getting sick, every day, for hours and hours.

"Do you have any idea when you might be due?" the midwife asked.

Ailbe shook her head. She wasn't sure how long all this was supposed to take. She didn't have any siblings. That... *bastard*, he was her only cousin, and he was eight years older than her. Wasn't it a year or thereabouts? That couldn't be right. That seemed like an outrageously long time to grow such a tiny thing.

"Do you know when you conceived?"

Ailbe looked at the floor. Oh yes, she knew that one.

"July. July the... tenth, I think it was."

"Thank you. That's helpful. You'll be due mid- to early April; that'll be nice. Is the baby's father your boyfriend?"

"No. He's my cousin."

"Ah. Grew up together, did you?"

"Not exactly, no." Ailbe had lied before, about not worrying about anything – she *was* worried, a bit, about one thing in particular. "Nurse..." she said, apprehensively.

"Hmm?"

"Because he's my cousin, and we're related, is there going to be… something wrong with it? The baby?" She tried to hide the wobble in her voice. "Is it going to be blind or deformed or something?"

"Cousins, that's very unlikely, no," the midwife said. "It's more of a problem in… closer relations. Don't worry."

"It'll still be adopted, won't it, even though we were cousins? Are cousins?"

"Yes, your baby will still be adopted. Don't worry yourself, Ciara."

Ailbe was happy with that. The nurse would have been to school a good deal longer than Ailbe had been. She was far cleverer than Ailbe and knew all sorts of things that she didn't know, so she was happy taking her word for it. She was relieved.

"Your blood pressure is a bit high," the midwife said. "We'll keep an eye on that."

"Okay."

"So, it's £100 to be collected ten days after the birth; otherwise, you'll remain until your child is adopted. You'll be assigned work by the Sisters in the convent until four weeks before your due date. Then, you'll be moved here, and sleep on the ward in the hospital, and help out with the babies here. If you don't go after the ten days, you'll go back to the convent, continue to work and visit your child in the nursery. All babies are breastfed for the first year, no exceptions. All right?"

Ailbe felt like she'd been hit by a bus. She tried to process the information she had been given, but it was a lot. The midwife had spoken quickly and in a tone that wasn't really hers, like she was embarrassed by what she had to say. She'd asked if that was 'all right'. Ailbe had not heard anything less all right in all her life. For starters, who on earth had £100 for such a thing? For seconds, she didn't want to have the baby. She didn't want to breastfeed it. She didn't want to visit it in the nursery and get all attached and mammy-ish and speak in a baby voice to it and then be kicked out onto the street, for her trouble, at the end. The midwife had said she would 'remain until the adoption'. And then what? Suppose Maire was, right at this very moment, marrying Fionn in a church somewhere and didn't come back for her after all? What was she supposed to do after that?

"Nurse, am I in prison?" Ailbe asked. The midwife didn't smile but, after all, Ailbe hadn't really meant it as a joke.

"You are free to leave at any time," the midwife said hopelessly. It sounded rehearsed, something she'd said many times. Of course Ailbe was free to leave; they all were. But where on earth could they go?

"Yes. All right," was all Ailbe said.

*

The nun who had met Ailbe the previous night was in charge; that was quite obvious from just a few minutes in Bessborough. The other nuns in the convent went by a name – Sister Niamh, Sister Regine – but she was known simply as 'Sister', as though she were the only one. It was as if giving her a name would humanise her and put her on the same level as the other nuns there, and she would not have put up with that. Sister might just as well have been the only one, thought Ailbe, as she noticed the other nuns cowering away from her almost as much as the girls did. The majority of the work was

59

done by the pregnant girls themselves – the laundry, the kitchens, the cleaning and maintaining the back gardens. They were expected to work all day and knit silently all evening. A couple of the girls worked over in the hospital building, tending to the new mothers, bathing and dressing the babies and taking them over to their mothers to be fed. Ailbe hoped to goodness she wouldn't be given that job.

She was placed in the laundry, washing the sheets and tablecloths and other linens in various states of soiling. It was in another red-brick building, separate from the main house and the hospital. Ailbe was alarmed at the range of bodily fluids that found their way onto sheets during pregnancy and birth.

Even in November, it didn't take long to get overwhelmingly hot in the laundry and some of the girls, in the later stages, often felt woozy. They were not allowed to open the windows, and they were not allowed to talk. Ailbe considered that, if it was this bad in November, the summer would be a hundred times more unbearable – but, actually, she might not still be here. Maire might have come back by then. So, she was relieved to think she might not have to find out.

Ailbe would also discover later that evening, to her chagrin but not completely to her surprise, that she was totally dreadful at knitting.

CHAPTER ELEVEN

Bridget felt more anxious than she could remember feeling in years as she sat with her head against the wall that separated her room from the spare room – Maire's room now; she'd have to get used to that. She remembered when Fionn was born; she'd been twelve years old. He was placed in her awkwardly circled arms after Ruth had held him, and she was informed by John that this was her nephew. She was now an aunt. She had felt terribly grown up and responsible.

And now, that tiny human for whom she had felt so responsible was next door, in her spare room, breaking some poor wee girl's heart. She had never felt like this about her own flesh and blood; it wasn't something they did in their family. Be upset with one another, that is; Mother just wouldn't have it. But this – she shook her head. If there was one thing she couldn't stand... She needed both hands and feet to count all the women she'd known in her life who had been led along by a man who said he wasn't married, or that he was but he'd leave his miserable wife any moment now, only to turn around one fine day and call it all off – then complain to their lovelorn that they were now 'making things uncomfortable'.

Although, Bridget had to admit, it did rather sound like the girl was coping. She was giving him a tremendous haranguing.

When Bridget heard Fionn's heavy footsteps down her stairs and the front door shut gently behind him, the girl started to wail. Bridget admired that she had held on until he was gone – she, herself, had never been one for crying in front of a man. She flew into the room and wrapped the girl up in her arms.

"Don't," Maire sobbed, "don't, I'm—"

"You're mine to look after now, Maire," she said gently, as she squeezed the girl close to her body and rocked her like a baby. "I'm so sorry. I'm sorry. You just... cry. All you want."

Maire wailed and wailed.

Bridget clung on, as Maire soaked her sleeves with tears, until she was finally calm and they sat together at the foot of the bed.

Maire hiccupped. "I loved... I loved—"

"I know," said Bridget, holding both her hands in hers. "We always do, dear. It's a terrible waste of our good health."

Bridget had brought up a tray of tea and homemade scones. She'd tiptoed downstairs early that morning after an unsettled night, listening out for the slightest sound from Maire's room, and busied herself in her kitchen baking this and that. It was the only thing she could think of to do to keep her hands busy, and she thought they might be helpful around this sort of time.

"Eat this," she ordered.

Maire looked pale and stared into space. She shook her head.

"You're in shock, dear, you need to eat," Bridget pressed.

Reluctantly, Maire took the plate and nibbled from one half of a scone nearest to her.

"Have some of that tea too. Good," said Bridget. "That's the way. So," she continued, after taking the other half of scone for herself, "I think we'd better talk all about it."

Maire gave a brief and awkward account of how she and

Fionn had met and what had happened since they met in July, which Bridget nodded along to as though she didn't already know. Maire told her about Ailbe, and how it had happened to her. Bridget crossed herself and said she was very sorry. Then, Maire was happy to listen for a while. Bridget chatted away merrily about her life as a nurse; no, there was no husband, it'll just be us, she told her, and we'll be grand.

Maire was relieved to hear that.

Bridget said that Fionn was a good boy, but a foolish boy – she was not happy with him just now and Maire was free to say what she wanted about it.

Maire laughed slightly through her tears.

Bridget told Maire how her sister Ruth was a glorious woman, and her husband Donal would dote on a child. They'd be marvellous parents; Maire needn't concern herself unduly about that, but it hadn't been easy for them. They'd seen rather more loss than was fair, Bridget said.

Maire was sad about that. It seemed so unfair, for them to long for a child all this time and yet both her and Ailbe were now carrying babies they didn't want.

Well. That they didn't anticipate, at least. Ailbe had said outright that she didn't want hers, under those circumstances especially. But Maire had never said that.

Bridget, sadly for Maire, had never heard of Bessborough either and hadn't had any idea that such a place existed for sure, so she couldn't answer any of Maire's questions about what life was going to be like for Ailbe. She could, however, answer Maire's questions about life here in Dublin, and Maire had a lot of them.

"So, is this my room, for the whole time?"

"Absolutely."

"Are you sure you don't mind me being here?"

"Don't be silly, dear."

"Can I read the books?"

"I had hoped that you would."

"Shouldn't I be getting sick? Ailbe was getting sick."

"Count your blessings on that one, my sweet."

"Are Ruth and Donal nice?"

"You tell me when you meet them tomorrow. Or the day after tomorrow. Or next week. Whenever you're ready."

"Is it going to hurt?"

"Yes, I'm afraid so. A lot, probably. But I'll be with you."

"What's Fionn's wife like?"

Bridget paused. Maire's eyes glassed over, but she stared at Bridget determinedly. Bridget avoided her gaze and looked out the window.

"Are you sure about that one?" she asked gently.

Maire nodded vigorously before she changed her mind.

"All right. Well. She's... very pretty. Beautiful, really. They met at university when Fionn was getting his medical degree; she was working in one of the university offices doing something or other. She took a shine to him and they got married as soon as he'd completed his medical training. Everyone in the family said he should wait because she was the first girl he'd ever really—"

"Yes, but what is she *like*," Maire interrupted. She didn't need the whole tale of romance to add colour to her nightmares. She didn't know what she'd rather hear – that Fionn was in a loveless marriage to a miserable old battle-axe, and had sought comfort in her, Maire's, arms, or that the poor woman was an angel and therefore Maire had a sister in their shared agony of Fionn's wicked betrayal. Surely, it had

64

to be one or the other.

"She's..." Bridget faltered. Her and Ruth had been brought up to never speak ill of people, particularly members of the family, if at all possible. However, she could only imagine what her late mother would have had to say about Mrs Fionn Conghaile, given half a chance. "She was a bit pushy," Bridget conceded at last. "It was she – we think, anyway, Fionn would never actually admit to it – who insisted on moving here with him and, of course, they couldn't move if they weren't married and so..." Bridget tailed off. She wasn't sure what might set the girl off crying again. "She's nice. Very accommodating to the family. Always remembers to send birthday cards and things like that."

"Are they happy?"

"This would indicate not, I suppose."

"And the children?"

"Hmm. Boys, the both of them," Bridget said, patting Maire's hand.

Maire thought about two miniature Fionns, dressed up for their first Holy Communion. Her baby would have brothers – not that it would ever know.

"John and Colm, John was named after my brother John, Fionn's father."

"Is he still alive?"

"Oh yes. His wife, Fionn's mother, isn't though."

Maire nodded with mild interest and stared at the carpet. She realised she'd never actually asked Fionn about his family, though he had asked about hers. She'd told him all about her two younger sisters – they were surprise twins, hence money being rather tight at home – and her mother and

65

father, both schoolteachers. Now she knew he had a living father, a dead mother and at least two aunts. Plus a wife and two children that he'd casually kept to himself.

"Maire..." Bridget was saying.

Maire looked at her; Bridget looked worried.

"You mustn't repeat this, but no one else is going to say this to you, so I want to," she said.

Maire was nervous. "What?"

"You don't... you don't *have* to do this." Bridget peered at Maire who had gone instantly very red. Then she turned away and looked at the floor, then out the window, then at the wall.

"Yeah... I think I do, though," she said defeatedly.

"No, you don't. This is still your baby. There is no... *law* that says you can't keep your baby, even if you are on your own. All of these decisions have been made without you. You don't have to do it just because it's what Fionn wants."

Maire was surprised to hear the bluntness of the words and realised that, actually, she hadn't thought of it like that. Since she'd realised she was pregnant, it had all been about trying to resolve the situation, as though it were a terrible mistake that needed to be undone, rubbed out with an eraser, in some way. Even the hasty marriage she had hoped for was, in the first instance, to cover it up. She'd told Ailbe first, then written to Fionn and told him, who had written back hastily with instructions about the car and where to wait for it. In the face of her despair about Fionn suddenly blowing cold, she'd just been quietly grateful that he'd arranged something, anything, that didn't involve her being homeless in the village, being gossiped about and condemned by everyone who had, up until now, always really liked her. Or, heaven forbid, having a termination and angering God forever. Or, being beaten half to death by her father, like Ailbe had been.

She had fleetingly believed last night that her and Fionn were going to be together, get married and be a family, and that that was why she was here. She'd barely had time to adjust to the idea of that not being the case. The mere idea that she could say 'actually, no, thank you' and maybe persuade her parents to take her back; maybe pretend her baby was her mother's later-in-life surprise child, was a bit more than she could reasonably deal with.

Bridget was now looking worried that Maire might just say she agreed with her after all and hop on the next bus out of Dublin – and break Ruth's heart, all over again.

"I know," Maire said at last. "But... I don't think I can do it on my own. It's not the right time. It's not the right circumstances. He was right. It should be Ruth."

"Are you sure?" Bridget asked. She touched Maire's hand tentatively and, to her surprise, Maire took hold of it firmly and held it.

"No," Maire said, and smiled. "No, but it's the right thing to do. You and I aren't idiots, Bridget."

"We are not." Bridget smiled and then sighed. She looked down at their entwined hands. "So we understand each other. Don't tell Ruth I said that."

Maire nodded. "Never."

"Good. So, how about a nice hot bath?"

*

Later that afternoon Maire sat at the kitchen table with a pen and paper. She had cried in the bath for an hour and Bridget

67

tried to pretend she hadn't heard. She had sat outside the door for a while, feeling a bit like crying herself, wondering whether to go in and try to comfort her. She decided against it. Later, she busied herself peeling vegetables and hummed along to the radio as Maire wrote.

Dear Ailbe,

I don't know if you'll ever see this. I hope you do. I can't imagine how it's going to feel to do all of this without you. I'm so sorry. I obviously didn't realise we were going to be separated.

I'm in Dublin with Fionn's Aunt Bridget. He's married. He's been married the whole time and has two little boys already. If you do get this and are able to write back (I've written the address on the other side), please don't say I told you so. But you can think it. Because you did.

Bridget's sister Ruth has lost five babies before birth and ~~she's having ours~~ *Fionn thought it would be better if Ruth and her husband adopted this one, save me having to bring it up on my own. And then the baby stays in the family, which I suppose is good. She lives next door to this house, where I'm staying with Bridget. I've not actually met them yet, but I will. Bridget's nice. She's a nurse, so I'll be in good hands for 'the duration'. I didn't like it when the man said that; it sounded like we've been sent to prison. Which I suppose we have.*

~~I'm sad.~~ I'm fine and everything. I don't have to do it on my own and, once all this is over, Ruth is going to have her baby that she's always wanted by the sounds of things, and I'm… well, actually, I don't know what I'm going to do yet. I don't suppose I can go home. Good thing there's plenty of bar work here in Dublin.

I really hope you're all right. I pray so much that you're all right. That nun didn't seem very welcoming and so I hope the others are nicer to you. Bridget said your baby should be born in March and mine could be April or May and, when we've done it, I'll get some money together to come and get you. Or you can come and get me. You'll be finished first.

See you soon, Maire.

"Are you writing to your mother?" Bridget enquired gently. Maire shook her head without looking up at her.

"No. To my friend, Ailbe. In the convent."

"Oh." Bridget didn't know what to say about the convent. It was a shame they couldn't both have come; she could have got another bed in that room perhaps. She'd never officially heard of such a place in all her years of nursing, but she had suspicions that they must exist – and if her suspicions were further correct, she imagined they were not going to be pleasant. But she didn't want to tell Maire that. Maire seemed very fond of her friend and she was upset enough as it was.

"I don't think my mother would want to hear from me," Maire said sadly.

Bridget didn't know what to say to that either.

"I left them a note," Maire continued, "to say what I'd done and that I was sorry and that they wouldn't have to see me again. And my month's wages as well."

"Where will they say you are?"

"I don't know." At this moment, she didn't particularly care. Maire didn't say anything else. She folded her letter and put it carefully into an envelope. She reached into her pocket for Fionn's parting gift, flattened it out on the table and began copying the letters onto the front. She'd been correct. They'd gone right towards Cork.

"I'm sure… I'm sure they will miss you very much," Bridget said.

Maire shrugged. It didn't seem to her like anyone missed her really – Fionn didn't seem to have done.

"Sure."

CHAPTER TWELVE

It was Thursday and Bridget was fussing on the landing.

"Are you sure you want to do it today, Maire?" Bridget was asking. She hovered awkwardly in Maire's bedroom doorway as Maire pinned up her masses of curls with pretty clips. "We can leave it, wait a few more days, if you're not ready?"

"Yes," Maire said. "Yes. Today. This morning. Now."

Bridget nodded and slipped quietly downstairs. She picked up the phone in the hallway and dialled Ruth's number. She answered on the first ring.

"I'll bring her over just now," she mumbled.

Ruth made a squeak and hung up the phone.

"Well, you look just lovely," Bridget said enthusiastically, as Maire came down the stairs in the only change of clothes she had brought with her. Bridget had lent her some make-up to cover up the circles and blotchiness from her crying, at Maire's request. She had pinned up her hair and brushed her teeth. It was a shame about her nails but that couldn't be helped now. Her heart was in her throat.

"Let's go then," she croaked.

Ruth's front door was already open when they stepped outside. Bridget checked the street before allowing them to scuttle quickly from one house to the other. Maire tried not to be offended.

Ruth's house was a mirror reverse of Bridget's, attached by a shared wall. Ruth's living room was on the left, where Bridget's was on the right. Both had kitchens at the back and a long hallway. Ruth and Donal stood smartly dressed at the foot of their stairs, looking like they were waiting to greet the *Uachtarán*. The house smelled clean and looked immaculate. Maire's face flushed and her palms started to sweat. Bridget shut the door behind them and anchored herself to Maire's side.

"Maire," she said gently, "this is my sister, Ruth, and her husband, Donal."

They both smiled at her. Maire smiled back. She nodded politely at them. She hoped they wouldn't want to shake hands because hers felt unnaturally clammy. She didn't know what to say. She looked at Bridget for help.

"I'll make tea!" Bridget said enthusiastically and pushed herself between Ruth and Donal to busy herself in their kitchen. Ruth smiled warmly at Maire again.

Maire felt mortified and terribly alone. She was pregnant which meant they knew that she had... and with their nephew... They probably remembered him as a child. She felt disgusting. She didn't want to meet their eyes – but they seemed determined to meet hers.

"Please, come and sit down, be comfortable in here," Ruth said, gesturing towards the living room.

They let Maire in first and followed her. Maire sat where Fionn had sat, a little over a month ago. Ruth and Donal sat where they had been sitting that day too.

"Maire is an unusual name," Ruth said. "Very pretty."

"I... I suppose it is. Thanks."

"Did you sleep okay?"

Maire had not; she'd slept dreadfully, in fits and starts. "Very well, thank you." She looked at Donal, who was still yet to speak to her.

Ruth looked at him too. He coughed.

"You have… beautiful hair," he said, nodding to himself. "I hope the baby has that much red hair." He smiled innocently at Ruth who was shaking her head at him in disbelief.

Maire stifled a snigger. She quite liked them already. "I'm sorry," she interjected. She wanted to apologise for getting pregnant when she hadn't wanted to. She wanted to say she was sorry for doing so easily what they had tried for so long to do, and had failed, time after time. "About your children. Bridget told me. It's just… really awful. I am sorry."

Ruth and Donal were quiet. They held hands.

"Thank you," said Donal, on behalf of them both, "for calling them our children."

The clock on the mantelpiece ticked.

"Your house is nice," Maire said.

Bridget bustled in now with a teapot, a tray of cups and a plate of biscuits.

"Thank you. We've been very happy here for a long time."

"Are you all… is your family rich?" Maire asked tentatively. She'd been wondering about this for a couple of days. Their houses seemed so big and full of things. There was so many of them in the family – and it sounded like at least three of them had been to university, no questions asked. They both had phones in their hallways. Maire's family hadn't had a phone at all – they had one in the village that everyone used, near the post office.

"What makes you say that?" Ruth asked. She looked amused.

Maire gestured at the ceiling and the walls, for want of better words to explain.

"Our mother left me my house," Bridget explained. "They were a bit older and had long paid it off. And Donal's father left him this house. He is an only child."

"An only child?" Maire asked. "That's a shame," she said, thinking of her little sisters at home and how cute and jolly they were.

The room was silent. Ruth was looking forlornly at Maire's belly.

"Oh," she said, "I'm sorry. I didn't mean... I bet it's grand being an only child. The baby will have... all your attention. That'll be... just grand."

"You all right?" Bridget mouthed at Maire. She nodded. Bridget nestled in next to her on the sofa.

Bridget was better at fuelling conversation than they were without her. They talked about how Ruth and Donal had met as neighbours when they were children, how long they'd been married, how long they had tried to have a family. They told her about their other siblings and all their children, the whole network of aunts and uncles and cousins and brothers and sisters that made up the Conghaile family. Maire talked about her work in the bar and her mother and father, and her twin sisters, although she was sure they wouldn't be very interested in all that. Donal talked enthusiastically, and at length, about his flooring shop. He'd left the Saturday boy to run things this morning. Ruth told Donal not to be so boring. It made Maire laugh.

Ruth and Donal said they were sorry for her trouble. She said she was sorry for theirs.

"We're dreadfully upset with Fionn, just now," Ruth reassured Maire.

Maire didn't say anything.

"You deserve better, dear, and you'll get it one day," Bridget added.

Ruth looked uncomfortable. They were never supposed to speak ill of the family; Mother had always said so. Ruth didn't like to do it. Bridget was less concerned.

"I hope you'll be very happy," Maire said. She didn't want to look too sad and have them feel bad for her. She didn't want Ruth and Donal to think she resented them – and, after all, it was Fionn who had thought of this for them. "As a family."

Donal bowed his head as if in reverence to what she had said. Ruth started to sniffle slightly. Donal took Ruth's hand and Bridget took Maire's and gave it a squeeze.

"Thank you, Maire."

CHAPTER THIRTEEN

Ailbe was tired, but then, so was everyone else. The girls were all awakened every morning with a deafening bell that was hung on a rope in the main hall downstairs, mere minutes – it certainly seemed that way to Ailbe – after she had finally drifted off to sleep. Milly was still crying every night. Ailbe had managed to find out after a couple of weeks that she was only fourteen; she had a sixteen-year-old boyfriend in Waterford, whom she had loved desperately. He didn't know she was pregnant or where she had disappeared to. Milly had asked Ailbe in a quiet, terrified voice if she knew which part of her body the baby was going to come out of. It was much the same story for most of the girls that Ailbe had spoken to – even though, of course, they weren't supposed to speak. None of them really realised that what they were doing was going to lead to a baby. But, thought Ailbe, how could they? If they were never told, they would never know.

Still, breakfast was something to look forward to; it was actually more of a portion than she used to get at home and that wasn't always guaranteed. There was also tea – ready brewed with milk in, in a gigantic pot. They scooped it out with cups like witches from a cauldron. She couldn't remember a time when she could rely on breakfast being available when she woke up. She liked to express her gratitude, where gratitude was warranted.

Breakfast aside, however, what she really hated was getting up for Mass, which was compulsory at eight o'clock every single morning regardless of how little sleep they might have had or how cripplingly pregnant they might be.

They filed in in silence, like the criminals they were told they were, and the priest gave lengthy sermons about sin and redemption and their 'earned suffering'. Some of the girls cried every morning – silent, shoulder-shaking sobs – all the way through the service. Ailbe loathed it, every single moment – and, if that wasn't enough, they all then had to say the rosary together in the day room each evening, after a few tedious hours of knitting. Not only did Ailbe not have a rosary, she also couldn't remember any of the words. She'd been struck by a nun round the head and given a 'spare' rosary left behind by another girl.

Ailbe had worked out, on observation, that some of the girls were like her and some of them really were not. She felt most sorry for those ones. No one – except Maire, naively – had ever expected Ailbe to amount to anything. This was exactly what the world had expected of her and, God save her, she hadn't let them down there. But the others, the nice girls from good families who went to good Catholic schools with the striped socks and satchel bags – she could see the looks in their faces. This wasn't what was supposed to happen to them. Their parents were disgusted and disappointed and embarrassed, and they wouldn't see them. Some of the richer girls got phone calls, but not many. They would be the ones disappearing after ten days and leaving their children to be reared by those left behind – not that she begrudged them that. And, of course, some of them weren't girls at all; some were grown women in their twenties – one was thirty next week. But they were all treated like they were twelve years old under Bessborough's roof, as though they were infected with a sickening leprosy and were in the best place to keep them hidden away – for which they were

77

expected to be damned grateful.

Ailbe was washing the floors today. She wolfed down her soda bread and margarine with gusto. The others picked at theirs and turned their noses up at it before gingerly picking away at the corners with reluctance. Ailbe didn't mind floor duty as she could do it by herself and no one would really speak to her. The huge house had acres of floor to cover, and it would take all day, which was another day ticked off in her book. By the time she stopped, it would be time to eat again and, if she was lucky, she'd be just tired enough to crash out tonight and sleep through. It also gave her time to think about Maire and where on earth she might be.

Ailbe had considered during her long first nights here that there were two realistic possibilities as to Maire's location. She hadn't come here, and there'd be no sense separating them if she was going to go to a 'facility' exactly like this one – if there even was another one. So, either Maire had been right, the doctor person – Fionn, or whatever – was taking her to Dublin to have her baby with him, and they were going to get married before she showed too much and have a whole fleet more kids afterwards. Or, more likely, Ailbe had been right and Maire's baby wasn't going to be Maire's baby for very long. She was probably being sent to England while she still had time to get the procedure done. She knew Maire would be writing letters. She just didn't know exactly where they were.

That dinner time, Ailbe sat with Vida. Vida was a few years older than Ailbe and had long dark hair like her. They were in different dormitories but worked in the laundry together. What she had just said made Ailbe's skin prickle.

"You…" She didn't know what to say. "You've been here

before?"

Vida nodded as she sucked margarine off her knife. She didn't look too down about it.

"Ah yeah, must be eight or nine years ago now, that I came the first time," she said. "Believe me, it's better here now."

It had never occurred to Ailbe that a person would get into the same situation twice. She actually hadn't considered that the home would take the same girl twice, but then, if Bessborough was given money for each body that crossed the threshold, perhaps they didn't really care whose body it was, and whether it'd been there before. Perhaps they were duty-bound by the cross they all wore to take everyone who knocked on the door; Ailbe wasn't sure.

"What do you mean, it's better now?"

"Oh, well, we had this uniform," Vida went on. "That was hideous. Really emphasised this whole prisoner-of-war thing they have going here. Punishments were far worse. I once had to stand in that corner for six hours one day." She gestured towards the other side of the room.

"While this pregnant?" Ailbe said, bewildered. "What did you do?"

"Hoh. More pregnant than this. I cried because my heartburn was really bad," Vida said. "My fault really, shouldn't have been making a fuss. They don't like that; it scares the others. Mass was longer then as well. And we had to stay for three years and work and raise the wains, before they sold them off. You should have seen the state of the girls on that day."

Ailbe didn't know what to say. Three years of being here... it made her blood run cold. That was truly a prison sentence. Although they mostly had to be here, because being anywhere else wasn't really an option, the midwife had told her and any new arrivals since that they were 'free to leave at any time'. Vida said they *had* to stay. Three years of your life, gone, just like that, scrubbing the floors in here.

Ailbe couldn't imagine feeling any love for her cousin's baby that was currently encroaching on her person, but she also couldn't comprehend spending three years with a child – three years of being its mother – and not feeling *some* sort of pain when it was taken away, after all that. How could anyone? And for the ones that had loved their boyfriends, and then loved their babies... Ailbe couldn't imagine. It made her sad but relieved that she couldn't imagine.

"Anyway, like I said, it's better now," Vida was saying. "The day before you arrived a girl was picked up by her mother three days after having the thing. I guess they paid through the nose for that, but still."

Ailbe had pieced together that outside money had value here. She didn't talk a lot but she did listen. Some money got you an occasional phone call – even though the girls were told there wasn't a phone. Some more got you pain relief when you needed it the most. A good deal more meant you had a few days' bed rest and then someone who could bear to look at you came to collect you at the end. There were very, very few visitors, only under the most exceptional of circumstances. Only a few of the girls seemed to get letters in the post and all of the post was opened by Sister beforehand. Ailbe hadn't yet heard of an amount to be paid to allow them to keep, and leave with, their babies.

"So, how come you... how come you're...?"

"Pregnant again?" Vida finished, sensing Ailbe's

discomfort at her own curiosity.

Ailbe nodded.

"Well, they sent me home, didn't they," Vida said, with an air of defeat that wasn't usually her way. "Sent me back to the same old man and what do they exp—"

"That's enough!" bellowed Sister, in her deep and croaky voice.

They hadn't realised Sister had come in. Ailbe jumped. Vida didn't flinch but simply rolled her eyes.

"You've both got work to do, now *get on with it.*" She sprayed spittle at the girls as she spoke, and marched away, slamming the dining room door behind her.

Ailbe eased herself quickly to her feet.

"It's always us," Vida hissed, catching Ailbe's arm before she tried to leave. She was clinging on, and it hurt. "It's always us. All these babies have fathers. All these babies have some bastard da somewhere. With any luck mine will be dead when I'm out this time. But it's never them, Ciara. It's always going to be us. Remember that."

CHAPTER FOURTEEN

"Bridget!" Maire was shouting, as soon as she heard the key in the front door. "Bridget! Bridget!"

Maire was perched awkwardly on the sofa with her hands pressed tightly against her tiny bump. She looked pale and panicked. Bridget rushed in still wearing her coat and shoes, and still clutching her keys.

"What? What's wrong?"

"It's the baby," Maire said, and she started to cry. "I think-I think—"

"Take a deep breath, Maire," Bridget said. "What's—?"

"I think something is wrong with the baby," Maire whimpered. "I can feel all these strange feelings and I just don't think it's right." She sniffed and rubbed her belly.

Bridget paused and set her keys down on the table.

"What sort of feelings?" she asked.

"Well, it's like… a sort of… fluttering. It feels all kind of fuzzy and strange. Do you think it's something wrong with its heart? Have I given the baby a heart attack? How could I do that?"

Bridget placed her hand next to Maire's and tried not to laugh. She felt the slightest movement under her fingers and Maire started to exclaim again.

"That! It's that! What's wrong?"

Bridget smiled. "Maire, the baby is kicking."

"Kicking what?"

"Kicking you!"

Maire looked down. Something that had feet and legs was moving around inside her. She'd done that. She'd grown those feet and legs all by herself.

"Oh."

Bridget started to laugh.

Maire looked at her and started to cry and then laugh as well. She tried to haul herself up.

"What are you doing?" Bridget said, as Maire made for the hallway.

"Phoning Ruth!" Maire said, eyes sparkling, as she dialled the number.

*

That evening, Maire was reading one of the many books Bridget had recommended, on the sofa in the living room. Bridget was plucking at her harp. Maire loved the sound; she'd never heard a harp played before, not in real life. Brannigan's had bands all the time – people playing fiddles and banjos and bodhrans, the occasional flute and concertina. Her father had played the violin, poorly, but the sound always quite amused her. She loved the harp; she decided that now. It was glorious.

"That was lovely," she said, when Bridget finished a piece. "What was that?"

"Oh, nothing really," Bridget said. "Just something I made up when I was at school."

"You wrote that?" Maire said incredulously. "It was beautiful!"

"Oh no, it's only a little thing," Bridget insisted. "Here, would you like to try?"

Maire jumped up immediately; she'd always wanted to learn an instrument. Bridget stood up from her stool and had

Maire sit on it. She explained how the thickness of the strings would affect the sound. Maire wanted to just run her hands up and down all the strings at once, hear the rising and falling scales, and marvel at the sounds she made without knowing how she was doing it.

"You should practise while you can," Bridget said. "In a few months you won't be able to reach half the strings!"

Maire looked down. She had just started to show in the last couple of weeks. Ruth was beside herself with excitement. Maire, less so.

"Bridget, have you ever been with a man?" Maire asked. Bridget didn't look as surprised as Maire thought she would. She knew it was a nosy question but, after all, Maire was going to have to give birth in this house, to Bridget's nephew's baby, no less. They should get comfortable, sooner rather than later.

"No," she said simply. "No, I'm not very interested in all that."

Maire had considered that, by virtue of the fact that Bridget was unmarried, she wouldn't have been with anyone – but that was no guarantee of anything. As she knew well.

"Didn't you want to get married?" Maire pressed.

"No," Bridget said again, assuredly, but quite happily. "No, I like my house; I like my things; I like my space. Marriage is for people like Ruth. I might have enjoyed the whole... mothering thing, perhaps. But I think I'm a bit old for that now."

"Isn't Ruth older than you?"

"Yes."

The conversation ended there. Bridget smiled, an authoritative smile that let Maire know this particular topic of conversation was now at an end. Maire hoped she hadn't offended her; she liked Bridget an awful lot.

Maire looked around the room. Above the television set was a wall plaque that read: 'In the world you will have tribulation. But take heart; I have overcome the world.' Maire knew that scripture, she thought – she'd heard it before.

"I like that," Maire said simply.

Bridget looked at where Maire was looking and nodded. "Yes, John 16:33, it's my favourite," she replied. She often looked at it when... well. When she had tribulation. No wonder Maire had been drawn to it as well.

"Shall we say our rosary together?" Maire said brightly.

Bridget nodded. "That would be lovely. I'll pop upstairs and get them," she said, and disappeared upstairs to their bedrooms.

CHAPTER FIFTEEN

Ailbe was walking back to work from her usual morning of terrible sickness when she saw Vida, Camille and some of the other girls starting to form a huddle at the foot of the stairs. They were peering around the corner, towards the far end of the hallway that led to the front door, and speaking quickly in terrified whispers.

"What's happening?" Ailbe asked. All their faces were glum.

"It's Sandra's turn," Vida whispered.

Ailbe didn't know who Sandra was. "Turn for what?" Ailbe asked.

Camille shushed her.

From the convent's back door that led to where the hospital and nursery was, a young woman of about nineteen emerged from the outside, carrying a baby girl of around a year old. Ailbe surmised that this must be Sandra. She had bright blonde hair, which her child appeared to have inherited, although Sandra's hair hadn't been washed for a while. Sandra was absolutely sobbing her heart out.

Slowly Sandra walked the full length of the corridor, carrying her child. With every heave of her shoulders the child bounced slightly, and assumed it was a game. Sandra's daughter had been dressed in a knitted cardigan that looked quite new and had a pink bow in her hair. She was babbling and grabbing fistfuls of her mother's hair in her tiny hands. At the front door was Sister, and a well-dressed couple.

Sandra's sobs got louder as she reached the front door at the end. Sister prised the baby out of Sandra's arms as soon as she was within reach and held her out to her new parents at arm's length, facing it away from her own body, as though the baby were filthy.

"Mama," the baby said, reaching her arms back to Sandra. "Mama!"

Sandra was despairing. She couldn't speak. The woman of the couple took the baby from Sister, who tried immediately to wriggle free from the woman's arms. She had to pin the baby tightly to her chest to stop her trying to escape. They both looked down their noses at Sandra with judgemental sneers. The man crossed himself and shook his head at her. The baby had started to cry now too.

"Thank you, Sister," the man said, and he encouraged his wife to turn away and exit the building.

"T-T-Thérèse!" sobbed Sandra. "No, Thérèse! I'm not ready. I'm not… I'm not… I'm not ready…"

The couple walked down the steps and towards their car without looking back. Sister shut the door quickly before Sandra could attempt to follow them.

Sandra continued to wail, leaning against the wall for support. "No, my Thérèse, no!"

"Oh, they're not sticking with the 'Thérèse'," said Sister smugly. "Stop crying. You knew this day was coming. You should have prepared yourself. You had plenty of time to 'get ready'."

Ailbe couldn't believe what she was seeing.

Some of the girls had started to shrink away, weeping softly; a few had memories of having done it themselves before. Most lived in fear of having to do it with their own children, someday soon.

Ailbe gaped at Vida in disgust. Vida just nodded.

"Oh, Ciara, come with me quick; she's going to go," Vida said quickly.

"Go where?" Ailbe asked but she was already sprinting to the door alongside Vida as she spoke. They each caught an arm of Sandra as she went down, hard, onto the concrete floor.

Sister made no effort to help Sandra; instead, she simply barked at them about not running inside. Not that they were particularly encouraged to run anywhere. Vida glared at Sister with a seething hatred as Sister walked away, shouting at the rest of the girls she found hiding in the doorway to stop gawping and get back to work.

Supporting Sandra as best as they could, Vida and Ailbe struggled to their feet and carried her between themselves to her bed, upstairs in the dormitory. She cried and screamed for her child the entire way. They passed other nuns on the way, who avoided their gaze and didn't acknowledge Sandra at all. Sandra had been back sleeping in the convent since Thérèse was born, two beds down from Vida in the room one over from Ailbe's.

Outside they heard car tyres scraping away on the gravel; Sandra must have heard it too. They laid her down as gently as they could manage on her bed; Sandra pulled up a corner of the blanket and sobbed into it. Mercifully, there was only one window in the dormitory and it didn't face the front. Sandra screeched and wailed inconsolably. She made sounds Ailbe had never heard before, from human or animal.

"I can't believe they made her do that," Ailbe muttered.

Vida was silent.

"Did you have to do that?"

"Of course," Vida said. She swallowed hard. "Most of us

will, eventually. That's why you want to get collected as soon as possible after. It was harder after three years instead of just the one... last time... They pretty much walk themselves out at that stage." Vida touched her belly.

Ailbe had never seen Vida be emotional before and she wasn't sure what to do. Vida was a soldier. Ailbe depended on that; seeing Vida like this sent shivers of discontent right into her soul.

"Worst day of my life," Vida muttered.

"Amputation without anaesthetic," Ailbe said gloomily.

"Exactly."

They watched over Sandra for a few more minutes and then went to get more sheets from the laundry. She had cried so much that she'd made herself sick.

*

That evening, another new girl arrived. She was dropped off by her mother, who kissed her unhappily and then turned away and walked up the long drive away from the house without looking back. The girl was small, blonde and introduced herself cautiously as 'Emmaline...?' as though it were a question. She had a bright face and a bonny countenance; she could have been fourteen or forty; no one was sure. She joined the other girls in the dayroom after tea for the knitting, at which she was already extraordinarily proficient.

Emmaline was given the same spiel they had all received about not talking to anyone about anything from her past – no mention of where they were from, under what circumstances they had come to be here, any details of the paternity and especially not their real names. Emmaline appeared to have forgotten all this the second she got her boisterous feet under the table.

"I'm from Wexford," she said, settling down on a small chair opposite Vida and Ailbe.

They looked at her and said nothing.

"I'm five months gone already. My mother kept me at home because my daddy was away, but he's coming back soon and we don't want to upset him. I'm getting married after this, so I am; he's in the army," she said proudly. She was wearing an engagement ring with a tiny solitaire diamond. "Where are yous from?"

Ailbe put down her knitting, not that she was making any progress with it. "We're not," she said slowly, looking over her shoulder for Sister. "You know, we're not really supposed to talk."

Emmaline just smiled. "Oh, I know, but I think that's a bit daft really," she said brightly.

Vida smirked at the mere thought of one of them decreeing Sister and her rules to be daft. Not that she didn't agree.

"We're all going through the same thing, aren't we? We should all try to be friends. You're doing that wrong, by the way. Did you know? You've dropped a stitch."

Ailbe raised her eyes to heaven, put down her knitting and sighed audibly. It wasn't the same thing. Her and Vida were here under vastly different circumstances to Emmaline. Emmaline, who appeared to believe she was on holiday here. Emmaline, who had a mother willing to not only keep her for five months in her condition, but to bring her here and kiss her goodbye. And she had a fiancé who did not appear to have abandoned her. Sandra was upstairs; she hadn't eaten or even stopped crying yet. Ailbe wondered if Emmaline even knew that she was going to have to leave here without her baby? She wasn't acting like it.

CHAPTER SIXTEEN

Ruth and Donal were equally covered in flecks of grey paint. Their second bedroom – the equivalent to the one Maire was sleeping in in Bridget's house – had been Donal's childhood bedroom and then their first marital room. When Mr Quinn had died, they waited over a year before moving out his things, buying a new bed and changing the wallpaper.

Ruth had wanted to paint the nursery a light grey and she had bought yellow curtains and a yellow lampshade to brighten it up. She had asked Donal to make stencils, which he had, painstakingly drawing and cutting in the evenings after work, for hours on end.

The baby wasn't due for another five months but Ruth had insisted they start the preparations now; Donal thought it was a bit soon but, of course, he hadn't dared say that. The crib they'd bought three weeks ago was still in the enormous cardboard box it had arrived in, waiting to be assembled. Donal flicked paint at Ruth from across the room and she laughed.

"When do you think we should tell them?" he asked, gliding his paintbrush up the wooden doorframe. Ruth wanted those grey as well.

"Tell who what?" asked Ruth, taping her stencil to the wall.

"Tell the baby they're adopted. I think we should tell them, don't you?"

Ruth felt her blood run cold as he said it. That wasn't at all what she had been thinking. She was prepared to guard this secret with her life. This child was a miracle baby, born to them in middle age after a series of tragic losses because the Lord had at last blessed their family when they were truly ready. Ruth hadn't even realised she was pregnant, had hardly looked pregnant; it was just one of those... miracles. She had the story all worked out.

"No," she said, desperately. "*No!*"

Donal stopped what he was doing immediately. He didn't like to upset Ruth, not at all. He hadn't meant to. He dropped his brush down onto the dustsheet on the floor and embraced her quickly.

"Okay," he said, "okay, I'm sorry—"

"No, not *ever*," she cried. "Never, because the baby will leave us, Donal, it'll leave us! And go and find its *real* mother and we'll be childless all over again!"

Donal was sure that wasn't true, but he wasn't going to be the one to contradict her again. He'd clearly upset her enough as it was. Ruth had felt so alone all these years, he knew. She had no other friends except Bridget. As all her schoolfriends had grown up, married, and produced broods of bright, noisy children, she'd pulled away from them and refused to keep in touch because she couldn't bear to watch. It had been hard for her; he understood that.

"Okay," he said again. "Okay, we won't tell. We'll tell Bridget and John that they're not to say anything and it'll be... just our little secret, okay?"

"Okay, she sniffed, squeezing her hands around his back. "Okay."

"All right then," he said, wiping a tear off her cheek with his thumb. "I'll make the tea." He scurried off downstairs to the kitchen.

Ruth followed slowly down the stairs and reached for the

phone in the hallway. She dialled Bridget's number.

"Bridget," she said in a low voice. "We're never going to tell the baby that it's adopted."

"All right," was all Bridget said.

"You mustn't ever tell anyone," Ruth implored again.

"All right," Bridget said again.

"You have to tell Maire that's what we're doing. You know her better. It'll be better coming from you."

There was a brief silence.

"*All right*," Bridget said, as though through gritted teeth, and she hung up the phone.

*

Maire hadn't been surprised that Ruth didn't want to tell the baby where it had come from. Since finding out who Fionn really was – what he really had, all along, and what he'd arranged – she had assumed that the baby had already stopped being hers.

Bridget was relieved – she desperately hated to see Maire upset – but she was also sad that Maire had taken such a dim view of the situation so early. But what point was there, Maire had said, to cling on to false hope?

"He's not marrying me. We're not a family," she had said.

When Bridget and Ruth had their first private conversation about their separate roles in Fionn's dilemma, they had agreed, very strongly, on one particular thing: Maire was one of them now. No matter what she'd done or how it had happened so Bridget was greatly saddened to hear her words.

"Look at them," Maire had continued, gesturing towards

the shared wall to Ruth's living room. "They're meant to be a family. It isn't fair what they've been through."

Bridget didn't think it was fair what Maire had been through either, but she didn't want to say that. Maire had been in a very despondent mood lately, about the pregnancy, about everything.

Maire had never thought about the baby making contact with her later in life. She found it so hard to imagine the baby as anything other than... well, a baby. She didn't have to worry about teething and toddlers and school places. All she'd thought about was being pregnant, hiding the fact that she was pregnant, and then giving birth to the child that wasn't really hers and handing it over to Ruth – who would be thrilled. There was no more to it than that. She couldn't really imagine what she was going to do half an hour after the birth, let alone twenty years from now.

Maire and Bridget were sitting in Bridget's living room, in separate chairs. Maire had just announced that, when the baby was born, she thought it would be best if she didn't hold or really see the baby at all. Bridget was taken aback.

"But it's... it's—"

"No, it isn't," Maire said. She was reading a book and she didn't look up from it. She didn't want to argue with Bridget about it. There was obviously a feeling growing in Bridget that she, Ruth and Maire were all going to raise the baby between them, like a little coven of benevolent witches, and they'd all be equal mammies together. Maire knew that wasn't going to be the case. She would have to leave eventually. It was time Bridget accepted it too. "I don't want to hold the baby," she said firmly. "What's the point? Ruth should hold the baby; it's Ruth's baby."

"You might feel differently when it's born, Maire," Bridget said.

Maire shook her head. "No."

Maire considered whether she actually *did* want to hold the baby, and see the baby, and kiss its tiny forehead and stroke its fine, downy hair; she was just fighting against it now because she knew that would make it harder in the long run. Getting attached would be the worst thing she could possibly do. This was Fionn's child. Her child that she'd made with Fionn. She'd spent a long time since last November trying to stop herself from loving him; it was much, much harder than she had ever realised and, at this point, she wouldn't say she had been successful, either. The baby, her baby, was a whole level above that. She couldn't see it. She wouldn't see it.

"Would it be all right if I went to confession?" Maire asked. She desperately wanted to go outside and go to church. They said the rosary together every night and Maire really loved it, but she'd been to Mass every week her entire life and she missed it desperately. She'd been reading Bridget's missals but it wasn't the same. She had so much to confess, after all. She had to go. "Please?"

Bridget bit her lip and didn't say anything. Ruth had decided to tell Father Kelly that she was pregnant and on bed rest on doctor's orders; therefore, she couldn't come to Mass herself. He was even dropping round communion for her and sitting at her bedside, praying over her to protect her from the dangers of geriatric motherhood. Bridget cringed every time she saw him tootle good-naturedly up the drive. Bridget had stopped attending Mass in solidarity with Maire, and they prayed at home. She didn't suppose Ruth had told Father

Kelly about *that*.

"Maire, you know we can't really have people see you," Bridget said. "I'm so sorry. But you can talk to me. Is there anything you'd like to talk about?"

Bridget had such a kind face; she had been so gentle and sweet to Maire since the night she'd arrived. Maire knew Bridget would do anything for her – except this. Anything except let her out.

"Sorry, yes, I know; that's all right," Maire said. She forced a smile for Bridget and Bridget smiled kindly back.

"Shall we have a tea?" Bridget asked, as she always did.

Maire nodded. Bridget scurried off to the kitchen and Maire went back to her book.

CHAPTER SEVENTEEN

Not even twenty-four hours after arriving, Emmaline had succeeded in becoming the most actively avoided person in Bessborough, save for Sister herself. Despite fierce shooshing from Sister Regine twice during their nightly knitting the day before, Emmaline had chatted to anyone who would listen throughout the evening, had said the rosary in twice as loud a voice as anyone else and continued to gossip about her life and brag about the good looks of her handsome soldier fiancé all the way up the stairs to the dormitories. Mercifully for Ailbe, and the despondent Sandra next door, Emmaline was lodged elsewhere.

They could still hear her the following morning as the girls all sleepily dressed for Mass and started making their way downstairs. It was as though she was actively offended by silence. Ailbe adored silence – it was the only way she had ever known she was safe. If her house was quiet, it meant she was alone, and she would hopefully see the evening out. It was when there were voices, evidence of other people, that she knew she was in trouble. Emmaline was stealing the silence that brought Ailbe her only peace, and Ailbe was greatly perturbed.

Emmaline's chirpy voice punctuated the yawns and drowsy mutters all the way to the chapel.

"Goodness, you look tired. Are you tired? I slept like a log, so I did. It was a long journey from Wexford yesterday; travelling is tiring. Don't you think travelling is so tiring? Even though you just sit there doing nothing. It's funny, isn't it?"

Nothing was funny at Bessborough, thought Ailbe, as she – for the first time ever – wished desperately for Sister's presence to force Emmaline to be silent.

"I'm seeing the nurse after Mass, so that's exciting, isn't it?"

Emmaline always seemed to be asking questions, which made things difficult for the other girls, who knew they weren't supposed to answer her. Emmaline did at least quieten down for the filing into the chapel, which commanded a certain reverie about it that even Emmaline couldn't ignore. Ailbe still heard her whisper 'wow, look at the size of that crucifix' as they got down on their sore knees to pray. Ailbe still loathed Mass every bit as much as she had always done, but at least this morning she was grateful for the forced silence of it all. Be thankful for ye small mercies; she thought she'd heard that somewhere before.

It was so predictable that it was almost laughable, thought Ailbe – and Vida as well – when Sister stopped Ailbe leaving the chapel and told her to escort Emmaline down to the hospital to visit the midwife.

"And then take her to the laundry with you afterwards; she's going to be working in there." Sister raised her eyebrows smugly at Ailbe before she swept away down the corridor and out of the building.

Ailbe groaned once she was out of sight and almost immediately Emmaline was at her side, asking her what the nurse was going to be like. Vida was trying her hardest not to laugh as Ailbe stomped off to the hospital with Emmaline in tow, who was wittering on about the service being far longer than it was at home, and the bruises on her knees she was probably going to have tomorrow, and they did rather seem to hammer home the 'earned suffering' thing here but we were all God's children, after all, and we'll all be forgiven for our transgressions eventually...

*

Ailbe leaned against the wall outside the nurse's office to wait for Emmaline. She'd palmed her off to the nurse for a bit, so she was her problem now for half an hour or so. Ailbe could still hear the rise and fall of Emmaline's muffled voice through the brickwork, and the tiny efforts of the midwife to get a word in. Ailbe didn't like coming here. It smelled like disinfectant and all she could hear was babies – crying babies, cooing babies, laughing babies. And the occasional moaning mother-to-be in labour with little to no help or company.

Ailbe wasn't concerned so much about the birth – Vida had explained the mechanics of it and she was satisfied with that – but having to live here in the hospital and keep visiting the baby and breastfeeding. Oh God, now she really didn't feel up to doing that. It just seemed unnecessary if the babies were all going to be taken away anyway. What was the point? She didn't like the idea of it at all, it was a bit... close, for her liking. Vida said it had been hell for her, the first time – and if Vida said something was hell, it really, really was. She didn't say that sort of thing lightly.

From the midwife's examination room, there was silence. Ailbe thought that was remarkably strange. Perhaps Emmaline had fainted at the sight of her own blood being taken in the tubes or something like that; some of the girls hadn't liked that at all, although Ailbe wasn't bothered. The door opened and a pale, dishevelled and much quieter version of Emmaline appeared in the doorway. She hovered there and didn't come out into the corridor, hanging on to the doorframe like she was treading dangerous waters and afraid to drown. She looked Ailbe dead in the eyes with a thousand-yard stare, like she knew she was there, and also didn't, at the same time.

"Did you know...?" she asked, as though she had just seen a ghost. "Did you know they take our babies away?"

Ailbe said nothing but reached out her hand and led her quietly to the Sister's office to use the telephone they were always told wasn't there.

*

"How could she not have known?" Vida asked in a whisper, folding her sheet. She felt sorry for poor Emmaline now. Emmaline had genuinely thought she was coming to a rest home for pregnant women, to have her baby under God's glorious watch until her fiancé picked her up for their wedding; this must be a crushing disappointment for her, to say the very least. She was one of those rare ones that had been absolutely thrilled to be pregnant.

Ailbe shrugged and carried on pinning up the wet sheet she'd just cleaned; she was struggling to get the blood out of it. "I don't know. I suppose her mother didn't tell her?" Ailbe said. "Thought it would be easier if someone here told her instead?" She didn't know what people were told before they came here; Ailbe, of course, hadn't been told anything. "She's probably on the phone to her mother just now, giving her hell."

That would be an unpleasant call, for both of them, Vida and Ailbe agreed. Of course, it was possible her mother didn't know either and she'd taken the advice of some well-meaning family priest, by sending Emmaline here. Perhaps she was expecting her magical grandchild to appear this summer, just in time for her to be the mother of the bride, and now her heart was broken too.

That was not the case, as Vida and Ailbe found out that evening when they sullenly took up their knitting. Emmaline was already there, sitting alone in an armchair, knitting furiously from a dark purple wool. Her eyes weren't focused but the irises ran back and forward, left and right, as though she were reading a book with immense speed. She had the face they'd mostly all had at some point – the face of a person who had been crying hysterically for many hours. She wasn't wearing her engagement ring anymore.

"Emmaline," Ailbe whispered. "Emmaline, are you all right?" She knew it was a pointless question, but they'd all been quite unkind to her and she'd had a terribly rough twenty-four hours after all.

Emmaline didn't look up from her invisible book and her furious knitting. "We're not supposed to talk," she snapped bitterly, and didn't say anything else.

CHAPTER EIGHTEEN

The Conghailes had a Christmas tradition. As there was so many of them, they took it in turns in family groups to hire a large hall somewhere near to where they lived on the first weekend of December, and they had an enormous Christmas party for the family. Everyone brought food and drink and presents for the children; if there wasn't already a tree somewhere in the room, someone would bring one and decorate it, just for that night. They found stations playing Christmas songs on the radio and they danced happily together. Then, all the family units largely kept to themselves on Christmas Day and St Stephen's Day to eat and drink themselves silly and exchange presents.

Over the years Ruth, Donal and Bridget had been to Baldoyle, Sandyford, as far down as Dunlavin for Fionn's youngest brother, and up to Donegal on a couple of occasions for John, as well as having hired out the church hall themselves when it was their turn. Ruth, Donal and Bridget counted themselves as a single family unit. Of course, no one had ever made the journey to Belfast to see Dermot and his family, and it was only Bridget who ever invited him down – they never came – and Liam had stopped coming too once he'd emigrated. This year it was only a short hop over to a function room in Rathmines, given that numbers were dwindling these days, but none of the three of them would be in attendance.

Ruth thought about what had happened in this year's summer. She had written to John to say she'd lost another one, the last one; could he tell everyone for her, she had asked, so she wouldn't have to answer lots of questions at Christmas? Now, Christmas was here, and she was expecting. She was expecting every bit as much as Maire was – and because Maire was showing, it meant the family couldn't see Ruth. She'd written again, once Maire had arrived, to the entire family to tell them all that she was pregnant and expecting a baby in the spring. John knew the truth, but no one else.

Maire was melancholy as Christmas approached. She'd never spent Christmas without her family before; not one Christmas morning had ever passed in which she had not woken up in her own bed, with her sisters in bunk beds beside her, and their handmade stockings stuffed with sweets and little hand soaps and other knick-knacks their mother had found. Daddy cooked Christmas dinner; he always had done, and it was always delicious. They sang carols in the living room by candlelight and sometimes Granda had come up from Cork to stay the week. Mammy would have knitted them all jumpers. Maire was unhappy, deeply unhappy, but she didn't want to let Bridget know that.

She'd been with Bridget now for seven weeks, give or take. The first week or so had been awkward but they'd settled down into a routine together and, on the whole, Maire was happy with her situation. She hadn't been sent for an abortion; that hadn't even been mentioned. Bridget clearly knew a lot about pregnancy and childbirth and brought home stacks of books for Maire to read so she'd feel prepared. Bridget had sorted Maire out some clothes, as she only had one change. Maire tidied up and hoovered the carpets, tinkered with Bridget's harp and read a lot of books. It was... nice. But she had hoped, on her long journey here, to be married to Fionn by now, pulling a wool jumper over her growing bump and decorating a Christmas tree in his little doctor's house, both together. Every event was the death of another hope; she prayed that, soon, she'd run out of big events that had tied unpleasantly to her dreams.

Not that decorating Bridget's tree wasn't fun; it was. Bridget had been drinking sherry and was bright red in the face, telling Maire every story of every bauble in immense detail. Bridget was laughing. The radio was playing Christmas carols. Bridget had promised Maire they would have their own Midnight Mass together at home. Ruth and Donal were coming to Bridget's house – their house – for Christmas Day and, despite herself, Maire was quite looking forward to it. Bridget had managed to wangle Christmas off from the hospital for the first time in more than fifteen years, and she was determined to make the most of it.

When Maire awoke on Christmas morning, she could smell cooking and baking from the kitchen already. It was the same as at home and it made her feel slightly happier; all that was missing was the merry sounds of her sisters' voices. She went downstairs in her nightgown and found that an extra present had made its way under the tree since she'd been to bed the night before. There was a tag in Bridget's lovely handwriting that said, 'Dearest Maire'.

"Oh, Maire, morning, Merry Christmas!" Bridget called out as she walked into the kitchen.

Much to Maire's surprise, Bridget embraced her warmly and kissed her cheek. Maire realised that she hadn't been kissed in a long time. Perhaps this Christmas would be a nice one after all. She poured herself tea from the pot and looked on as Bridget checked things and stirred things and peered through the glass of her sparkling clean oven door. She was drinking orange juice out of a wine glass – at least, Maire assumed it was orange juice.

"Ruth and Donal will be here soon. Get dressed, or Donal will be all blushes."

By the time Maire had dressed and had run a comb through her curls, they had arrived, carrying a plate of freshly made hot bacon sandwiches for breakfast. They munched away and laughed together, and Bridget eventually ushered them all out of her kitchen to stop them taking up all the space. Maire listened joyfully to stories of Ruth's and Donal's childhood Christmases, sometimes shared, as it was just Donal and his father over the fence and Mariah only had the girls, and sometimes Dermot, at home.

*

That evening, Maire was marvelling at how full she felt, and Bridget was laughing at her.

"Seriously, Bridget," she said labouredly, "this belly is only really… twenty percent baby." Maire was warm by the gas fire, full of Bridget's delicious cooking, still chuckling at family stories of Dermot's Christmas Eve drunkenness and awful, last-minute gifts. She was happy, far happier than she had ever expected to be. She admired her little bump affectionately. Although she wouldn't be there to see it, the growing baby was going to have a lifetime of the most marvellous Christmases. It gave her comfort.

"Oh, Maire, you didn't open your present," Bridget said, crawling on her knees under the tree and retrieving it. "It's not quite as big as Ruth and Donal's I'm afraid, but hopefully you'll like it."

It was true; Ruth and Donal had surprised Maire immensely by buying her a gift for Christmas too: her very own suitcase to put all her new clothes in for when she left so that she didn't have to leave them behind. They'd also put a copy of *Cathleen Ní Houlihan* in there for her, in case she finished all of Bridget's books. She'd been just delighted.

Bridget gave Maire a small box wrapped up in tissue paper, secured with a neat gold ribbon tied into a bow. Maire hardly wanted to open it; it looked so beautifully done. Inside was an antique-looking box, which, when she opened it, glinted at her.

"It was my mother's," Bridget explained, as Maire examined the gold coin-shaped item on a rough gold chain. It had a small cross at the top, a hand either side, and a dove emerging, pointing downwards.

Maire had never seen anything like it before. When she turned it over, it was engraved with a large letter 'M' in elaborate calligraphy.

"Mariah?"

"That's right," said Bridget. "It was her confirmation medal. It's been blessed."

Maire frowned and stayed quiet. She didn't know what to say. It seemed exceptionally precious – a family heirloom, no less. What was she, little old Maire, to do with this?

"It's... lovely," Maire said. "But don't you want to keep it? If it was your mother's?"

"Not especially. She left behind stacks of jewellery, but this... I thought... I just thought you might like to keep it to remember us by," Bridget said sadly. "I know you've not been here long, but what you're going through, what's happened to you… and they bought you a blasted *suitcase* to send you on your merry way—"

"I like my suitcase," said Maire. She did. She hadn't thought of it like that. Surely they hadn't either? To her it seemed like something innocent that would have been Donal's idea. Anyway, none of this had happened *to* her – she'd jumped in bed with a man when she knew she shouldn't. Most of the time Maire felt chronically as though she had no right to be here at all.

"I just… don't want you to forget us," Bridget said. "You're one of us. You mean the world to us. To me. Of course, if you *want* to forget us, put all this behind you, we completely understand—"

"No," Maire said. "I mean, yes, I want to put it behind me someday; it is what it is, Bridget." She sighed. She'd stopped crying about Fionn at night now, although she still felt sad whenever she thought about him. "You're the only reason I'm not in a hospital in London, having terrible things done to my insides. You're the only reason I'm not with that awful nun at Bessborough. I'll never forget what you've done for me."

Maire was sad that Ruth and Bridget hadn't liked their mother very much. They'd never actually said it, but she had picked up little things. There were no photos of her in the house, and Bridget had photos of *everyone*. She was rarely mentioned and, when she was, Maire noticed Ruth in particular start to twitch and look sad. Maire loved her mother. She was a simple woman, a kind one but very strict with the girls. She wanted to 'keep them right', as she always said. More than that, she was very involved with the church. Maire had assumed that, despite her mother's enduring

108

kindness, her failure to keep Maire right would have broken her heart. She missed her mother terribly.

Bridget felt awful. She was meant to just be making the girl comfortable and keeping her safe for Ruth's sake, and now she was all but ready to adopt her. She was going to make it worse for all of them; she knew that, but she couldn't help it. She wanted to keep Maire in the house with her forever. She was such a dear girl and the world had been unkind to her. Bridget's own nephew had been abominably cruel to her. The people outside their house were scathingly hideous to girls in her situation. She knew that even Ruth found the whole situation very uncomfortable – but she was getting a baby out of it, so she said nothing. Bridget had just wanted to help because that's what she always did.

"Are you sure you like it?" Bridget asked tentatively.

"Yes," Maire said, nodding enthusiastically. "Yes, it's perfect. I'm going to put it on right now."

Bridget helped her.

CHAPTER NINETEEN

Ailbe was rather sick of bread and margarine. She'd had it every single morning for the best part of four months. In fact, she was getting rather sick of everything. Three more girls had done the dreaded walk to the door with their children in the last two weeks. You could hear the sobbing and crying in every corner of the convent on those days, and she'd just about had enough of it. Emmaline had cried so noisily at the whole affair that she'd been given the standing-in-the-corner-until-teatime punishment that Vida had rather thought was defunct now. Emmaline had cried exponentially at that as well and had her punishment extended by an hour for her trouble.

Three more pregnant girls had arrived quite recently and would eventually succumb to the same inevitable fate. There were whispers around the dormitories this morning that one of the babies had died after a four-day labour; apparently, he was secretly buried somewhere in the grounds last night. Bessborough's residents had little to no opportunity for contact between the hospital and convent once mothers were transferred there, so they weren't sure yet which one of their own had been the mother.

Ailbe was not praying – she didn't believe in that – but hoping, hoping earnestly and desperately that Maire would come for her before her child was adopted, so she wouldn't have to do the walk herself. Not that she was going to love the thing, none of that. She just didn't want everyone to watch while she did it. Although the sight of it was horrific, the girls couldn't help but watch. Helen's was almost as bad as

Sandra's; with no family to go to, Helen had no choice but to stay and rear her son Dylan for the best part of three years. She'd held his little hand all through the walk to the door and, as Vida had said, he'd basically walked himself out. Excited by visitors he didn't recognise, the little boy had loosened his hand from his mother's grip and run, innocently, straight into their arms. Sister had shut the door and ordered Helen away before she could say goodbye. Helen's grief had been beyond tears.

"He... he let go of my hand," she had stammered, pale and withered, frozen to the spot. "He let go of my hand!"

For their part, the nuns were afraid that if they didn't seem to be treating the girls as though they had done wrong, which they had, and punishing them accordingly, they themselves would be punished, too – in this world, and the next. Just as the girls had no choice, neither did the convent congregation, it seemed. But Helen's grieving was so awful, some of the nuns seemed to be moved from their usual hardness when observing her despondency. Not Sister, though – she'd simply asked Helen if the ten minutes of a man's pleasure had been worth it and sauntered off.

On the days when it had been Maisie's and Deirdre's turns to do it, Ailbe had hidden herself in the day room out of respect; but there was no escaping the sound of the mothers' desolate wailing, wherever Ailbe was. This new rumour about the dead baby had also disturbed Ailbe greatly; she didn't think babies died from being born anymore. She'd thought that was something that happened a long time ago, before nurses and doctors were trained properly and knew things. The shock of hearing about that in this very building had stopped her in her tracks.

111

She asked Vida if any of the mothers had ever died here.

"Where do you think your 'spare' rosary came from?" Vida responded bitterly.

*

Christmas came and went without mention; they only knew Christmas had even occurred at all because one of the new girls mentioned that the last time she'd seen her boyfriend was Christmas Eve. She'd hoped to surprise him with the news, and then they could get married quickly, but she hadn't heard from him since. Ailbe thought it was strange that an institution so dedicated to (obsessed with, really) the Christian principles would just completely ignore something as important as Christmas but then she didn't understand much of what went on. She just put up with it, like everyone else.

Every day was largely the same in Bessborough and so Ailbe grew to observe Sister's daily patterns with interest. They were, as to be expected, meticulously regimented. She left her office in the morning to attend Mass; then she came to the dining room to glare at them all over breakfast, and then she went and spent her mornings over in the hospital, bullying the young midwife and sneering at all the new babies. The rest of the nuns passed their mornings either at prayer or tending the front gardens. She could do it; she felt quite confident of that.

When Sister had left the dining room, Ailbe followed her out silently and listened for the closing door that meant she had left the building. She watched her through the glass panel in the door, striding away down the path with purpose. She didn't look like she was coming back for some time.

Post arrived for Bessborough once a week. There wasn't always loads of it but Ailbe had noticed Sister, or sometimes somebody else, meet the postman and put the bundle of post in the office. Sister Regine went into town once a week and sometimes took parcels and letters with her. It had been her who met the postman this morning. Somewhere in the office was the incoming mail for the convent.

Ailbe checked the deserted hallway for onlookers and slipped silently in through the office door. She'd never seen the inside before as the door was always closed, but it wasn't locked, which was a possibility she hadn't planned for. That was lucky. There was a large mahogany desk and bookshelves lined with huge ledgers. She knew they contained all the records of the women and children that had been here before her, because her own details had been taken from her and written down by a grumpy slightly younger nun in glasses on her first day. The ledgers were huge in size and vast in number. It made Ailbe feel unwell. There was a wastepaper bin, which was empty, a small window, and a huge crucifix on the wall. As with most places within Bessborough, it was silent.

Ailbe searched every shelf and every drawer and was starting to feel defeated. She hated all the religious paraphernalia about the place: a Mother Mary here, a crucifix there. How dare that woman act like she was *literally* holier than thou with all her meaningless junk, yet refuse antibiotics and doctors' referrals needed by the poor girls who were bleeding and weeping and oozing over in the hospital, just out of spite.

Ailbe was all but ready to give up when she noticed a

sewn bag, like those the girls were often instructed to take down to the bins; it was hidden down the side of the desk, squashed between that and the bookcase. She pulled it out and rummaged in it – inside were dozens of handwritten letters addressed to the girls. Some of the names she recognised. Like, for instance, her own. She and the other girls had been walking their own letters down to the bins for months without knowing.

Some of the girls received letters – generally the ones who came from the better families, the ones that could afford to be taken away sooner after birth, and the ones whose babies wouldn't be marched out to Irish strangers but were instead taken to Shannon airport and sold to second-generation Catholic Irish-American families across the sea. Vida had told Ailbe all about it. Sister opened all their letters first and passed them on if she found them suitable; Ailbe had long wondered what happened to the ones that Sister read but didn't like.

She pulled them out one by one and dropped the ones addressed to her – Maire had rather sensibly written 'Ciara' on the front envelope instead of Ailbe – at her feet. Her heart quickened and adrenaline flooded her body; she had letters, a dozen at least, from Maire. She found one addressed to Milly and took that out too; it was only small and fitted in Ailbe's pocket. She hadn't actually thought of how she was going to smuggle all of these letters up to her dormitory, but she decided to worry about that when she'd finished and had counted how many there were. She had always known it. She knew Maire would have written her letters and that wicked woman was hoarding them somewhere. She was just grateful they hadn't been put in the bin immediately.

114

"What do you imagine you're doing, Ciara?" Sister said coolly.

Ailbe jumped out of her skin. Sister was truly the stealthiest woman in the world. She stood in the doorway, towering and taking up all the space of the doorframe. They locked eyes and Ailbe didn't move or speak. It was really no good in making excuses; it was obvious what she had been doing. And frankly, Ailbe thought, why shouldn't she do it? This was theft. Not her crime – Sister's. This was Sister's theft of their own property.

"How…? How could you?" Ailbe seethed. "How could you do this to us? How could you *do this to us*?" Ailbe had witnessed so much in four months. She had seen daily, unimaginable cruelty that the girls were all told they deserved. Their earned suffering. Sister's comrades handed their children over to strangers while their unmedicated bodies refused to heal. She wasn't frightened of Sister. This betrayal of their humanity was a step too far for Ailbe and she wasn't going to stand for it – for herself, or for any of them.

"Ciara, I am going to ask you to keep your voice down and to pass those to me," Sister said coldly, as she shut the door behind her with her foot. She barked and shouted frequently but, when she whispered, the others found it terrifying.

Ailbe stooped down and handed fourteen letters with her name written on the front in Maire's delicate handwriting to Sister, who dropped them all into the empty waste paper bin. She took up a wooden box that was on the desk and, without breaking eye contact with Ailbe, lit a match from the box. She dropped the lit match into the bin. Ailbe said nothing.

She made no sound. She didn't want to give Sister the satisfaction.

Sister picked up her dreaded rod from the desk. Maire's whereabouts, her stories, her reality that Ailbe knew nothing of blackened and furled and smoked before Ailbe's eyes. Sister beckoned Ailbe near her.

"You... *girl*," she hissed, "are headed for some terrible, terrible things."

CHAPTER TWENTY

"If it's a girl, I know just what I want to call her," Maire said, smiling to herself as she dried a cereal bowl.

Bridget had to wash and Maire had to dry because her bump was now so big, she couldn't reach the taps. Her belly had popped out like a bowling ball since Christmas and she joked constantly about it being twins. Bridget dropped her dish into the sink; it slopped soapy water over the edges and dripped onto her feet. Maire had seemed in a better mood lately; her hormones seemed to have levelled out and she was back to feeling excited about every kick and every hiccup of the baby. But Bridget hadn't expected this, not at all.

"You've been thinking of names?" she asked tentatively.

"Yes! I promise it's a good one. Very Catholic. I think." Maire giggled and blinked at Bridget, who had stopped singing along to the radio. She looked uncomfortable. She twitched her apron.

"Oh. Um… Maire…?"

"What?"

"Well, the thing is…" Bridget began, and looked down at the floor.

Maire stared at her; she didn't like it when Bridget was like this.

"The thing is Ruth and Donal will be wanting to name the baby, won't they." She spoke quickly, then glanced up at Maire, who wasn't smiling anymore. "It's just, they're going to be the baby's parents. So they'll probably want to give the baby its name themselves."

Maire stood silently. Bridget opened her mouth and

117

closed it again. The radio crackled on.

"Oh," said Maire at last. She felt a flood of embarrassment. "Of course. I'm sorry." She avoided Bridget's eyes and folded up the tea towel gently, placing it on the side.

"Don't be upset dear, please—"

"I'm not upset!" Maire barked. She looked at Bridget and softened her face. She forced a smile. "I'm not upset," she repeated. "I just didn't think of it like that. Of course, you're right. I'm sorry." She smoothed and patted the damp tea towel she'd folded. "I think I need the toilet again. This baby…" she huffed, forcing a smile for Bridget and waddling out of the room as fast as she could.

She locked the door and sat on the edge of the bath, her heart racing. She couldn't decide if her overriding emotion right now was anger, sadness or embarrassment. Of course Ruth and Donal would want to name their own child. They probably had a whole list written out in a drawer somewhere, for every time they'd… Well, anyway. It was their baby. She was just the soil, growing the roots. It was they who would have the flower. She was upset it hadn't occurred to her previously, when she was busy telling herself over and over again that it wasn't her baby anyway; now she felt tired.

She didn't want Bridget to think she was upset with her; it wasn't her fault after all. It was just so… disappointing. Pregnancy and the entire situation with Fionn had turned out to be one grave disappointment after another. But this was what she was brought here for, why she had the privilege of Bridget's cooking every day and her own bedroom and all the books she could read in a lifetime. It was her job to grow the healthy baby that they'd tell everyone was theirs. Once

Maire was gone.

The phone was ringing. Bridget answered it on the first ring which told Maire that she was standing right next to it, at the bottom of the stairs, probably staring up at the locked bathroom door waiting for Maire to come out. Well, she was going to stay here for a bit longer, Maire decided. She did need to pee after all.

Then she heard Bridget scream.

As she hauled herself down the stairs as fast as she reasonably could at her size, Maire saw Bridget standing perfectly still on the spot, holding the telephone receiver limply by her side. There was a high-pitched voice barely audible at the other end, still speaking. Bridget was completely white and her mouth was wide open.

"Bridget, what's—?"

"It's Dermot," she said, barely above a whisper. "My brother Dermot. He's dead."

CHAPTER TWENTY-ONE

Ailbe was lying on her bed. She'd arrived with a black eye so she thought she might as well leave with one. Sister had done her best; Ailbe had taken her beating in silence while she was forced to watch Maire's letters burn. Ailbe had been beaten before and, actually, this wasn't one of the worst – but it was still, admittedly, quite bad.

Downstairs, someone was doing the walk. Ailbe wondered who it was today. They weren't normally collected this late in the day; after about three o'clock, all the mothers with babies in the nurseries breathed a little easier that today wasn't their day. They were never given any warning, of course. The screams and wails of a mother giving up her flesh and blood were all the same, whoever's mouth they came from; she couldn't work out which one of them it might be, and whether it was someone she knew. The child was crying as well as the mother this time – that always made it worse. Ailbe wondered how the new parents could sleep at night knowing they'd prised a screaming child out of the arms of its mother – a child that clearly didn't want to leave her. She wouldn't find out who had lost theirs today until she saw one of the other girls, and they wouldn't be up for a while yet. She shut her eyes and wished she could shut her ears too. The terror and ordeal of it all was so debilitatingly awful.

She thought she might have dislocated her shoulder; she definitely had bruising around her face and somewhere on her head was a wound that was refusing to stop bleeding. She thought of the poor girls in the laundry that would have a nightmare of a time trying to wash the blood out of her sheets tomorrow – ugh, she felt terrible. Sister hadn't hit her near her bump; presumably, someone had already put their order in for it. She couldn't be damaging the stock. Sister had caned her across her back, lots of times, so much so that Ailbe was still peeing blood. As the last of the letters turned to ash, she'd had one last hit across the back of the head for good measure that had made her see spots. Then, of course, she'd had to walk herself up the stairs to her bed. She was given the afternoon off work.

The main take away from it was that Maire had been writing. And she was still writing – one of those letters could only have arrived this week. The postmarks were Irish, not English; Maire was for sure still in Ireland. So, somewhere out there, Maire was alive and well. That was all she had wanted to know. Maire must have married that doctor after all, Ailbe surmised. She wasn't here and she hadn't been sent to England for the procedure, so he must have married her. Thank goodness for that.

The fact that Maire had kept on writing without a response from Ailbe, evidently for months now, meant that she wasn't angry with her; she didn't feel like Ailbe had abandoned her. Perhaps Fionn – was that the doctor's name? It'd been so long now, she couldn't remember – perhaps Fionn had told her what this place was and that she shouldn't expect replies. Maire was still thinking about her. Maire had not forsaken her. She was content with that. Nothing else, not the bruises or the bleeding or the humming pain, mattered at all.

It was evening now and getting dark; the sound of tired footsteps started to bustle in the distance. Vida had swapped with another girl to be in Ailbe's dormitory so she could keep an eye on her towards the end of her pregnancy. She burst through the door first.

"You fecking lunatic," Vida said, sitting at Ailbe's feet and surveying the damage.

"Hello to you as well," Ailbe replied.

"Ciara! Oh goodness, we heard what you did!" cried Collette. She was a second offender, like Vida, and therefore got more of Sister's wrath than most for her troubles. Collette had been slapped a couple of times, but nothing quite as severe as this. "What on earth were you thinking?"

The other girls wandered in in droves and generally chit-chatted, quietly of course, about the state of Ailbe. Finally, Milly dithered into the room.

"Milly," Ailbe whispered.

Milly waddled her very pregnant self to Ailbe's bedside. "Oh, Ciara," she said morosely, "you look awful."

"Thanks a million," Ailbe said. "Look, I've left you something under your pillow," she said. "Don't tell anyone."

Milly beamed at her. Ailbe tried to smile, but it hurt.

CHAPTER TWENTY-TWO

Donal fussed in the kitchen making the tea and made up a plate of biscuits that no one ate. Ruth and Bridget sat together, holding hands and quietly weeping. They rocked back and forth together as one, trying to comfort each other with muffled words that Maire couldn't decipher, and clutching a rosary between them. Maire hadn't asked any questions yet, and she daren't. Bridget had only fleetingly mentioned Dermot a couple of times before – the youngest of her and Ruth's three older brothers. 'The one that lived in "the North"'. She couldn't reconcile the grief she was seeing with someone who was mentioned so rarely. She just stared at them; it felt like her stomach was made of lead and her heart would beat right out of her chest from the sheer panic of it all. Her racing heart was making the baby leap and kick. *Not now,* she willed.

She'd only known one death before; her grandfather in Cork, who they visited every summer. Her father had taken the phone call, then sent Maire and her sisters upstairs to their room. They huddled together on the landing, not daring to breathe, as they heard their father speak in soft tones to their mother. They'd heard her scream and then wail. She'd wailed for days, and then gone to bed for a week and a half.

What little Maire knew about the North she'd learned about in school, and occasionally the family's grainy old radio had crackled stories about bombings and shootings and lists of the dead. Her father didn't like to talk about it, said it wasn't their problem anyway, and her mother had always just shrugged and said it was too complicated for her to

123

understand, let alone explain to Maire and her sisters. One Christmas – about five years ago, she thought – she'd crept downstairs for a glass of water and heard an argument between her father and his brother that seemed to be something to do with it; there had been bombings in Dublin earlier that year, near to where her uncle lived. Her father had said it wasn't their war and they had no business getting involved. Her uncle said if there was any risk at all of his wife and children getting blown up then that made it their problem. Something smashed and Maire ran back upstairs to bed. That side of the family didn't come for Easter the following year and, in fact, now she thought about it, they hadn't visited since.

It had never occurred to her that deaths in the North would affect people in the south. She wished her parents – her school, *anyone* – had educated her more about what went on there.

John phoned and Donal spoke to him on the telephone in the hallway so Maire was able to piece together a few more facts. The funerals would be held in Belfast so the children could attend. Dermot's wife, Leanne, had been in the pub with him and had been shot as well – along with six others. All their funerals were going to take place one after the other at the same Protestant church. Leanne's parents lived in Derry and were going to take all four of the children for the time being.

"More out of the frying pan and into the fire," said Donal, and scurried off back to the kitchen again.

Maire struggled out of the armchair and followed him.

"Ah, Maire," Donal said when he saw Maire enter and close the door gently behind her. "I'm so sorry about all this."

"No, I'm so sorry," said Maire, hovering awkwardly by the door. She'd only been in this kitchen once before. "Did, um…" She gazed around the walls for inspiration. "How did this happen?"

Donal scratched his chin. He gestured to Maire to sit down and pulled out the chair for her, holding her arm gently as she eased herself down. He opened and closed his mouth several times before he began to speak.

"It was Dermot and Leanne's wedding anniversary tomorrow, so they were out for lunch, I suppose." He didn't say anything else for a while.

Maire chewed her finger.

"It was getting tough for them up there. Dermot was interned few years back and nearly… then. He kept saying he wasn't a Catholic anymore, but they wouldn't believe him."

Maire didn't know what that meant and she didn't like to ask.

"It's not going to be… um… easy to make the arrangements," he said quietly, glancing towards the wall that the kitchen shared with the living room. "Dermot met Leanne in a Belfast nightclub; he was up there tiling a bathroom. Did the man a favour, being from the south and all. Leanne is, y'know, from the other lot," he said awkwardly.

Maire nodded.

"Mariah went mad. Refused to go to the wedding. He stayed up there with her and they had the four children. The British thought he was Catholic. The IRA thought he wasn't. I don't know what he was, apart from somehow everybody's enemy. You can't be shot by the IRA and then have a Catholic funeral. They probably didn't even realise he wasn't a… well, you know."

Maire thought she did know, but she didn't really like to say. She had moved her hands to her bump without even realising it, as she thought about the children. Orphaned one Sunday lunchtime, just like that. Now they had to leave their school and all their friends, and the home they'd shared with their parents. No more Christmas mornings with them, as a family. Maire missed her mother. God, she missed her mother.

"And Derry is—"

"Just as bad I think."

"Will you all go to their funerals?" Maire asked. "The three of you?"

"No," Donal said, without hesitation. "It's not safe. My Ruthie isn't going anywhere near that place. Anyway, we're going to the Aran Islands in a couple of days for our holiday. That'll be just what she needs, to take her mind off all this business."

*

That evening, after Bridget had sat at her harp and played 'Just a Closer Walk with Thee' and nothing else for the best part of three hours, she called out to Maire.

Maire had been playing Patience at the kitchen table, wondering at what point it would be reasonable or just plain disrespectful to leave Bridget to her grief, and to go to bed.

"In that cupboard," she said hoarsely, gesturing limply as Maire took out the only item in said cupboard – a dusty, boxed leather photo album. "These people will be your baby's family," Bridget croaked.

Maire stiffened at the words. *Not my baby.*

My baby.

The photos were mostly black and white but there were a few in colour. Bridget pointed out her parents, Seamus and Mariah, with two smartly dressed schoolboys and a scruffy boy with ice cream all over his face who she said was Dermot. One of Dermot holding Ruth as a baby and another of Dermot holding Bridget as a baby. And a tall, handsome man who, apart from a vastly bushy moustache, looked so much like Fionn he needed no introduction from Bridget at all.

"This is them," she said, taking the photo out of its sleeve and handing it to Maire.

It was that scruffy boy, except, now, no ice cream, but a suit. He had clearly grown taller but his face had hardly changed at all, and the girl in the wedding dress next to him looked like a teenager.

"She was young," Bridget said, as she noticed Maire's eyes hover over the bride. "Leanne was. Out celebrating her eighteenth birthday when he met her. She was nineteen and he was thirty-five when they got married; her parents weren't happy at all."

"She's beautiful," Maire said.

"Was. Yes, she was," Bridget muttered darkly. "Same age as me actually. He sent me the photo when I was at university; no one else has one."

"Why just you?" Maire asked.

"Because I was the only one," Bridget said, taking the photo back off Maire, "that didn't mind." She put it back into its sleeve and smoothed it over. "Ruth doesn't even know I've got this. Everyone else was a bit... disappointed. Old-fashioned, you know." She stared at the photo some more and then briskly turned the page and coughed. "Oh, this is Liam."

"The one that lives in America?"

"Philadelphia, yes."

CHAPTER TWENTY-THREE

The wind on the Aran Islands felt catastrophic. Donal, and only Donal, would think to come here in February when the weather was at its most appalling. The landscape stretched out, it seemed to Ruth, to the curves of the globe and beyond. Everything was a shade of green. The rocks stuck out precariously over the cliffs and peered curiously at the ocean below. She could see why ancient explorers thought that Ireland was the very edge of the world.

Ruth liked Inishmore. It was the site of the remains of the Seven Churches they'd visited on their honeymoon. They had decided to return with the camera, now they had one. Her and Donal, plus their five babies – they all had a church each, when she thought about it.

Donal rushed after another couple to ask them to take a photograph and Ruth breathed in the ocean air, wondering what it would feel like to be the last woman on earth. She was briefly alone here, just for a moment, and she thought about how, once the baby came, she'd never really be alone again. But that was what she had wanted, always – a baby, a family, and to never be alone. She looked up at the vastness of the sky, barely visible between bushels of thick clouds. She wondered if Dermot was there. She glanced out to sea and thought of her brother Liam, far away in America, and how this was the closest she'd been to him in five years or more. She wished that he would write to her, instead of just to Bridget.

Ruth had always hoped that heaven was real. Not just for herself, but for the ones she'd lost. A nun she'd met once at church had told her that her lost children were growing up in heaven with Jesus, and that was the greatest gift that could be given to them – although she was, of course, very sorry for Ruth's trouble. Ruth had thought about this for a few days, feeling better for a little while, but then, when she lost the fourth and fifth babies, she no longer felt it was helpful.

She went to confession and Mass like everyone else; it was a non-negotiable and there was no room in her mind, or her heart, not to believe. But she felt unjustly punished. She went to confession to explain how angry she was with God for taking away her father and her children. Human transgressions were easier – there was scripture for that. 'Father, forgive them, for they know not what they do.' But God knew what he was doing. God always knew what he was doing. Ruth just didn't understand *why* God was doing what he was doing. She did not understand why her three brothers had managed to have seventeen children between them and she'd had to tearfully go into the church and ask Father Kelly, twice, to cancel the baptisms she had so optimistically booked. She was lying to him now about her pregnancy. She tried to feel bad about it, but she couldn't. She hadn't booked the baptism yet and Father Kelly had simply nodded and said he understood. He would clear the church's calendar for them when they were ready.

So, yes, she was angry with God. He'd taken her brother and sister-in-law now too. He wouldn't give her a child but had taken both parents from four children. So many parents had been taken from so many children; so many children had been taken from so many parents – and not just here. All over the world. The world supposedly in the palm of God's hand. None of it was fair. She didn't know what to do or say or

130

think when she sat in the pews and recited the words she'd said every week for the whole of her life. She believed. But she wasn't happy. She wanted to praise and thank God for the coming baby – Fionn and Maire's baby. If only she could believe that something wouldn't go spectacularly wrong with that too and she'd end up alone once more.

Donal returned with a pair of German backpackers who were struggling to keep hold of their bags in the wind. Their faces were pinched red, but they were smiling and laughing with Donal. Donal wasn't normally friendly with strangers like that. Ruth laughed too.

Donal handed over his camera, pointed out the right buttons and then rushed to Ruth's side. The German was marvelling at the size of the camera. Behind them the ocean stretched on for miles, angry waves crashed against the cliffs, and the sun peeked through the rushing clouds. Donal put his arm around Ruth's shoulders. The man with the camera shouted ', "*Lächeln!*' and they did.

CHAPTER TWENTY-FOUR

Bridget was in a tizz. She couldn't bear to miss the funeral, but she didn't want to leave Maire alone. Ruth and Donal had gone off on their holidays to the Aran Islands and, if anything happened to her, Fionn was the only other person who knew where Maire was – and Clodagh by now also, as far as Bridget knew. If anything went wrong, Maire would rather die than call them – Bridget already knew that. Bridget, being the only one to have maintained proper contact with Dermot after his marriage, hadn't deigned to tell Ruth she was even going.

"If anything happens, if the baby comes and I'm not here, you must ring for an ambulance," Bridget insisted, writing down the phone number for the maternity ward at Bridget's hospital, plus taxi companies and everything she could think of.

"Bridget, you told me I wasn't due until the very end of April," Maire said.

"I know, but—"

"It's *February*, Bridget."

Maire acquiesced to being checked and measured three times a day for three days before Bridget finally caught the bus to Connelly Station to get the train to Belfast. She had some loose change to phone Maire from the payphone at Belfast train station, and she would phone her again when she was getting the train back if Maire was still awake by then; she wasn't to wait up for her. Maire had all but pushed her out the door and made her go.

Bridget hadn't been to a funeral in a long time. She had

been told, in passing, that a ninety-two-year-old great aunt had made her a tiny black crepe dress for her father's funeral, when she was four months old. There had been her mother's, of course, when she was still at university. She'd been given a special dispensation to delay one of her exams so she could travel home from Galway for it. That one wasn't terribly well attended; the family had come out of respect to the five children, but Mariah hadn't been widely well liked. Bridget had been invited to a couple of patients' funerals over the years as well when she'd nursed a particular person over a long period of time and got quite close to the family. They were always hard; she usually busied herself in the kitchens making hundreds of cups of tea at the wakes, or refilling wine glasses once the sun had gone down on their grief.

She felt lonely on the train. She was dressed in her dark clothes and it was probably obvious to other passengers where she was going, and what for. There must be funerals every day of the week in Belfast, she thought. They would be having Protestant funerals, so there'd have been no open house the night before, no open caskets with their hands clutching rosaries. She would go to the church, see those poor children; then there was a burial and a small wake in a first-floor pub function room. Then Bridget would slip away, back to the train station, for the nine o'clock train back to Dublin. She was frightened. She'd listened to the radio telling news about the North every day for the whole of the seventies and, even so, she felt woefully unprepared for what might await her there.

*

133

Maire was rifling through Bridget's wardrobe for a bigger coat. She had borrowed one of Bridget's loose, wool jumper dresses and put on her own thick tights with it. She neglected the belt; it made her bump too obvious. If she could do up the coat with a thick scarf around her chin and a knitted hat down to her eyes, she'd blend in and no one would notice her as anyone in particular. She hadn't been anywhere except Bridget's house for almost four months.

Maire found a parker-type coat with a big fluffy hood in the wardrobe in her room and put that on. She checked herself in the mirror with all her winter attire on and was satisfied; she didn't look pregnant at all. Did she look fat maybe? That would be better. She'd certainly gained some weight around her face in the last couple of months that hadn't gone unnoticed. She went downstairs, sat at the bottom on the third from last step and waited for the phone to ring.

*

Bridget phoned Maire from the payphone as soon as she was on the concourse at Belfast; she was, of course, fine. Bridget then got a taxi from Belfast train station to Dermot and Leanne's house. They'd lived on a small turning off the Shankill Road in a three-bedroomed terraced house. The boys had one room; the girls had the other. Bridget wanted to cry at the sight of the boarded-up windows, scorched walls and damaged shops that made up the streets of Belfast. She'd never seen anything like it in all her life. Armed British soldiers hovered around in the distance; they were extra alert when there were funerals. Small children stepped over broken glass and empty bullet shells like they were nothing.

Bridget supposed, to them, it was nothing. It was every day. Her four nieces and nephews had stepped over broken glass every day on their way to school for more than a decade. Bridget felt devastated and ashamed; of what, she wasn't sure.

A couple in their early sixties were standing with the children outside the house. Leanne's parents, Bridget surmised, and the dear children who had grown up yards since she'd last had a photo of them. They had pale faces; they held hands and stood in morose silence as the cars came with the coffins. Bridget didn't know if she ought to be here after all. She represented the family that had abandoned Dermot, because of Leanne.

Leanne's parents and the children got in the cars behind the coffins; everyone else was walking as the church wasn't far away. Bridget blended into a sea of grieving friends, relatives and small children who weren't totally sure why they were there and what they were doing. It was freezing cold, and it started to rain.

*

Maire put on her old boots she'd arrived in; they were tighter now where her feet were swollen. There was a spare key in the bowl in the hallway. She pressed it firmly into her pocket, had a good look out the frosted glass panel for onlookers as Ruth and Bridget had done before when she'd gone from house to house, and when she was sure there was no one, she stepped outside.

Maire was quite sure no one had appeared as she left the shared driveway of Bridget's and Ruth's attached houses and so she was content to walk up the road and not feel conspicuous. She admired the road; she had come up this street in a car with no idea where she was, where she was going, or how much longer she'd be pregnant. She'd got out of the car, into the house, and had barely been outside since. It was cold. She was delighted to have the opportunity to be cold. Of course, she didn't know exactly how to get to the church, but she'd seen it out the window and heard the bells from the garden, so she knew it wasn't far. She could see the bell tower already, poking up between the roofs and chimneys.

A left and a right turn was all it took to bring Maire face to face with the first church she'd seen in months. She was glad; it had started to drizzle. She'd only ever been inside two churches before: St Anne's, of course, at home, where she'd gone three times a week since she was two weeks old, and St Stephen's in Cork city when they'd gone to visit her granda. This one was called St Katherine's. She assumed they'd all be roughly the same inside and she'd know what to do and where to go. She meandered up the path, glancing at the tombstones, and slipped in through the big wooden door.

*

"A warm welcome to you all on this very cold day," a priest was saying gloomily.

Bridget recognised the inside of the church from the photograph she'd kept and shown Maire; Dermot and Leanne were married in here. Their coffins were side by side at the altar, where they would have stood on their wedding day. If they were married in here, they would have christened all four of the children in here as well. Bridget knew that no parent should have to bury their child, and the despair of Leanne's parents was evident, but no child should have to bury both their parents on the same day either. No one in this church could imagine the extent and complexity of their very specific, horrendous grief. No one was really listening to the priest; everyone was looking, distraught and forlorn at Dermot and Leanne's row of orphaned children.

*

Maire decided it would be better if she didn't take her coat off once she was inside the confessional, just in case. It wasn't all that warm in the church anyway; no one would think she was strange. There was only one other woman there and she was shutting the door to the box just as Maire came through the doors of the church. Maire would have to wait for a while; she hoped the other lady didn't have too much to confess.

The last time she'd seen Fionn – not that awful time but the last good time; the one before the awful time – she'd let herself daydream about their wedding. This church would be magnificent for a wedding, she thought. It had more than a dozen stained-glass windows and a long, long aisle. The organ alone was something spectacular. There were plenty of pews for a big Irish Catholic family like Fionn's. Along with hers of course, although there weren't as many of them as there were the Conghailes. They would make two uneven sides of the church.

She wondered who the last bride to swish down this aisle was and how her father had felt. Maire missed her da. She'd been a little bit afraid of him; they all were, but he was a nice man on the whole. She'd always liked to think that no matter what wrong she did, her da would forgive her and be there for her. He'd always be proud of her, really. But this was something unforgiveable. She didn't have to ask, and she hadn't done. She'd just disappeared into the darkness one night, with Ailbe, never to be seen again. They were probably glad, Maire surmised, that she had gone.

The lady was out. She obviously didn't have much to feel bad about; she hadn't been in there long at all. She didn't make eye contact with Maire as she strode purposefully to the front of the church and knelt in the front pew. Maire heaved herself up, slowly settled in and closed the door of the confessional box.

*

Bridget loathed burials. The children shouldn't be here, she thought firmly. This was too much for them. Their daughters were sobbing, noisy red-faced gagging sobs that sounded more like screams of pain than tears. Leanne's mother was trying to comfort them, but she was in no better shape herself. Leanne's father stood silently in a long black wool coat, with a hand on each of the boy's shoulders. They were silent, like him. Soon they would be moving to Derry to live in their grandparents' house, attend a new school – three of them anyway; their eldest was working now – and step over more broken glass and bullets in a different city. Bridget shut her eyes. She wasn't going to show herself up and cry for the brother she rarely made time for; her loss was nothing compared to theirs.

At the pub, Bridget didn't know what to do with herself; there was no domestic kitchen in which to hide and make the tea, as she would normally have done. Some of Dermot's friends were starting to drink now, laugh sometimes, in small groups as they shared anecdotes and stories. Leanne's friends huddled together and drank wine at tables, talking quietly. The younger children had been taken home. Bridget's nieces and nephews sat together in a small booth, eating crisps and not speaking. Below, the pub ran as normal. People laughed and joked and watched Manchester United play on television; Bridget wanted to march downstairs, turn off the TV and scream at them all *'How dare you watch football when my brother is dead?'*. She hated how the world kept turning after a death; it just wasn't fair. The whole world should be grieving Dermot and Leanne. Their orphaned children were just upstairs.

No one had spoken to Bridget or asked how she knew the family. That was a question people asked at weddings: 'How do you know the bride and groom?' People were less interested in your connections at funerals. She wanted to go home. She wanted a whiskey; she wanted to cry, and she wanted to go home.

*

"Forgive me, Father, for I have sinned. It has been five months since my last confession." Maire was embarrassed to say it; Father Jeffrey at home had never heard her say more than two weeks before. She wondered if he'd realise he didn't recognise her voice; she had an accent very unlike the Dublin accent and he must know all his parishioners on voice alone.

The priest coughed slightly but let her continue. "I had an affair with a married man. I didn't know he was married, Father; I swear on the cross and on the Bible that I didn't know."

Father Kelly didn't say anything. He didn't make a sound, or fidget, or gasp, or anything. Maire hadn't known what she'd been expecting. Did she think he was going to poke a crucifix through the wooden filigree holes and strike her with it? Maybe the last lady had confessed to murdering someone, and nothing Maire could say was likely to be of interest after that.

"It was a... a... sexual affair, Father," she said, blushing at the word. She'd never used that word before. It had been so long since she'd confessed and she had never, ever said anything about it before. But there was no holding back now – what was the point? God knew her sin and she couldn't lie her way out of it; she was just making her own charge sheet even longer if she did that. Father Kelly still didn't say anything. She took a breath. "We used... these things as well. To try and stop a pregnancy. A friend of mine, her family, gets them illegally, and she gave them to me. And we used them. But they didn't work."

She heard the priest's soft voice at last, now.

"So your confession is that... you used illegal measures to prevent pregnancy from sexual intercourse, but, nevertheless, you are now pregnant?"

"Yes." Maire burned, inside and out.

"But you are not married? He is married to another?"

"I am not. And, yes, he is."

The priest paused. Maire didn't want to say anything else. She felt a hundred times lighter. She missed the days of going

140

to confession when she was little, to 'confess' that she'd been lazy with her homework and had been less than tolerant to her infant siblings; it did at last feel good to get it all off her chest. Like she'd said, she was happy to swear on the cross and on the Bible that she hadn't known Fionn was married. That part, and that part alone, wasn't her fault. She'd been so terribly, terribly weak-willed and she expected to hear all about it from the priest just now.

"My child," the priest said gently. "There are places for young ladies like you. I can give you an address for an institution run by the Sacred Sisters where you can go and safely deliver. You can get there on the train."

"Thank you, Father, but that's actually… why I'm already here."

*

Maire could hear the phone ringing as she hastily unlocked the door with the spare key. She couldn't not answer it; Bridget would have a fit. She answered it just as Bridget was about to give up at the other end and have a meltdown of panic.

"Are you all right?" Bridget asked, as soon as she heard Maire's voice. "You sound out of breath."

"Oh, I'm fine. It's just… effort, isn't it, getting out of the sofa at my size!" It wasn't totally untrue; it had taken some effort to get off her knees and onto her feet in the church. "Are you all right? I thought you wouldn't be back until later."

"I'm fine," Bridget lied. "I'll be on the train shortly. See you tonight."

CHAPTER TWENTY-FIVE

The day after her beating, Ailbe was moved to the expecting mother's ward at the hospital as she had been told on her first day she would. It was a bit early, she thought, but suspected she was being moved to keep her out of the sight of the other convent girls, all of whom were quietly claiming her to be something of a hero. That, and the sight of a beaten face, was probably considered to be frightening for the others, when complaining over heartburn was enough to warrant a punishment for potentially alarming the masses.

Ailbe had found out through Vida – who seemed to always know everything about everyone – that the dead baby's mother had been seventeen-year-old Jacqueline. She wasn't told where he was buried and, as he'd been born dead, Sister hadn't allowed Jacqueline to see him even once. She was now under unofficial house arrest and constant observation to stop her running outside to look for his hastily dug grave. Vida had also discovered, by her stealth and general nosiness, that as there was now no baby, no more money would come into the convent for her keep. Jacqueline was being sent home tomorrow.

Unfortunately, Ailbe's new living arrangements meant she now had to tend to other people's babies instead of just washing their sheets, and her work was reassigned to the day nursery. She had been dreading this. She had never held a baby before and hadn't intended to. Also, after the shattering experiences with Sandra and Thérèse, and Helen and Dylan, she didn't want to go anywhere near someone else's baby. She felt evil and complicit, just at the thought of touching them.

The first thing that she had to do was help the midwife wash all the babies. It had to be done every day, so she prepared herself for a few more weeks of holding them under the armpits, as far away from her as she reasonably could, while the midwife sponged them down. The midwife did the majority of the washing on the first day, while Ailbe held them out like wet socks and looked out of the window at the grizzly winter.

Six weeks on, she had made some progress with the whole enterprise – making a buzzing sound with a sponge to make the babies laugh. She dressed them in the knitted clothes their mothers had made for them. Some were better at it than others; she pitied the poor wee things that were squeezed into tiny cardigans, composed of bizarre and unmatching colours, much too small for them. Emmaline hadn't spoken to anyone properly in weeks since her phone call home, but her knitting was so good and so quick that she produced armfuls of beautiful things and donated them to whoever was sitting around her at night. Ailbe, of course, had remained terrible at knitting. She could only do squares, and only in one colour. Vida, too, did hers twice as quick and passed half-completed things over their laps to Ailbe when the nuns had checked in and inspected their work. Sister raised her eyebrows at Ailbe but didn't say anything. She rather hoped, when her time for the walk came, that it would be dressed in something Vida or Emmaline had knitted.

*

On a remarkably rainy day that could have been in March or

143

April, she wasn't sure which – all she knew was there were daffodils growing outside – Ailbe recognised that she had been in labour since that morning and was, therefore, starting to face the inevitability that, at some point, she would have to say something. Being friends with Vida had several benefits, not least of which was that Vida had already been through labour herself twice now and Ailbe had often been present when Vida gave advice to the others, so Ailbe knew a lot of the ins and outs. Knowledge is power, Vida used to say – fear makes it worse. Vida and Milly had given birth to little girls on the same day three weeks ago; Bessborough had only one midwife, and she'd run between the two. Vida was back in the dormitory now; Milly had been collected by her mother.

Ailbe knew that early labour could take all day, so she thought she might as well get on with things in the meantime. Ultimately though, she knew it could only end one way and, after her waters broke on the floor she'd just spent two hours scrubbing, she waddled herself to the midwife's room.

The midwife, though disciplined and foreboding in her own way, was a good deal kinder to the girls than the nuns were. Since Ailbe had been moved to the hospital, she'd seen her a lot, and she always smiled at them. No one but her had smiled at Ailbe in months. Also, the midwife didn't look as though she enjoyed Mass all that much either. Ailbe liked that. When Ailbe told her she'd been having pains all day, she sucked her teeth and raised her eyebrows at her.

"You know you should've told me right away," she said. She took Ailbe's pulse again.

"I was all right," Ailbe said. Beads of sweat were starting to form at her hairline, and she had to admit that it was starting to get quite painful now. She regretted missing her tea. She quite fancied it now that she was here.

Two hours later, her contractions were washing over her with a mesmerising agony. She felt sick with the pain. The midwife told her to think about other things and take lots of deep, big breaths to help keep the pain at bay. But the pain just wouldn't stop. She didn't know what else to think about. Memories of life before Bessborough brought her little joy. She thought about Maire; yes, that helped. Maire with her mad red curls and her giggly, girly laugh and their long walks across the moors to keep Ailbe away from home for as long as possible. To keep Ailbe safe. Their friendship, and that alone, had brought her the only joy she'd ever known, or was hereafter likely to know. She imagined Maire with her, holding her hand.

The sun had long gone down when Sister swished into the room. Ailbe couldn't help but groan at the sight of her through her surges of pain.

"It's lovely to see you as well," Sister said bitterly. She pushed Ailbe's knees apart without asking and studied her intently.

Ailbe hated it. She looked away. Another contraction came and she felt like her belly was going to explode. When she touched it, it felt like a rock. She felt very, very hot.

"All right, I want you off that bed," Sister was saying.

Ailbe huffed.

"What? Now?"

"Yes! Now!" Sister pulled the chrome commode into the middle of the room. "On here."

"Where's Sister... the other sister, the midwife," Ailbe asked.

145

"Getting some rest. Presumably, if you take as long with this as you do everything else around here, she'll be with you all day tomorrow and we can hardly spare her," Sister complained. "So. On here. Hurry up."

Sister didn't move to help Ailbe, so she struggled up and off the bed herself, then waddled over to it. It was immensely uncomfortable and bitingly cold, as she had expected. Another contraction, already, and it was hideous. Ailbe opened her mouth and screamed. Sister slapped her.

"Don't you dare!" cried Sister.

Ailbe felt shocked. Her mouth was still open, but no sound came out. The pain of the contraction detracted considerably from the pain of the slap but her cheek still burned with a rush of blood. She glared at Sister.

"We don't allow *any of that* here, and you know that. Suffer the consequences of your sins *in silence* and have some *dignity*, for the Lord's sake!"

She swept out of the room and slammed the door behind her. Ailbe pulled the curtain and stuffed the end into her mouth so she could bite on it when she wanted to scream out. She felt tears prickle at her eyes. Just this once, she thought; just this once, she'd have a little cry for herself.

*

Ailbe watched the sun rise from the commode after ten excruciating hours. She knew labour could be long and, of course, she'd expected it to be very, very painful, but she hadn't realised it would be so... *boring*. So monotonous, repetitive, and so incredibly lonely. She thought back to Jacqueline, whose baby had died, the baby that was buried

146

anonymously somewhere outside. Jacqueline had done this… exactly this, this agony, this torture, for four days. She was surprised the girl hadn't died along with her son; Ailbe surmised that she probably would have wanted to.

Ailbe heard a patter of feet outside and realised it must be time for Mass, for the others in the ward upstairs. Mass was still compulsory from three days after birth. She looked at the sky and thought about God. She scowled at the clouds. What a monster He was. As she thought it, the previously ceased rain started to splatter against the window once more and the door opened.

"Ciara, how are you getting along?" She heard the midwife's voice.

As soon as Ailbe saw her, she broke into a smile of relief. She hadn't realised, until that moment, just how much she hadn't wanted to be alone anymore.

Another contraction quickly took away her smile.

"Oh dear," said the midwife, "let's get you back on that bed and have a look."

Ailbe didn't mind so much when it was the midwife looking. Especially seeing as she had marginally good news.

"Ooh, that's excellent. Let's have a little push, Ciara, and in an hour or so, you'll be a mammy."

Ailbe didn't feel like a mammy. She didn't want to be a mammy, not to this baby, not to any baby anymore. Her and Maire had talked about it. She had thought that, if she was lucky, she could find a way to get out of the village, find a decent job working for someone who didn't hear her surname and instantly recoil, live with Maire and have a life. Be happy. Find a nice-looking sort of man that wouldn't mind going to London for a registry office wedding and perhaps have a couple of boisterous kids. She liked that idea before. But not now. Not after all this.

She felt immense pressure between her legs. She was so hot, and so tired.

"Now?" she said to the midwife.

"Now," the midwife replied. "That's it! And again!"

This continued for, as the midwife had promised, about an hour. Ailbe asked 'now?'. The midwife said 'yes'. Ailbe pushed, although she didn't know what she was doing or how she was doing it. The midwife gave her short, direct instructions. Ailbe felt a growing burning, an indescribable burning, and then the unmistakeable feeling of something being ripped apart.

Her jaw slackened in preparation for the roar of a lifetime, but the midwife had already shoved her hand across Ailbe's face to muffle her scream.

"Let's not have Sister back in here upsetting you," the midwife said. "Take a deep breath. I know it hurts. I know it hurts."

Ailbe wanted to screech with the pain, but she daren't. She didn't want to look down, but she was sure there'd be rivers of blood; she could feel it pouring.

"That's it, that's the head and shoulders, Ciara. Well done!" the midwife chirped.

Ailbe could feel it. She knew what she'd done. It was amazing.

"And there we go!" the midwife said and, suddenly, a stuttering screech filled the room.

Ailbe realised it wasn't coming from her own lungs this time. The agony ceased almost immediately; it was miraculous. The midwife plonked a purple, blotchy, messy

148

bundle of arms and legs on Ailbe's chest. A long grey tube was hanging out of him and disappeared back between Ailbe's knees. She marvelled at the baby. She marvelled at herself. She panted and felt like she wanted to cry. She also felt like she wanted to laugh. It was a peculiar, but not unpleasant feeling. She wasn't sure what to do.

"What a handsome wee one he is," the midwife was saying.

He. She'd had a son. She hadn't really thought about that, hadn't really cared, until now. A little boy, for her trouble.

"Let's have him here and have him weighed."

The midwife cut his cord and Ailbe rested her head back on the bed and shut her eyes. He was still crying. She felt bad for him, pushed unceremoniously out of his home like that. He was probably quite happy in there. She was so relieved. She had done her job. Only a healthy one could scream the house down like that. Some parents somewhere were going to be absolutely delighted with him; she was proud of him already.

"Seven pounds, three ounces," the midwife said proudly. "That's terrific." She wrapped him up in a towel and brought him back over to Ailbe.

Ailbe didn't think twice about instantly taking him in her arms and cradling him. She looked into his tiny face. He slowly stopped crying and squinted open his tiny eyes to look at her. Their eyes met. She felt an extraordinary wave of something she had never felt before. He was just grand.

The door swung open and in stormed Sister, eyeing Ailbe and her newborn son with suspicion. She looked at the floor and screwed up her face, tiptoeing with pointed disgust around the puddles of blood that were gathering there.

"How much then?" she asked the midwife curtly.

"Seven three, Sister," the midwife answered sheepishly. "Ciara did—"

"Is that all?" scoffed Sister. She jerked her head at Ailbe. "All that fuss for not a lot."

Ailbe would have had something to say if she had slept in the last thirty hours, which she hadn't, and if she wasn't cradling what she was sure was the most perfect human being to have ever lived.

"Where's the rest of it?" Sister said scornfully, looking around the room.

"She hasn't delivered the afterbirth yet; he's only a few minutes o—"

"We don't have all day, nurse, for the love of Christ," she snapped. "Tell her to get on with it."

"Yes, Sister," the midwife muttered. "Sister, Ciara has a second-degree tear. She needs probably seven or so stitches. May I insert—?"

"No," Sister said. "She's all right." And with that, she left again, the door banging noisily behind her.

Ailbe looked at the midwife, who braved a smile for her.

"You are all right," she repeated to Ailbe.

Ailbe nodded. "I am. I am all right."

*

The midwife, a girl called Collene, and another girl, Sally, helped push Ailbe's birthing bed into her empty space on the new mothers' ward. Each bed had a tiny cot beside it; she was going to be here for ten days with her son before he was placed in the nursery and she went back to work. She would just wait for the day when she was called to dress him and make the walk with him to the door. She knew the format; she'd seen it enough times during her time here. No one had even bothered to ask her if her family had put up the £100 that meant she could leave next week; it was fairly obvious that she had no such family, with no such fortune. In any case, she wasn't bothered about that. Maire would be here in a few months, probably, after she'd had her own baby, and they could both start again.

So, Ailbe had decided, she was going to make the most of these ten days; then it would be time for nerves of steel. She was good at that bit. Hand him over to his real parents with all the bravery she had. It wasn't his fault; he hadn't asked to be made – in violence, or at all. The least Ailbe could do was hand him over to a deserving couple, with a nice house (she hoped) near a good school. She hoped, earnestly, that they would raise him to be a far better man than any of the men she'd ever known. They could probably do that a great deal better than she could, Ailbe thought, and that alone brought her comfort.

Still, she had to admit, he was incredibly sweet. Handsome indeed, like the midwife had said. She had been frightened of who he might look like, but he seemed to resemble her only. She lay on her side as it was more comfortable; he was lying with his head turned slightly in her direction. He opened his eyes and they looked at each other. She smiled. Sally had brought her tea and toast and Ailbe had enjoyed that immensely. She wanted to sleep, but she didn't want to miss the slightest movement of his tiniest toe. He had a full head of very dark hair. She was so enamoured by him that she didn't notice Sister swish in and regard the room with

151

a general distaste.

"Have you thought of a name?" she barked at Ailbe.

Ailbe looked blankly at her. "Er... no, I... I only had a girl name," she admitted.

Sister rolled her eyes. "What is his father called?" she asked.

No way, thought Ailbe. *No way in Hell*. "I don't remember," she said triumphantly, smiling, savouring Sister's horror and disgust. *Why not give the woman what she expects*, thought Ailbe, *just this once?*

"It's the seventeenth today," Sister said. "Call him Patrick. That should make things easier. Middle name can be whatever you like but make a decision today."

She wandered over to the next bed to pick on Margaret and her eight-day-old daughter. Margaret was having a hellish time with the breastfeeding and Sister seemed to enjoy making her feel worse about it. The midwife had diagnosed Margaret with an infection and mastitis, but Sister refused, point blank, to obtain antibiotics for her. Margaret had also needed multiple stitches, which Sister wouldn't allow.

Ailbe hadn't cared much for what day or even month it was here; they were all the same anyway. But she supposed Sister was right – the seventeenth of March, so it was. Ailbe settled back into her pillows – you got two in here which was a rare treat – and resumed staring at her son. Her son, her little love.

"Hi," she whispered. He made a sucking sound in his sleep. "I'm your mamma, so I am." He looked like he was smiling too. Ailbe's whole body flushed with happiness. She'd never felt happiness before, not like this. She searched his face and found that he looked so familiar, like she'd seen him every day of her life. Until she realised, of course, that she had. "Hi Patrick," she whispered. "You know, you look ever so much like me."

She hadn't thought she'd be allowed to name the baby at all, so she was bewildered at the responsibility of giving him a middle name. Except she couldn't think of one... Ma... Mo... Mi... She couldn't think of an M name. Maire's father had been called Cillian, and he'd been kind to her sometimes when no one was looking. Kinder than anyone else in the village, really. He'd been a good teacher as well; she had always tried her best for him.

"Sister!" Ailbe called out. Sister looked over at her and appeared gravely inconvenienced.

"What now?"

"Cillian, please," she said, looking over at the tiny baby beside her bed. "For the middle."

"Hmm. Good choice," Sister said.

Ailbe was surprised; that must be the first decent thing Sister had said to her since she arrived. They both peered at the baby with the brand-new name. If Ailbe wasn't mistaken, Sister was almost smiling, in spite of herself.

"Oh. You need to sign this," Sister said, handing Ailbe a sheet of paper and a ballpoint pen. It was already filled out; just the section where Sister needed to write *Patrick Cillian* in was blank.

"What is it?" Ailbe asked. She'd never signed her name on anything before. She wasn't sure how she would even do it.

"It's a dispensation order. For the adoption," Sister sneered.

153

Ailbe recoiled from it in horror. "Already? Today?" she asked incredulously.

"Well, no, he's not being taken *today*," Sister said, rolling her eyes. "But it's better if you just do it now. For the records."

Ailbe wondered why she couldn't have signed this particular piece of paper on any day from November, when she had arrived, as opposed to today, the very day of her son's birth. She looked over at him, sleeping peacefully in his cot. Ailbe reminded herself that this wasn't really her baby. He had always been meant for another, and soon he would be. She sighed as she scribbled *Ailbe Donnelly* on a dotted line. Sister snatched the paper away as soon as she had done so and folded it up. It disappeared in a flash into the folds of her clothing.

"Can I hold him?" Ailbe asked.

"He's yours," Sister responded, with a huff of derision.

Ailbe dived into the crib with both arms outstretched.

"For now, anyway."

CHAPTER TWENTY-SIX

"Maire, come and sit by me, I want to talk to you about something."

Bridget had been fondly listening to Maire play the harp – well, two thirds of the harp; she couldn't reach the furthest notes anymore – with happiness and sheer admiration. She had picked it up with amazing speed. Every day when Bridget had got home from work, she found Maire, sitting at the stool, concentrating like a mad thing on the sheets of music and plucking furiously at the harp. She'd learned to read music in a week and a half. Bridget marvelled at her.

Maire hauled herself up and dropped heavily into the seat beside Bridget on the sofa. She'd be there for the night now; it was getting harder and harder to get Maire in and out of furniture. She was starting to look very tired.

Bridget handed her a stack of paperwork and brochures. Maire glanced at it all and looked at Bridget with confusion.

"What's this?" she said, wearily, and Bridget grinned.

"Have you given any thought to what you're going to do when you leave here?" Bridget asked gently.

Maire had not. She'd been hoping that day wouldn't come. She'd arrived here in love with Fionn, pregnant with Fionn's sweet child. She was going to have to leave without either of them. She'd have to leave without Bridget as well, dear Bridget, who was like a mother and a sister to her all at once. It wasn't something that she liked to think about.

"No."

"I assumed as much. So, I've done some thinking for you. Have you considered continuing with your studies?" she asked.

Maire gaped. A year ago, it was all she had thought about, every single day.

Bridget continued. "A lot of Irish girls go to England to study nursing, you know. There's more universities and colleges there, more hospitals and, frankly, millions more people getting sick for you to work on."

Maire didn't know what to say. She looked down at the paperwork. They appeared to be application forms of some sort.

"I don't... understand," Maire said at last.

"Maire, you are such a clever girl," Bridget said tenderly. "You're much, much cleverer than me. I want to help you. I will not have you go back to being shouted at by drunks. You will go to England and be a nurse like me. A much better nurse than me, probably."

Maire was speechless. She didn't know what to say. She had nothing to give Bridget, nothing at all. She said so.

"Well, it's just as well I don't want or need anything," Bridget said. "Come on, Maire. You worked it out yourself as soon as you got here. We're not short of a few. I don't have anyone to spend my money on but myself. What am I going to do with it, have pockets sewn into my shroud?"

Maire still didn't say anything. Study. University. Become a nurse, get a job and somewhere to live and... put all this behind her. Forget about Fionn the way he had forgotten about her.

"And you can go and get your friend from the home in Cork," she said. "I'll make sure you have your tickets and somewhere to stay in London while you get settled. Anything you need Maire, you can just let me know."

"Ruth said... we weren't supposed to stay in touch," Maire reminded her.

Bridget frowned. Yes, that had been another of Ruth's demands. Maire had assumed they wouldn't anyway, but Bridget certainly had high hopes of watching Maire's life – her new life – unfold.

"Th-thank you, Bridget," she said at last. "Thank you." And then she burst into tears.

Bridget laughed and put her arms around Maire and told her all about the wonderful things she was going to do, all the learning she was going to do, how many lives she was going to touch. Maire grinned from ear to ear through her noisy tears. The baby, sensing its mother's rising, happy heartbeat, started to dance.

CHAPTER TWENTY-SEVEN

Ailbe was hot. Seriously, outrageously hot. Wasn't it only March still? She wasn't really sure. She hadn't been out of bed for a while. She remembered the cold when she'd first come here, how she'd been sure she would freeze to death before that first night was even over. And now, she was hot. Really, really hot.

She didn't feel very strong but she used one arm to bring the other nearer to her head. A stone-cold hand that she realised must be her own landed on her chest, and she felt the heat radiate from her burning chest to her frozen hand. It didn't make any sense. Where even was she, anyway? This wasn't her and her mother's room. This wasn't the room at Brannigan's, either. The ceiling had windows. That was strange.

Someone was talking to her. The curve where her shoulder met her neck was starting to hurt. She didn't quite understand what they were saying but, so far, no one had asked her to get up and do anything. It must be time to leave soon. She'd outstayed her welcome for sure, wherever she was; whatever she'd had to drink, it was too much. Maire would be angry with her, so angry with her. She'd told her off about her drinking before. She knew Maire was right; she didn't want to end up like her da.

There were shapes she couldn't make out moving around her bedside. They looked like shadows but they were white. Her breasts hurt. Her privates hurt. Her stomach hurt. She wanted to reach out to someone, wave at them, tell them she couldn't remember what had happened, but her arm felt too heavy to lift. She felt like she wanted to go to sleep.

Oh, God. Had she wet herself? Her thighs and legs and privates were wet. She wanted to reach down and feel but her arm didn't seem to be moving on her brain's command.

She also wanted to tell them that she was hot. She opened her mouth and was sure she'd said the words, but she didn't hear them come out. Her mouth felt dry; she desperately needed a drink. She felt a cold, rough hand on her forehead, and then it went away, and then another one. Someone pulled the sheets off her and the voices got louder. The light coming in from the windows was too bright; she wanted to tell them to turn it down. Turn it all down, because it all hurt.

CHAPTER TWENTY-EIGHT

Maire was, what Bridget would call, 'having a day'. She knew about the changes to her hormones because Bridget had explained months earlier; she'd brought home all sorts of books and pamphlets for Maire to read, and she had read them diligently, but she still couldn't quite get a handle on it when it came. Sometimes she cried; sometimes she couldn't think straight and could hardly remember her own name. Sometimes she flew into a terrible rage and complained about nothing in particular at an exceptional volume. Bridget, being rather used to irritable patients, made tea and let her get on with it.

Today, Maire was crying. It was her due date, and she was crying. She was sobbing so much her back ached and her throat hurt. She wanted to rip Fionn's heart out of his body for what he had done. She hated Ruth and Donal for being so perfect and raising her baby, the baby she hadn't even had yet. They had painted walls in *their* house for *her* baby, and she hated them for it. She hated everyone for everything, and it wasn't fair. Her mother was supposed to sew her a lace wedding dress. Where in Hell was her mother now?

Bridget came home from work to find Maire sobbing on the kitchen floor. Bridget hauled her up, despite her weight, and sat her down gently on a kitchen chair. She put the kettle on.

"I don't want to do this anymore, Bridget," Maire wailed. "It's not fair."

"I know, my love. I know," Bridget cooed, stroking Maire's head. Her already masses of curls had grown longer

160

and thicker with pregnancy.

"You don't know," sobbed Maire. "You don't know."

Bridget was silent. Maire was quite right – she didn't have a clue. Bridget had never conceived a child, lost a child, given up a child. She knew nothing of Maire's pain, and for that matter, Ruth's. She was well aware of it, every year or so when Ruth had lost another one, and then another one. There was nothing she could say to either of them to ease their suffering.

Bridget made a pot of tea while Maire snivelled into tissues at the table. She remembered how much Maire had cried during her first few days in the house with her; it had broken her heart then, and it did again now.

"The thing is, Maire," she said gently, sitting down opposite her, "what you're doing is simply extraordinary. You're going to give an extraordinary gift. Something other people can't even imagine. You're giving the gift of a family. A family to people who, without you…"

Maire looked up at her and sniffed. She hadn't thought of it like that. Maire and her baby alone wouldn't be the family she had wanted. What could she do, carry it under her arm like a rugby ball, straight onto a ferry into England – and then what? Be at the mercy of their social system instead and the baby be taken from her anyway, into the arms of God knows who at God knows what orphanage? She had known all of this when she arrived here. She couldn't change her mind now. She had no alternative.

"Without you, darling, they don't have it. Without you…" Bridget tailed off. She didn't know what to say. John had five children. Liam had eight. Dermot, God rest him, had four. And Ruth had also had five, but she didn't have a family like

161

they did. Not the family she had wanted, anyway. Bridget had tried, and failed, to fill that void in Ruth's life. A sister was nice, but it wasn't a child. That was what Ruth had always wanted.

"A gift?" Maire repeated. She hiccupped.

"A gift," Bridget assured her. "A wonderful, glorious gift. A gift that, frankly, even God couldn't give them."

Maire nodded. She knew Bridget was right. No one was making her do this. True, she had no other options to speak of, but Bridget had asked her, months ago now, if she was happy to do it this way. And she had said that she was. Ruth and Donal were doing nothing wrong by wanting to love and raise her baby. She was just... having a day.

"I know it's a huge sacrifice for you," Bridget said tenderly.

Maire nodded.

"And your friend, Ailbe, too. But to think, in a few months' time you'll be in England, training to be a nurse. And then you'll be giving all sorts of gifts. The gift of health, and *life,* Maire. Life! Let Ruth change the shitty nappies."

Maire started, and then laughed. She'd never heard Bridget swear before.

"And you two go and live your lives."

Maire didn't really know what that might look like, but she liked the sound of it. She was excited about nursing. She would detour to Cork first, of course, to get Ailbe. She hoped to God Ailbe was all right.

"What do we say, my girl?" Bridget was asking. *"I have said these things to you, that in me you may have peace."*

"In this world you will have tribulation," Maire recited. *"But take heart, I have overcome the world."*

162

Bridget squeezed her hand.

"That's it. That's the way," Bridget said gently. Another tear escaped from Maire's eye and she wiped it with the back of her hand.

"I loved Fionn," she said hopelessly. "I wanted to live my life with him." She looked down at her bump and thought of the child – half him, half her. Soon to be living proof of her love for him – and his betrayal of her. "I really, really wanted him."

Bridget squeezed her hand. "I know, love," she said, just as hopelessly. "But there'll be someone else. It might not feel like it now, but there'll be someone. London is a big place, my girl."

*

Maire sat up in bed and listened to the rain hammer on her windows. She'd pulled the curtains because it was dark but she didn't really feel like sleeping yet. Besides, it was that time of the week.

Dear Ailbe,

I can't believe you probably have a two-month-old child by now. If you've written back, I've not received any of your letters; maybe they ration the paper there, or keep you busy with other things. I hope you're all right. I wish we could be together so you could tell me about the birth and what happened; how did it go? How much did it hurt? Did you have a boy or a girl?

I'm dreading it to be honest. Bridget is a nurse. I think I told you that before, so I'll be in good hands and everything.

163

But I wish we could talk about it and you could tell me what it was like, and if you're okay, Ailbe. Are you okay?

She thought about what Bridget had said to her a couple of weeks ago, when she was having her day. About making a sacrifice and giving a gift. If Ailbe was struggling – which, if she was, she'd never admit it – it'd probably help her. She wrote it all out, what Bridget had said. She hoped this time she'd get a reply.

When she woke up the following morning, the bedsheets were wet. Maire was mortified.

"Bridget!" she called out. Her legs were wet too. Oh God, she was twenty years old. Was she really going to have to say this? "Bridget! Bridget, I think I've... I've wet the bed."

Bridget came rushing in, still in her nightgown.

"Show me."

"Urgh, Bridget, no, you don't want to see—"

"Show me, Maire. It might be your waters."

Her waters. She hadn't considered that. She started to panic.

"*Don't* panic," said Bridget, who had apparently become telepathic after all this time with Maire. "Yes. Waters. All right, my dear, the slightest twinge of tummy cramp, you need to let me know."

If Maire's mother had been available for comment at the time, she would have told them that, in their family, the babies turned up late but then they turned up fast. Without this information, Bridget had been watching Maire like a ticking bomb for the past ten days, and now that her waters had gone, the pains started right after breakfast, which Bridget had not expected. In her experience, first babies did come late, which Maire's was, but they also took an age to make an appearance from the first twinge to their first cry, which Maire's absolutely was not.

Bridget had telephoned Ruth who came over right away. Maire wanted to do it in her bedroom; it had been her safe place. She liked the bed and the fact that she could see out of the window from it. Ruth spread old sheets over the bedding and the floor, while Bridget got her bag out of the car, in which she had stockpiled a number of items throughout Maire's pregnancy to make the delivery easier for her at home. She was most pleased with getting away with a couple of syringes of pethidine, which she was sure would help Maire out considerably.

Maire's contractions came thick and fast, with only very small breaks in between them. Bridget examined her as quickly as she could between the surges and found that Maire was already halfway along before lunchtime. Ruth held Maire's hand, brushed her hair off her forehead, gave her sips of water to drink. When Bridget gave Maire the first stab of pethidine in her thigh, she was overcome with gratitude to which Bridget laughed, and Ruth looked daggers at her. Maire moaned and groaned and cried as the pain got worse. This part, Bridget had already told her, was going to be the worst bit. She held Ruth's hand and looked intently at her.

"You can do it," Ruth said, with as stern and committed a face as Maire had ever seen on her. "You can do it. You clever girl. You brave girl. You can do it."

*

Donal sat on the floor in the nursery with his head against the

165

wall. He could hear Bridget's and Ruth's muffled voices on the other side, and low moans from Maire; he couldn't make out words, but he could tell by the ebb and flow of their noises, the intonation of the sound, that Maire was near the end already. They were cheering her on, encouraging her over the finish line. He had never felt so useless in all his life.

He looked around the room. He'd painted the walls grey and made elephant-shaped stencils at Ruth's request, painting them yellow. He'd built the crib himself. His father had been excellent with wood – Donal was devastated that he wasn't here. He would've built a much better crib, with his own hands, in his own workshop. At forty-four, Donal felt as nervous and unprepared for this day as he had on his first day of school. *What do I do, Da*? he prayed. *What do I do?*

*

Bridget was telling Maire to give it one more big push.

"I can't!" she wailed. "I can't. It's too—"

"You can, and you are," Bridget said. "Baby's on its way. Come on, Maire."

She pushed. It hurt. It burned. They'd run out of pain relief an hour and a half ago.

"That's it! Good girl!"

"Good girl, Maire!" Ruth chimed in. She rubbed Maire's back encouragingly.

Maire hadn't the heart to tell her that she would much prefer it if Ruth was at the other end, not touching her, just shouting encouragement from a safe distance over Bridget's shoulder.

She pushed and pushed, and then she heard it. That

166

mewing sound she remembered from over a decade ago, when her sisters were born in the kitchen.

"Haha!" said Bridget triumphantly, holding the baby up to show Maire and Ruth. "It's a wee girl!"

They gasped. "A girl! A girl!" they said together, and Ruth kissed Maire's face and head over and over again.

Maire was exhausted. She didn't mind being held and kissed by Ruth now. She felt like she'd earned it.

"Thank you." Ruth was blubbing between kisses. "Thank you, darling, praise God, thank you. Thank you."

"Ruth, come and cut this. Did you bring the scales up?" Bridget asked.

Ruth said she hadn't. She snipped at the cord between Maire and her daughter and gazed at it in awe.

"Wow," was all she could say.

The baby was turning red and starting to screech.

"Oh goodness, she's got some lungs on her," Bridget said. "Ruth, the scales?"

Ruth flew out of the room and down the stairs. Bridget wrapped the baby swiftly in a towel and took her to Maire's head. Maire peered into the folds of fabric and smiled. She sure looked like her da.

"Are you sure?" Bridget whispered. They could hear Ruth clattering around with pans downstairs, looking for the scales.

Maire looked at the baby's face. God, she was gorgeous. A whole head of red hair. Donal was going to be pleased. Maire couldn't have been prouder.

"Yeah," she sighed. "Yes, I'm sure."

Maire closed her eyes as she heard Ruth come back up the stairs. She kept them closed as they weighed the baby and

167

marvelled at all her eight pounds, three ounces of gloriousness; someone was shooshing her piercing cries. She was settling down.

"Is she sure?" she heard Ruth whisper. "She definitely doesn't want to—"

"No, she's sure," Bridget responded. She whispered: "Congratulations, Mammy."

Maire snapped her eyes open just in time to see Ruth's tear-stained face blow kisses at the baby in her arms. She turned away to walk out of the door. Maire strained her neck to see as much of her as she could. Maire heard her mewing, and then she watched her go.

Donal had been told to listen for the cry. He could let himself in then as long as he stayed downstairs. He straightened his tie in the hall mirror before he left and grinned happily at his reflection.

Ruth was already at the foot of the stairs when he burst hurriedly through the front door. She carried in her arms the pinkest, serenest, most cherubic baby he'd ever seen, wrapped up in one of Bridget's tea towels. They'd foolishly left all the blankets they'd brought at home. He stared at the baby for what seemed like hours of his life, with no wish to stop. Ruth gently passed the bundle into his own arms. He beamed. Tears streamed uncontrollably down his face and onto his shirt.

"We've done it," he whispered. "Ruthie, we've done it." He ran his finger along the baby's chubby cheek. Ruth was glowing. He'd never seen her look so elated, not since their wedding day. Maybe not even then.

"It's a girl," she said, smiling. Donal's mouth fell open.

"I didn't... didn't even think—"

"To ask? Didn't even care?" Ruth chuckled.

Donal laughed. He beamed at his tiny girl. "Didn't even care," he repeated, wiping away his tears with the back of his hand. She was heavy. Already he started to panic at the thought of this little one in a wedding dress. A girl. A little girl. "There go our plans for another baby Dermot," he said, and Ruth smiled sadly. Yes, they had discussed that. "Oh, can we name her Penelope, after my mam?" Donal looked like an excited child.

"Yes! I love that," said Ruth. "Can she be called Penelope Mary, *not* after mine?" They laughed together.

Donal liked that name very much too.

"Also," Ruth added in a whisper, "Mary does sound a bit like…" She gestured her head upstairs.

Donal nodded morosely in agreement. He looked up at the ceiling and crossed himself, muttering a prayer for Maire. Ruth did the same. Beside them in the hallway was Bridget's cluttered cupboard full of framed photographs; they would have to take one – a dozen! – as soon as they got Penelope home, to add to Bridget's clutter. Donal kissed Penelope's tiny forehead. Then Ruth did likewise. As they turned to leave, from the bedroom above, they heard a muffled, wounded wail.

CHAPTER TWENTY-NINE

Maire had never felt so warm and content in her life. The sun was streaming through the window of the room at Brannigan's and illuminating everything it touched; it glinted off Fionn's watch on the nightstand. It bounced off the mirror. She smiled. She was so happy.

"Fionn," she said slowly. He had been absent-mindedly stroking her hair for quite some time. He always did that afterwards.

"Hmm?"

"Do you think we will get married?" She took a deep breath after she'd said it and held it. She'd wanted to ask this for weeks now and it didn't seem like there was ever a good time to say it. But now she needed to know. Ailbe had told her never to look desperate. Was it desperate to enquire about marriage?

"I would love it if we could get married," Fionn said, without a second's hesitation.

"You would?" Maire turned to look up at him and beamed.

"Yes, I would love it if we could get married," he said again. "But are you sure you don't want to live a little first? You know, go to the trouble of turning twenty-one, perhaps? Maybe... get a different job?"

Maire laughed. A job. There were no jobs here; he knew that.

"I'm twenty-one next year, Fionn."

"And yet, still only nineteen now."

"But you'd want to? Get married?"

Fionn was quiet. He kissed the top of her head and lingered there.

"Of course I would want to. I'd love it if we could."

Maire smiled happily to herself and snuggled further into his chest. That was all she had wanted to know. It didn't have to be soon – although, if her instinct was right, it actually *would* have to be very soon. She'd tell him that part when she was sure. For now, though, she was getting away with this, with Abigail's and Ailbe's help. Her parents would be shocked, of course, that they hadn't known she'd met someone, but they didn't need to know about all this. She pictured her wedding dress. Lots of lace. Her mother would make it for her. A train that swished down the aisle of St Anne's as Fionn waited for her at the other end – and flowers! Lots of flowers. Her sisters would be bridesmaids, of course. And Ailbe. It was going to be wonderful.

"If we don't get married…" Maire began.

Fionn fidgeted. "Yeah?"

"If we don't get married, I don't want to marry anybody else," she said triumphantly.

Fionn didn't respond. Maire watched the sunbeams dance on the wall opposite them; a light breeze gently billowed the net curtain from the window. She watched it and thought of her veil. Her father would lift it for her, and she would smile.

"I don't, really," she urged again.

Fionn kissed her, languorously, as though it was the last time they ever would. She wanted to remember this, remember it perfectly for the rest of her life.

"I love you," she said.

He kissed her nose. "And I love you," he replied.

The sun was streaming through the window of the room at Brannigan's and illuminating everything it touched; it glinted off Fionn's watch on the nightstand. It bounced off the mirror. It was glorious, and yet, Fionn had never felt worse in his life. When it was happening, he felt good – elated, really – loved. Warm. Happy. It wasn't like that with Clodagh. He burned from head to foot with the shame and guilt of thinking of her now. He had no right to say her name, or even think it. Maire was leaning on his chest, happily sighing away, while he ran his fingers through her curls to straighten them out. She liked it when her hair was messy afterwards; she giggled when she saw it. He didn't like it. He wanted to absolve her of his crime as soon as they were done.

She had asked him if he thought they'd get married. He knew the question was coming; she'd had a look about her. He could see it on the corner of her mouth just desperate to escape. Of course she was going to ask about the future. Why wouldn't she? He couldn't keep getting away with this; it was monstrous and, the longer he allowed there to be silence, the more opportunity she had to pluck up the courage to ask. And now, she had.

"I would love it if we could get married," he said. His heart started to quicken and then he examined his words. *If. If we could. If only we could.* He hadn't lied. He hadn't said yes, or no. He'd said the truth; he would love it if they could. But they couldn't.

She smiled now, that smile he had seen the first time he ever saw her. Fionn couldn't handle that smile; it was his favourite thing in the world. She was beautiful. It made him want to cry sometimes. She was always smiling when she was with him. He felt horrible. Clodagh never smiled. Not at him, or the children, or at anyone.

She asked again. He repeated his words for her. But she was so young, he reminded her – didn't she want to... *live* a little? Escape him, and his wicked, terrible actions? He was terrified that she'd say yes. But she should say yes. If she got another job, she might meet someone else and forget all about him. The thought of her with someone else, marrying someone other than him... It made his heart hurt and bile creep up his throat. But she deserved happiness, and he couldn't give it to her; what right had he to be jealous of her marrying another, when *he* had been married to Clodagh for almost five years already? They'd never get married. Sooner or later, he'd have to tell her the truth and break her heart, and she would never forgive him.

"If we don't get married, I don't want to marry anybody else," she said.

He shut his eyes. She had said *if* too; maybe she understood, and he was the one misunderstanding the situation. It was the best thing, and the worst thing, she could possibly have said. What could he say now? He mustn't lie to her. He couldn't encourage her to leave him; it would break him. He kissed her for as long he could, in the hope that she would stop talking about this now. But he wanted to remember this day, this kiss, for the whole of his life.

"I love you," she said.

"And I love you," he replied, and he meant it, with all his heart. It was an honest answer. He couldn't lie to her anymore. He was being monstrously, abominably selfish.

He wasn't due to visit the village again for another four

weeks but that was too long; he'd put her through enough. He'd come back in two weeks – he wasn't ready yet – and surprise her, then break her heart. Ruin her life.

"I really do, Maire."

A suitable answer. An honest answer. That was important.

CHAPTER THIRTY

Fionn had parked his car on a side street a short distance from Bridget's house. He knew he could be there and not be seen by them, even if they happened to look out of the window right in that direction. There was a very handy tree that a very belligerent neighbour had been refusing to trim properly for the last year and a half. He hid by that.

Donal had phoned his office this morning and said, "It's going to be today by the sounds of it," and hung up.

There had been a brief agreement made months before that he would be told, when the rest of the family was, that Ruth's baby had arrived, and he'd meet the baby just like everyone else, at the baptism or some such event. But Donal had always been soft and reasonable to a fault, and Fionn hadn't been too surprised to have received some warning after all. He'd apologised and abandoned the surgery and his patients, citing a family emergency (which, truly, it was) and had driven at speed to get there. He'd been there now for several hours. He wasn't sure what he was expecting to see, or what he would do if her labour continued into the following day. He hadn't really thought; he'd just wanted to be there.

He'd been at a few births. It looked grisly to him. He was truly in awe of women and their physical capabilities; nothing had made him feel like more of a spare part than a woman in labour. Even at Little John's and Colm's births, even as a doctor, he had hovered in the corner while the women supported his wife; the women used words he dimly recalled from years ago at medical school that he'd since forgotten. He had held Clodagh's hand when they told him to. He had followed their instructions. He'd hated to see Clodagh in pain, and he hated the thought of Maire in it too. Clodagh had screamed at him that her suffering was all his fault. He supposed Maire's pain was definitely all his fault too.

He pulled out the envelope he had kept in his pocket since it had arrived at the surgery seven months or so ago. It had come the day before he had planned to leave again for the villages, to break things off with Maire and tell her the truth. He loved Maire's delicate handwriting on the outside and on the paper within. He held it and read it again for the hundredth time.

Dearest Fionn,

Thank you for organising the car for Ailbe. She's so relieved. Yes, she's Catholic, of course, we all are. That's not a problem. Can you tell me where it is that she's going to go? I want to make sure she's going to be all right.

I can't wait for you to come back, and I'm going to need you to come back sooner than you had planned to because... we're going to have a baby. I know it; I'm sure. I wanted to wait until I was absolutely sure before I told you because I know this is really, extremely unexpected, especially seeing as you used those things. I don't know which time it was. The last one before the last one, I suppose. I hope you won't be angry with me. I don't know what I did to make this happen.

When you were here last, we talked about getting married and I was so happy, Fionn, so so happy, because all I want to do is marry you and be with you forever. Not just because of this, not because we have to, but because I really, really want to. My parents will forgive us eventually. I know I'm very young, but I want this, I truly want this, with you. You always say everything will be okay and I believe you, that we'll be okay. You can phone the pub most evenings to speak to me if you want. I'm working a lot at the moment. Or write back and let me know when you'll be back to get me.

I love you. I love you so much. We're having a baby!!
All my love, forever,
Maire xxx

He didn't want to cry again – a grown man, weeping in his car. What kind of lunatic would he look? He coughed gruffly and put the letter away. Perhaps he should get rid of it. All it did was remind him of his hideous response. He hadn't phoned the pub; he was much too cowardly. He'd written a sharp letter back, telling Maire to get in the car with Ailbe on the date he had said and to pack some things, just a few, and that 'the arrangements were made'. He'd taken it to town himself to post it, to make sure it got there overnight. He didn't say he loved her. He didn't say everything would be all right. He didn't say anything like that. He knew she was upset and panicking, because she had written back almost immediately, pleading for an explanation, pleading for confirmation of his love. He hadn't answered that one at all.

Oh, he was just the worst man alive. He put his head in his hands and ruffled his hair.

Out of the corner of his eye he saw movement. He strained to his right and squinted over his steering wheel. It was Donal, peering out of Bridget's front door to check for onlookers. He beckoned behind him and from the house

177

emerged Ruth, cradling a bundle of fabric, with a child inside that he couldn't see. They disappeared into their own house and shut the door.

CHAPTER THIRTY-ONE

In the open doorway of a place they only knew as the convent of the Congregation of the Sisters of the Sacred Hearts of Jesus and Mary, a couple from Kerry stood nervously in their best clothes. The call had come a few weeks earlier than they had been expecting, but they were ready. They'd been ready a long time now. They had been greeted by the Sister, who had politely enquired about their journey and bestowed blessings in abundance for their marriage and future as a family. Brenda was particularly pleased with this welcome; she loved and admired nuns deeply. This one especially seemed greatly pious and very pleasant. The Sister radiated holiness. Brenda felt happy. She turned and smiled warmly at her husband, but he wasn't looking. He was too busy craning his neck to see if their baby approached yet to notice and smile back at her. Brenda pulled her big coat more tightly around her, to hide more of herself. It was their day, at last.

Another nun appeared from the bottom of the stairs holding a tiny boy in a knitted grey-and-yellow jumper, wrapped loosely in a blanket. He had dark hair and was lying serenely asleep, but his little hands were flexing on their own, like he was reaching for something. Brenda couldn't contain her grin as they approached. He was quite little but looked very healthy, which she thought was good news.

Sister took the baby from the other nun, and then passed him swiftly over to Brenda. Her heart was full. She fell in love immediately. Her husband stroked the baby's tiny head and marvelled at his masses of hair. They cooed and kissed and cradled him.

"How is his mother?" Brenda asked quietly. She had thought the mother would be here too, to pass over the child and show her consent. She had worried about that part of the proceedings but had hoped to see the woman all the same – she, after all, had made Brenda a mother today.

The nun smiled pleasantly, as if warmed by Brenda's concern. "The child's mother fares very well," said Sister formally. "She has already been collected by her family, who have forgiven her for her sins." Sister smiled sweetly.

Brenda was surprised but said nothing. It wasn't her place to question these sisters of Christ; who was she, really, to question anything about this? The nuns seemed terribly pleasant. It didn't look like a bad place at all: a big house with a rose garden.

"Very well then," Sister continued. "Have a safe journey, and God be with you."

Brenda and her husband nodded gratefully at Sister and happily carried away their son to the awaiting car. They'd decided to keep the name he had been given by the convent; they rather liked it. It was as Irish as they came.

Sister shut the door and turned to the nun who had performed the walk on the currently incapacitated mother's behalf.

"Thank you, Sister Grace, for stepping in there," she said. Even when expressing gratitude or pleasure, her words still came out as cold and unfeeling.

Sister Grace nodded. "Sister, do you think we ought to have lied to them like that?" she asked meekly.

Sister fumed internally. This particular Sister was young, brand new to the congregation, and Sister disliked her already. "I do not feel, Sister Grace," Sister said frostily, "that *you* should be thinking anything." She marched down the corridor and sharply ordered the girls who were hovering, mouths open and bewildered at the bottom of the stairs, back to work.

CHAPTER THIRTY-TWO

Maire knew it wasn't deliberate and couldn't exactly be helped, but sharing a wall with her recently adopted child was more of an ordeal than she could bear. Penelope – they'd taken to calling her 'Penny', for short – was crying, her hungry cry, and Maire leaked milk all over her nightgown and the bed sheets every time she did. After a while she'd hear the sound of Ruth's muffled voice, soothing and singing while Penny screamed inconsolably. Then Donal's footsteps, his voice for a while, then Ruth's again. Eventually Maire would fall asleep, clinging to the pillow she pressed around her ears, and wake up to the same sound in the morning. She wondered if they realised she could hear.

She didn't have long left now until she was due to leave. Her discomfort and pain were subsiding more every day; it was easier getting in and out of the bath. She'd almost stopped crying – not quite, but almost. She ate toast and watched television. She wanted to finish *The Silver Tassie* before she went anywhere; she was quite enjoying that. When Bridget came home from work, she'd tell Maire about the patients she'd seen. What would Maire do? What course of treatment would she recommend? Maire was nearly always right. She was ready to go.

On the one hand, lying in bed damp and itchy from breast milk for a child in a different house was about the worst thing she could imagine. She was still bleeding a muddy liquid almost constantly. The rawness of handing over the baby she hadn't even held was still there; it clawed at her, that tiny red face bundled in tea towels and the mewing sound she'd never forget. Then she had been in Ruth's arms, and that was that.

But, on the other hand, she considered, she wasn't the one trying to sing a screaming baby back to sleep. That sound, so far removed from the delicate mewing she remembered on that first day, was grating. It irritated her, drove her almost mad. It was like a car alarm that wouldn't turn off. Now, more often than not, she felt her mind had blackened to it all; it was hard to believe now that she had loved Fionn as much as she did. She often stretched out in the bed and thought how lucky she was he'd gone back to his grumpy wife. They deserved each other. And that screaming. Constant, endless screaming. It was enough to drive anyone to distraction.

She'd been asked if she wanted to see Fionn again before she left, to say goodbye, and she'd said no. She hadn't seen him at all since the day after she'd arrived, and she didn't know if he'd seen the baby. She didn't care. At some point Penny would be introduced to the rest of the family as Ruth and Donal's own and it wouldn't matter anyway. Penny had two half-brothers whom she'd call cousins all her life. It didn't matter, Maire thought; she never saw her own cousins and her family was no longer her family because of what she'd done. Ailbe's cousin had done this to her. Family didn't stand for a damn thing; it was all a terrible, terrible lie. There was no such thing as unconditional love; Bessborough wouldn't exist if there was. Bridget could keep pretending that she loved Ruth with every bone in her body if she wanted to, but Maire was sick of that as well. She was sick of it all.

*

It was a week or so later, when Maire was reading the

183

newspaper at the kitchen table, that Bridget shuffled in, looking distracted.

"What's that?"

"Hmm?" Bridget looked where Maire was looking. "Oh." She looked down at Ruth's camera in her hands and feathered her fingers over the buttons. "It's Ruth and Donal's camera. She asked me to take the film to town with me to have it developed but there's still two shots left. She thought it was stuck but I don't think it is."

"Oh." Maire continued to stare.

"And I thought... well... just..." She looked down at the camera again.

"But, Bridget, you said—"

"I know what I said," Bridget snapped. "I know. And I'm sorry. And Ruth would be furious – well, not furious, love, no," she added quickly, seeing Maire's face. "I just..." Her eyes filled with tears. "I've just really liked having you here. And when you're gone..." Bridget couldn't finish. She buried her face in a tea towel she snatched from the nearest chair and Maire ran to her.

She didn't want to go either, not really, but she was excited about London and learning about nursing. She was tired of hearing Penny screaming through the walls. She missed Ailbe and was desperate to liberate her from Bessborough. She shushed Bridget while she sobbed noisily. She wanted to sob noisily too, but there had been so much of that. She was so sick of the crying. She didn't want to make it any worse.

Later, when they had dabbed at Bridget's puffy eyes and hung the tea towel up to dry, Bridget showed Maire how to look through the tiny window of the camera and which

184

buttons to press. They would take one each, and swap when they were developed. Bridget pulled herself up next to her fridge and smiled broadly; she wanted Maire to remember that much at least. When it was Maire's turn to be photographed, Bridget asked her to smile too. Maire considered it had been quite some time since she had smiled. She thought about her tiny girl – well, Ruth and Donal's tiny girl. She had only seen her for a second, but she had seemed lovely. So lovely.

"That's it, Maire! That's a lovely smile," and Bridget smiled too. The light lit up her face as the shutter snapped.

PART TWO
1986–1994

CHAPTER THIRTY-THREE

The new baby was stretching in his sleep. Penny was curious as to what babies might dream about; he looked like he was smiling, so he must be enjoying it.

Little John and Colm were already running in the garden, while Clodagh stood in the kitchen bragging to Bridget and Ruth about Little John's incredible talent for football; Colm's marvellousness at the violin; not to mention Fionn's extortionate pay increase now that he'd given up the locum work, and the smoothness of the journey over in their brand-new Vauxhall Astra. They were buying a new house down in Ballsbridge, much bigger than the one they were in now. Oh, and baby Michael was sleeping through the night already and breastfeeding had been a complete breeze.

"What do you think, Penelope?" Fionn asked, crouching down beside Penny as she stared, mesmerised, as Michael yawned.

"He's so little," she said.

"Yes, he is," Fionn said gently. "You were that little once; can you believe it?"

Penny could believe it; she'd seen a photograph. It was in a frame in Auntie Bridget's hallway. Clodagh sounded like she was coming back and so Penny inched away from baby Michael.

"Don't get your face so close, it'll scare him," she barked at Penny.

"Hello, Auntie Clodagh," Penny said politely. She realised Auntie Clodagh must have forgotten to say hello to her when she came in. "How are you?"

"Clodagh, she's fine; he's asleep," Fionn muttered when Clodagh didn't respond to Penny.

"Can I hold him?"

"Absolutely not."

"Of course you can," said Fionn, glancing at Clodagh, who scowled at Fionn and pointed a bony finger with a long red nail at Penny's face.

"She is too young. And she's clumsy."

"Oh no, I'm very nearly six years old," Penny said proudly. "And I'll be very, very careful. I promise."

"I know you will Penny, and Auntie Clodagh knows you will too; it's just that Michael is very small," he said.

Penny nodded enthusiastically – she could see that.

Fionn told Penny to hop up onto the sofa and put a cushion under her left elbow and make a circle with her arms. Clodagh went back into the kitchen as Fionn lifted the baby and placed him carefully in Penny's arms. She beamed at him, and then at Fionn, and then back at Michael again. She looked at his tiny nose and tiny ears and little wisps of red hair, like Little John and Colm had. She liked Little John and Colm very much, but she wasn't always allowed to play with them. Penny had learned this week that Little John was called Little John because he was named after Uncle Fionn's father, who was not only called John but was also Mammy and Auntie Bridget's brother. Mammy's father and mother had lots of children and all of Mammy and Auntie Bridget's brothers had also had lots of children. In fact, the only ones, except Bridget, who hadn't had lots of children were her own mammy and daddy; they had just had her, and no more. But she had decided, just now, she was going to have lots of children as well. They seemed lovely.

Michael smiled again in his sleep and Penny decided he must be dreaming about football, because all the boys she knew loved football – the Irish kind, and the other kind that was on TV sometimes. All the boys liked a team called *Liver-pool* because some of their players were Irish and they played in red tops. She also decided that Michael, second only to her own mammy and daddy and Auntie Bridget, was her favourite person in the whole world.

"I'll have him back now, Penny; he's probably hungry," Clodagh was saying, and she swooped down and whisked baby Michael away back to the kitchen.

Penny considered that mammies must be very clever to know their babies were hungry even when they were asleep. She hoped one day she'd be a clever mammy like that. She thought maybe she'd have eight children, like Uncle Liam. That was her favourite number. Although it might be quite a lot of washing. Her mammy was always complaining about the washing and there was only one of her.

"So, Penelope, how's school?" Fionn asked.
Penny beamed. She loved this question. "Really good! I'm very, very good at counting and numbers. And skipping."

"You are? That's grand."

"And-and watch this!" Penny stood up and took a deep breath. "Penelope *is ainm dom. Tá mé i mo chónaí in Éirinn agus is é Naomh Pádraig ár bpátrún.*"

Fionn applauded and Penny laughed as she bowed deeply.
"Brava!" Fionn said.

Penny frowned. She thought it was *brav-o*.

"Fionn *is ainm dom,*" he said slowly, "*agus tá grá mór agam duit.*"

Penny thought hard. She didn't know all of those words.

191

She'd only learned five sentences or so thus far and she was immensely proud of that one in particular. She found Irish hard because she couldn't practise much at home. Perhaps she would be allowed to call Uncle Fionn on the telephone and practise with him. She'd ask Mammy about that later.

"You said, 'my name is Fionn'," Penny repeated.

"I did."

"What else did you say?"

"Ah now," said Fionn, straightening up from crouching on the floor.

He stretched and Penny heard his back click. It sounded painful.

"You'll have to go and ask your teachers. Tell them you need to learn more Irish."

Fionn wandered out into the kitchen, and Penny heard his voice join the others. She couldn't ask her teachers. She'd already forgotten the sound of the words.

*

Later that night, Ruth sat with her at the dining table, with pieces of paper spread out.

"Ruthie, she's five years old; she's not going to remember all this!" Donal had called out to her, pouring whiskey into a tumbler and settling down in front of the TV.

"Oh, I will, Daddy!" Penny had cried as she scurried in with a box of crayons. "I'm very good."

"Yes, darling, you are, very clever. And you get that from me of course," said Ruth, smoothing her hair.

They sellotaped multiple sheets of paper together and drew an enormous tree that stretched over all of them. Penny could colour it in as they went along, Ruth said.

"Now... what are Mammy's and Daddy's proper names?" she asked.

"Ruth Agnes Mary Quinn and Donal Gerard Quinn," she recited proudly.

Ruth grinned. "Perfect. And what's your name?"

"Penelope Mary Quinn but everyone calls me Penny because that's short for Penelope. Except for Uncle Fionn and Sister Margaret who always call me Penelope," she added, pursing her lips.

"Yes," Ruth said.

Donal fidgeted.

"But that is your proper name and when you get older and have to fill in forms you will have to write Penelope, not Penny. Which means you *will* have to learn to spell it properly."

Penny scowled.

"Don't sulk, Penny. Now, what were Grandma and Granda Conghaile's proper names?"

"Um..." She ran her finger lightly across their empty spaces. "I don't remember. They're from a very long time ago."

Together they wrote in Grandma Mariah and Granda Seamus, Uncle John and his wife and their five children (Fionn was the eldest), then Fionn's wife Auntie Clodagh and their wee boys Little John, Colm and Michael, as well as Uncle Liam and his wife, Uncle Dermot and his wife, and Auntie Bridget.

"They're my *cou-sins*," she said, elongating the syllables. This was a new word. She quite liked it. "So Uncle Fionn isn't my uncle; he's my *cou-sin* as well?"

"Yes."

"Why do I call him uncle then?"

"Because you're little and it's polite. Now, let's put crosses next to your grandmas, grandas and Uncle Dermot and Auntie Leanne," said Ruth.

"Why?"

"Because they're in heaven," Ruth said gently. "With God and Jesus and all the angels."

"Are they okay?" Penny asked.

Ruth smiled. "Yes, darling, they're okay," she said. "We just can't visit them, that's all."

Penny smiled back. Ruth looked a bit sad, so Penny tried to smile a bit harder.

"Good. So. How many children does Uncle Liam have?" she asked, looking for a green crayon.

Donal started to laugh from his chair. "I told you, Ruthie, this was a terrible idea. You'll be there all night."

*

Ruth looked proudly on at Penny as she carefully drew leaves on the tree and coloured them in. She was sad that Penny had no grandparents, though, and that she was learning to write their names without ever having seen their faces. Ruth hadn't had any either, but Donal had dim memories of an elderly grandfather, who smelled of pipe tobacco, bouncing him on his knee and teaching him to pull faces. Even if she had been ten years younger when she had Penny, it wouldn't have made a difference in that respect, so she couldn't blame herself for that, no matter how much she wanted to.

"Mammy, Irish is really hard," Penny said quietly. "When

194

we have to speak Irish all the time at school, sometimes I get upset."

Donal turned in his chair and he and Ruth looked at each other. She hadn't mentioned this before. In fact, Penny's teacher, Sister June, had remarked just a few weeks ago about how well Penny was doing in every area so far.

"Do you, poppet?" Ruth said gently.

Penny nodded.

"Well, it is very hard, but you're so clever, much cleverer than Daddy and I, and Auntie Bridget, because we can't speak any Irish at all!" Ruth said brightly.

Penny wasn't comforted. "Today, Cousin Fionn—"

"Uncle Fionn."

"*Uncle* Fionn," she said, "said something to me in Irish and I don't know what he said, and that happens all the time at school and I don't like it and it makes me feel stupid."

Ruth scowled at Donal. The all-Irish school had been his idea.

Any mention of Fionn made Donal fidgety and so he stood up to top up his whiskey. Ruth opened her mouth and closed it again.

"Uncle Fionn speaks Irish," Penny said.

"He does."

"Maybe I could call him on his telephone, and he could talk to me in Irish so I can practise," she said merrily. She thought it was an excellent idea, and she'd thought of it herself.

"Oh, I don't know about that," Ruth said straight away. She looked at Donal for support.

"No, Uncle Fionn's very busy, Penny," Donal agreed. "Remember, he's a doctor. He has all those patients to look after and then Auntie Clodagh and the boys too."

Penny thought about this. She was disappointed, but that was true. And Michael was very little and needed lots of looking after because he couldn't dress himself or brush his own teeth. She wasn't sure if Michael even had any teeth. But she liked Uncle Fionn, and they only saw him once a year or so.

"Hmm," Penny said. She pouted her lips.

"Keep trying hard on your own, Penny, and if you're still finding it difficult at Christmas, we'll have a think about it again then," Ruth said encouragingly. "Remember your teacher said you're doing very, very well."

Penny nodded.

"Anyway, I think it's time for bath and pyjamas, don't you little madam?" Donal said. "Come on, your carriage awaits."

Penny jumped up from her chair and leapt onto Donal's back, as she did every night. She laughed hysterically as he neighed like a horse and galloped up the stairs, her little feet bouncing at his hips. Ruth marvelled at him. Donal had turned fifty this year, and still he sprang around with Penny like a young man of half that. They'd have to arrange Penny's first Holy Communion next year. She could hardly believe it.

Ruth started to tidy up the table and put the crayons back in the box. They could pick this up again tomorrow night, and when Penny had finished colouring it in, she would pin it up in Penny's room, so she could see it all the time. Hopefully she'd learn everyone's names and, in doing so, she'd stop interrupting all their conversations with 'who?' every five minutes. Ruth had written 'My Family' on the top for her as a title, in big, clear letters in pencil, so Penny could go over it in marker pen. Evidently, she already had. Ruth turned the paper to face her. Over Ruth's handwriting, Penny had written '*Mo chlann*'.

*

On Monday afternoon, Penny had been summoned to Sister Margaret's office. Sister Margaret was in charge at Penny's school and children only got sent to her office when they had done something naughty. Penny searched her conscience for bad words spoken or naughty deeds performed. She was sure there was nothing she had done. She was turning her twitching hands over in her lap and biting her nails ferociously. She didn't like being in trouble. Especially with Sister Margaret – she liked her a lot.

Opposite her office was another office where children went when they were feeling sick and had to be sent home. Only women worked in there. The phone was almost always ringing, and it always smelled alarmingly of coffee. From where she was sitting outside, she could see Caoimhe Bell being sick in a bowl. It made Penny feel sick as well. Sometimes the women spoke English and sometimes they spoke Irish on the phone, depending on whose mammy and daddy they were speaking to. Penny had to remember to speak in Irish when she went in. She often got confused about it still.

"*Teacht i*, Penelope," called Sister Margaret.

Penny swallowed and stood up. She could go in now. Her legs felt slightly shaky, and she was worried she would fall over.

"Have a sit down there."

She sat in the big chair opposite Sister Margaret's desk. It

197

had cushions on it. Their chairs in the classrooms weren't like that. Sister had a hot cup of coffee on her desk, which smelled horrible to Penny and made her feel even more sick.

"Now then…" Sister Margaret was smiling at Penny.

She smiled back nervously.

"Miss Penelope. What's this I hear about *another* set of full marks on *another* maths test?" She spoke slowly so Penny could digest the words and remember them.

When she did, she was confused. She had thought that was quite good, what she'd done. "Yes," was all she said.

"And you were the only one who got full marks, which is the same as last week, isn't it, Penelope?"

"Yes."

"It's wonderful, Penelope, and we're all very proud of you," she said.

She took out a piece of yellow card and signed it with her fancy-looking pen. The end was pointy, and had a tiny hole in it, and Donal had one like that that Penny wasn't allowed to colour in with, so she knew it must be a fancy pen that Sister Margaret probably didn't colour in with either.

"Take this home to your mammy and your daddy. I'm sure they'll be very pleased."

Penny looked at the piece of card she had been given. It said '*bronnta ar*' and Sister Margaret had written *Penelope Quinn* on the line underneath it. Then it said '*as sár-obair i*' and Sister Margaret had written *matamaitic* on the line underneath that one. It had a star, and the words '*an-mhaith*!' printed next to the star. Penny grinned. She only knew one other person to get one of these, and that particular individual was currently bringing up her lunch in the school office. This would be on the fridge by teatime. This was excellent.

"And there's something else, please, Penelope," Sister Margaret said, in English.

"Yes, Sister?"

"Next week we're having some new children come to join your class. They are twins. Do you know what that means?"

"It means... they look the same and they were born on the same day, at the same time."

"Close enough. These are brother and sister twins, so they might not look the same. They are called Patrick and Mary," she said.

"We've already got two Patricks in our class," Penny retorted.

"I am aware."

"And a Mary."

"Right. Yes. I would like you to make a special effort to look after them and be their friends when they arrive. Show them where to put their lunchboxes, where to hang their coats, and keep them company at playtime. They've moved quite a distance and I need you to be very kind and make them feel extra welcome. Does that sound all right?"

"Yes," Penny said, going back to Irish. They weren't supposed to speak in English much unless they absolutely had to, and she knew the word for *yes* very well. She was pleased. New children sounded exciting. She could teach them all her favourite games. This day was turning out to be absolutely grand.

Sister Margaret went back to Irish too. "By the way," she said, "their *máthairtheanga* is *Gaeilge*."

Penny blinked. She thought she understood that.

"What is *máthairtheanga, i mBéarla,* Penelope?"

"Mother tongue. It means mother tongue. They speak

199

Irish at home!"

"They do," Sister Margaret said, smiling. "So, you can make friends and practise. Your mother called and said you were worried about your Irish."

Penny pursed her lips. She had heard – and understood – *friends, practise, mother* and *Irish*. She could piece it together from that. She nodded in agreement.

"Grand. That's settled then. We'll introduce them to the school at Mass tomorrow, and you can take them from there. *Ar shiúl a théann tú,* Penelope."

Penny jumped down from the big chair, proudly clutching her certificate in her hand, and trotted merrily back to her classroom.

*

Penny was right; it went straight on the fridge as soon as she was home.

"Well look at this!" Ruth had exclaimed, giving Penny a big hug and kiss. "What does it all say?"

"It says 'Awarded to Penelope Quinn for Excellent Work in… *Math-a-mat-icks*'," she said. "And there it says 'well done!'. And there's a star."

"I can see that!" Ruth grinned at Penny. "You are so clever. Let's pop it up here and you can show Daddy when he gets in."

"Can we tell Auntie Bridget?"

"She's at work, poppet. You can tell her on Sunday."

CHAPTER THIRTY-FOUR

Bridget was working far more now than she had done a decade ago. As she had told Maire, it wasn't like she needed the money; she did it because she loved it. She still did love it, but what she needed more now was distraction, company and something to do. She only saw Ruth, Donal and Penny on Sundays now. They liked their time together, 'as a family', and had made it clear that Bridget was not part of their new family unit.

All right, they'd never actually said it outright, but that was certainly how they made her feel.

When Penny had first been born, Bridget had Maire to look after and so she rarely saw the baby. Maire was utterly despondent; Bridget hadn't known what to do with her. Postnatal depression was bad enough on its own, without the added trauma of a broken heart in the first instance and then having given the baby away to boot. Maire had milk but no baby. She had raging mothering hormones but no baby to mother. Bridget had silently delivered Maire's afterbirth, cleaned up the sheets and the floor and the apparatus she had used, all while Maire howled and wailed, as if her whole world was ending. Bridget sat up on the bed with her and held her for hours and hours.

Maire had told her she wanted to go to Cork first, to collect her friend Ailbe from Bessborough, and then go on by ferry to Fishguard and take the train to London. Bridget had given her stacks of money to pay for them both to make the journey, and Maire had been immensely grateful. Bridget had taken down her John 16:33 plaque from the living room wall and buried it in Maire's bag when she hadn't been looking. Maire had promised to write, despite their agreement with Ruth, and she had done so, fairly regularly, amidst her studies and practical work.

Bridget had been so worried about the girls' journey that she had insisted on booking their hotel in London herself, and then she had telephoned every hour to ask if they had checked in yet. Eventually, the exasperated receptionist told her what she wanted to hear.

"Yes, they have checked in under the name Maire Connelly."

"Both of them? Irish girls? What did they look like?"

"Yes, madam, two Irish girls. One had ginger hair…"

Bridget cringed. She hated that word and the English would *insist* on using it.

"And the other had sort of… dark hair, I think? Very slight? Do you want me to put you through to their room?"

"No," Bridget had said. "No, I just wanted to check they had arrived safely."

"Are you their mother?"

"Yes," Bridget had said. "Yes, I am their mother."

*

Bridget was relieved when she first heard that; Maire must have got Ailbe out as well. She didn't know the girl but didn't like the thought of her there, in a place like that. God only knows what went on behind high walls in those sort of circumstances… She didn't want to speak or think ill of the Church, not at all; but she had heard stories. Sometimes.

In any case, Maire was doing beautifully now, after all she

had been through when she first left. The college and the hospital had been just thrilled with her and her progress; she'd finished with the highest marks and the best results of the entire cohort she had studied with. If Bridget could, she would have plastered them all over her house – put them on the fridge, like Ruth did with Penny. Maire was rotating around different departments at their last communication, and was talking about pursuing a Master's degree in one of the areas she liked best, part time, once she could. Bridget was bursting with pride at Maire's every sentence. She missed her desperately around the house; Bridget was awfully lonely these days.

In the years before Maire – and Penny, of course – Bridget and Ruth had seen each other almost every day. Now, she saw Ruth only occasionally during the week, as she had kept herself busy over these recent years with mother and baby groups, church picnics, swimming lessons and school events – everything she had ever dreamed of. She had made a new circle of friends with a new generation of mothers, and they sat around in coffee shops talking about their... well, actually Bridget had no idea what they talked about.

Bridget hadn't held Penny until she was almost five months old, long after she'd stopped saying goodnight to Maire's empty room out of habit, when Ruth had finally allowed someone that wasn't her and Donal to lay a finger on baby Penny.

The baptism had been an enormous celebration. Ruth was christening her first child at the same time as their brother John was christening his dozens of grandchildren. John hadn't been able to make the journey down for Penny's baptism and Fionn had attended the ceremony, briefly, sitting alone at the back and driving away from the church before the family had left. Ruth had pretended not to notice, but Bridget had, and made her notice known. Ruth had hired the church hall and spent hundreds of pounds on food and decorations. Penny's celebration cake had been bigger, at least two or three times over, than Ruth and Donal's wedding cake.

*

Bridget gloomily scribbled down the disappointing figures on the patient's chart. This one wasn't improving very much at all. He was in the ICU as the lone survivor of a horrific car crash up near the airport and had been in a coma ever since. If and when he woke up, the doctors would have to tell him that he was the only one here. The rest, he was terribly sorry to say, were all downstairs in the morgue. Bridget knew, for her part, that if she was to be woken up and told such a thing, she'd rather be put back to sleep and stay that way. She checked his oxygen level, which was ticking along adequately, and went to make a cup of tea.

She sat alone in the nurses' station with her mug and took out the letter which had arrived that morning, with an English postmark. She hadn't had time to open it as she'd crossed paths with the postman on her way out to work. She'd carried it in the pocket of her uniform all day and she'd only just, finally, got herself five minutes alone.

Dear Bridget,

I hope you're well and Ruth, Donal and Penny are all very happy and healthy. I was thinking it must be getting on for her first Communion soon, and I wanted to get her something for it. You say it's from you, of course. A nice Bible or a rosary or something, you choose. Enclosed is £20; let me know what you decide on and what she thinks of it. I hope it goes all right; I expect Ruth is throwing herself into making all the arrangements and planning a Queen's garden party!

Work is good. I've just finished a rotation in the respiratory ward, and it was fascinating. Something to think about, in any case...

Bridget slurped happily on her tea as she read about Maire's magnificence as a nurse. She was so proud. She had known this would be a good idea.

...we're thinking about a long weekend away to Brighton next month, a girls' jaunt – she's still not left London since we arrived; can you believe that? I'm sure you'd agree I think it's about time she saw...

"Nurse Conghaile?"

It was one of the medical students. She was a nervous wee one, not terribly sure of herself. But Bridget felt that, with some encouragement, she'd probably be all right. If only the doctors in charge of her thought that as well.

"Hmm?"

"Mr O'Sullivan doesn't feel very well."

"That's because he isn't, dear."

"No, he told me that he doesn't. I think he's... I think he's... awake."

CHAPTER THIRTY-FIVE

"You're adopted?"

Penny was silent. It was a shock.

"Yeah, it means my mammy and daddy *are* my mammy and daddy, but my mammy now isn't the one who grew me in her tummy. That was someone else. But they're still my mammy and daddy."

Penny stared at Patrick as he took another bite of the biscuits he had stolen from the kitchen. Penny had eaten hers already.

"But I don't really mind."

Penny had never known anyone adopted before. She didn't know if she was supposed to be happy or sad about it. Patrick didn't seem to be either. She and Patrick had played together every playtime and lunchtime for over a year, and he'd never once mentioned it. This was the first time Ruth had allowed Penny to spend the afternoon at a friend's house after school despite months of pleading, and they were taking the occasion very seriously.

Patrick and Mary didn't... *seem* adopted, Penny thought. There was nothing in their house that would suggest anything had taken place that was unlike her own family. It was all very mysterious.

"Oh," she said at last. "So is Mary adopted too?"

"No," he said through a mouthful of crumbs.

Penny wished he would swallow nicely and then speak, like she was told to do. Or did she wish she could speak with her mouth full too? She wasn't sure.

"I asked about that. My mammy and daddy didn't think

they could make a baby on their own, so they were going to get me from the lady where I was being born but I wasn't born yet. And while they were waiting, they made Mary on their own after all. It was a *miracle*." He said the last word proudly. "They made Mary themselves, but they really wanted me, and they chose me, which they said makes me extra special," he said, grinning. "But I'm not supposed to say that to Mary."

Penny thought about it for a moment. It had very recently been Father's Day and, at Mass, Father Kelly – who wasn't anyone's father, because he wasn't allowed a wife – had mentioned Joseph the Carpenter who adopted Jesus as his own wee one, even though actually he was God's wee one, and that he was an important person and an important father all the same. It seemed like a really good thing that he'd done, a good thing for God. Joseph taught Jesus to be a carpenter like he was. She imagined being taken to Da's carpet shop and learning how to carpet things, like Jesus. Penny smiled. Patrick's parents had done a lovely, good thing too, like Joseph had done.

Patrick saw Penny's smile and frowned at her. He hadn't said the worst part yet. "But I have to share my birthday with her so they could tell everyone we were twins." He sighed.

Penny thought that he didn't seem so happy about that part. "Why did they need to tell everyone you were twins?"

"I don't know," Patrick said, licking his fingers.

"Which one of you is the older one?"

"I don't know. Mammy won't tell us."

"Then how do you know it's your birthday you share? It might be hers."

"Might be."

"Is it a secret?"

"Oh yes," Patrick said, looking very serious. "We're not supposed to tell anyone or talk about it ever except with Mammy and Daddy. But I'm telling you because you're my very best friend." Patrick blushed slightly as he said that.

Penny was very happy. Patrick was her very best friend too, although she liked Mary a lot as well.

"Do you have any secrets?" he asked Penny in a whisper.

Penny thought hard. There was the small matter of the stolen biscuits before dinner. But apart from that… "No, I don't think I do," Penny said.

Patrick looked disappointed.

"But if I do ever get one, I promise I'll tell you it."

"Promise?"

"Promise."

They grinned at each other.

"Do you want to see my new goldfish? They're deadly," Patrick said.

She nodded and followed him to the hallway.

Patrick's goldfish were, indeed, deadly. He told her they were called Fleck and Bubbles and Penny laughed.

"Those are funny names," she said, and Patrick took grave offence.

"They are not," he said indignantly. "Go and play Cindy dolls with Mary if you're going to be a *girl* about it."

*

"Mammy, guess what."

Penny was sitting at the kitchen table doing her homework. Ruth stirred her soup on the hob and sniffed it

208

gently.

"What darling?"

"I know someone who is *ah-dop-ted*." Penny liked her new long word. She counted to herself; it was three *sill-ah-bulls*. "Mammy!"

Ruth had dropped her wooden spoon on the kitchen floor and splattered soup on the tiles. She was staring at Penny. Penny stared back at her. Perhaps she'd got the word wrong and said something rude. It wouldn't be the first time Patrick had taught her a rude word and she'd repeated it at home. Patrick was lots of fun, but he wasn't very… what was the word Sister June used? *Freagrach*. Responsible.

"Who…?" Ruth started. She could feel her heart beating in her throat. "Who told you… no, I mean, who told you that they're adopted, Penny?" She forced a smile and reached for a tea towel.

"Patrick," Penny said. "Patrick told me yesterday that he's adopted but Mary isn't, and he has to share his birthday with her."

"Which Patrick is that?" said Ruth, turning back to her soup and taking some deep breaths. She shut her eyes and willed her heart to slow.

"You know, Patrick who is Mary's brother. His da is a dentist. He speaks funny."

"The twins?"

"Yes."

"Ah, of course," Ruth said, smiling. "He doesn't speak funny, he's from Kerry."

"Sounds funny to me."

"Well, he's a very good dentist," said Ruth, smoothing Penny's hair. "It was very nice of Patrick to share his secret with you, but you must make sure you don't tell anyone else, yes? It's not polite to share people's secrets."

Penny nodded. She didn't have anyone else she wanted to tell anyway. After all, she was Patrick's very best friend. She went back to her homework, which she had almost finished, and thank goodness as it wasn't her favourite.

Ruth mopped up the floor with kitchen towel and quietly left the room.

*

A few days later, Penny was watching television with Donal as he read the Sunday papers, when Ruth pottered in and asked Penny what she wanted for tea.

"Mammy, why are you and Daddy so old?" she asked.

Donal laughed. Ruth did not.

"Excuse me, Penelope?" Ruth said sternly.

Penny was worried. She was only called Penelope by two people, neither of which were here. If Mammy did it, it meant trouble.

"Patrick and Mary's mammy and daddy are younger than you," Penny said. "And so are Caoimhe's. And so are—"

"Yes, all right, I get the picture," Ruth snapped.

Penny made a face and her cheeks started to flush.

Donal put his arm around her and looked up at Ruth. "Well, Penny," he said gently.

Ruth flopped into the other sofa and looked unhappily at them both.

"Mammy and Daddy have been married for a very long time, but it took us a very long time to make you. Some mammies and daddies make their babies very quickly and,

210

for some mammies and daddies, it takes just a bit longer."

"How long did it take you?" Penny asked.

Ruth raised her eyebrows at Donal.

"A very long time, Penny. Years and years. We waited a very long time for you."

"Is that why I'm the only one?" she asked sadly. "Patrick has Mary, Caoimhe has three sisters, and—"

"Yes, Penny, that's why," Ruth said bitterly. "You know, you shouldn't really be asking questions like this. It's really quite rude." She stood up and stormed out of the lounge.

Penny looked up at Donal for reassurance, and he kissed her little forehead.

"Don't worry about Mammy," he said. "Mammy gets upset that there aren't more of you. But because you are the only one, Penny, it makes you extra *extra extra* special to us."

Penny smiled weakly. She supposed that was okay. But she didn't have anyone to play with at home, which is why she went to play at Patrick and Mary's sometimes, and they often came here to play too. She would have liked to have someone to play with.

"So how do babies get made?" Penny asked.

Donal shut his eyes. Ruth was right – she shouldn't be asking questions like this; it led to very uncomfortable things. He hadn't prepared an answer yet; he'd thought she was still a bit young to be interested.

"Well, they're…" He paused.

Penny looked up at him expectantly.

"God makes them. And then he sends them down to us in mammies' tummies and they grow."

Much to Donal's relief, Penny seemed happy enough with that. Her school told her all the time that she had been made by God; they all were. So that was all right then. It made perfect sense.

"I've been here a long time now," she said hopefully – she was turning eight next weekend and that was a long time. "Maybe you'll be able to make another baby soon."

Donal smiled wearily at her. Ruth was fifty this year. She was going through the change and snapping mercilessly at everyone. He was almost fifty-three himself.

"Maybe. I'll keep you posted, shall I?" he asked.

Penny nodded. "Yes please."

They spoke no more about it. Donal changed the channel.

*

Ruth was experiencing hellish symptoms and the worst thing about it was that so many of them were the same as pregnancy. People assumed that because she'd had only one child, she'd only had one pregnancy, and one birth. She'd had five pregnancies that very few people knew anything about. One of them – the second one – she'd got as far as fifteen weeks. She'd been pregnant collectively throughout her life, roughly, for about a year. She'd resented every single period she'd ever had since her wedding day. Now, they were slowly disappearing before her eyes, and there was almost a muscle-memory-like reflex of shock and brief joy when she realised that she was late last time. Not now, though. Her body that had failed her every day for twenty-five years was now starting to slowly grind to a halt.

Ruth was hot. She didn't want to do anything about it because in approximately forty-five seconds, she'd be cold again. She stood in the kitchen and ran her hands under cold water until they started to feel numb. She didn't really care, the pain, the numbness; she didn't care. She wanted to glare at the walls just for being there. There was washing up to do and the sight of it, the smell of it, made her feel sick. She was sick of washing up. Donal never did any washing up. When she'd finished doing it all herself, she'd have dinner to cook and that would create even more washing up. It was all just a miserable, never-ending cycle of pointless stuff she had to do.

Ruth sloped back into the living room. Donal and Penny were watching TV happily together. She was so jealous of their relationship. Donal got to watch TV with Penny, bounce her around on his back and deal with her for just a couple of hours at night, when he got home from the shop. He had his dinner at the table with her while she did her homework, and then he read the stories and put her to bed. Penny appreciated all that. What she didn't appreciate was how her school uniform was always clean and ironed, how there was always a packed lunch for her every morning and a cooked dinner every night, how her little reading diary that was inspected by her teacher was always completed and signed, every day, by Ruth. No one ever said thank you for any of that.

She threw her weight into the other sofa with a huff. Neither of them took any notice. She wasn't even sure why she was surprised. No one was bothered about her. Penny giggled at something on the TV. Donal shut his eyes and started to doze.

Ruth stood up, grabbed her keys and slammed the front door. She was going to buy a dishwasher before the shops shut.

CHAPTER THIRTY-SIX

Bridget was at her wits' end. What good was it, being a nurse, if everyone just ignored her very sound medical advice every time she was asked for it? She herself had sailed merrily through the change eighteen months ago with just a small pot of Vitamin D pills and a tube of cream she hid in a drawer – but that didn't mean she didn't know what she was looking at where Ruth was concerned. She'd seen it a hundred times before; she knew she was definitely right – especially now that Ruth was slamming doors and bashing things around at such a volume Bridget could hear it in her own house.

Ruth was depressed; it was obvious to everyone except Donal. Or, more likely, it was terribly obvious to Donal as well, but he was pretending it wasn't happening because he didn't know what to do.

Bridget liked Donal. She reminded herself of that regularly because she wasn't about to start mentally bashing her own sister's husband. Mariah had refused to go to their wedding, but Bridget had been there, *delighted* to be there. She remembered that aspect of it very clearly. Donal was a bit of an oddball, but he made Ruth happy, and that was all that mattered. But as he'd aged, he'd just become... so terribly *lazy* with Ruth. Perhaps he was fed up of it now. He wasn't a shrimp like Mariah had always said. He was a jellyfish – mostly liquid-based, no spine, merrily drifting out to sea.

Bridget thought about everything she had done to keep Ruth happy over the years. She'd only gone to Galway to study; she might've gone anywhere else in the whole world.

214

She'd taken the first job she'd got at Richmond Surgical – of course, it was the Beaumont Hospital now – so that Ruth didn't feel alone after their awful mother had finally had the common decency to die. Ruth had been mysteriously despondent over the death of a woman who hadn't even spoken to her for the last eighteen months of her life. Bridget hadn't left that job in almost thirty years so that Ruth wouldn't feel abandoned. She'd had job offers, lots of them, that no one knew about; she'd turned them all down to stay with Ruth.

Perhaps it had all been a mistake. A huge mistake to keep moving the world for Ruth.

Now Bridget felt bad. Ruth was having a hard time and it wasn't fair that she was so hard on her. She just wanted the world to listen to her, because she knew that it wouldn't take much to alleviate Ruth's symptoms – because that's what they were, just symptoms, and symptoms can be treated. Ruth had everything she'd always wanted – a husband and family, a child who adored her, and Bridget next door at her beck and call. It would just be nice if Donal would pick up the slack so that Bridget could attend to her own life, now that she was nearing fifty and had devoted the first half-century of her life to Ruth.

CHAPTER THIRTY-SEVEN

Itching to throw another party since their last one for Penny's first Holy Communion had been rained off three years ago, Ruth insisted on hiring the village hall for her tenth birthday. Donal had taken Penny out to the park for the morning to keep her occupied, while Ruth and Bridget, and some of Ruth's young mam friends, decorated it with pink balloons and banners and pink crisp tablecloths. Bridget cut up sandwiches in the kitchen and made up cups of orange and blackcurrant squash.

Penny had wanted to invite her entire class to her party, which Ruth had said was quite all right – the more the merrier, in fact. The mountain of presents grew swiftly on the table as twenty-three nine- and ten-year-olds flooded the hall just before lunchtime. There was also some of the family: not Fionn's boys, as the oldest two were now fourteen and twelve and wouldn't be seen dead at a ten-year-old's birthday party. Michael was only four and Clodagh wouldn't bring him on account of him being so much younger than all the others, which Ruth had agreed was more than fair enough.

The girls all wore pretty party dresses in various shades of pinks and purples, with sparkly jelly shoes that seemed to be all the rage now. The boys wore little collared shirts and smart trousers. They all fussed around Penny, the birthday girl, who graciously said, "Thank you very much for coming!" to all her classmates, although Ruth had told her that's what we say at the end. Ruth looked at all the children and thought about her other five, who were not here.

She would have an eighteen-year-old, probably in its first

year of Trinity College, studying law or something clever like that. A sixteen-year-old playing Guns N' Roses at a deafening volume, deciding whether to do their Leaving Certificate and go and get a job somewhere as their elder sibling's punishing university regime looked a bit too much like hard work. Thirteen-year-old twins – good God, imagine twin teenage girls at home, if they had been girls, what with all these boy bands that were on the radio all the time now. And, of course, a ten-year-old, which she had. Ruth considered that if any of those children had lived, she might not have Penny with her now.

It was a difficult emotion for her to process. To wish for her other children would wish Penny away. To wish to keep Penny was to accept the deaths of five of her and Donal's children; for, absolutely, they were children, and they had died. She didn't like the word 'miscarriage'. It sounded like her fault. Like she had been carrying the babies carelessly in her arms and dropped them to their deaths. On this day, she felt happy. She felt young again. She still had a child in primary school; not many women her age could say that. She had been blessed with a miracle child at forty-two; that was an indisputable fact.

*

Bridget cut sandwiches from rectangles into triangles and then into smaller triangles. She arranged them neatly on a plastic serving platter. The children were laughing hysterically at the magician who had come to entertain them for an hour; she watched them through a little hatch in the kitchen wall. Ruth and Donal stood at the back, uncovering

217

the rest of the food. There was a *The Little Mermaid* birthday cake hidden in the kitchen behind Bridget for later and ten tall candles. The film had come out last year and Penny was utterly obsessed with it. Ariel had red hair too, she claimed proudly, and she floated around the house tunelessly shout-singing 'Part of Your World' so loudly that Bridget could hear it in her own house.

She thought about the ten years that had passed since Maire had been in her home. She was the closest thing to a daughter Bridget was ever going to get; she had rather hoped that she would have a similar relationship with Penny, once she was old enough. But Ruth was so possessive of her that Bridget couldn't get a look in; no one in the family really could. Bridget hadn't spent more than twenty minutes alone with Penny since the day she was born.

It was also undeniable that Penny was now the image of Maire. Ruth still said how much she looked like her side of the family; she bore an uncanny resemblance to her brother John, Ruth had said; it was absolutely remarkable. True, when Penny was a much smaller child, she had really resembled Fionn – well, John, as Ruth said – but now, she looked astoundingly like Maire. In just another ten years from today, she would be the age Maire was when Bridget had last seen her. It didn't seem possible.

Bridget carried the tray of sandwiches to the table where an enormous spread of buffet food was waiting. The children were clapping and waving goodbye to the magician and making their way briskly to the tables laid with paper plates and cups of squash. Ruth smiled merrily as Bridget wandered back to the kitchen to prepare the cake candles and make the bowls of strawberry jelly and ice cream. Donal put his arms

218

around Ruth and grinned at the canteen tables of happy children, eating his homemade scotch eggs, of which he was immensely proud.

Bridget had to get away. She didn't know where, or when, but somewhere, and soon. She was growing very tired of all this child-based merriment – for a child, she felt, she should definitely have been allowed to be more involved with. She had nursed this child's mother; she had delivered this very child, purple and screaming, into the world. Penny had been wrapped in a tea towel from Bridget's own kitchen. And now? Well. Now, next to nothing.

She lit the ten candles and carried the cake precariously in one hand. She tipped the light switch with the other to plunge the room into darkness. The children fell silent and turned to see what had happened. Bridget started to sing and they all joined in noisily.

"Happy birthday to you! Happy birthday to you! Happy birthday *dear Pen-neeeee,* happy birthday to you!" The children clapped and whooped.

Penny's whole face lit up as she recognised the red-headed mermaid on the cake that she so admired. She blew out all ten candles in one swift blow and beamed at her friends around the table, who applauded her heartily.

Donal kissed Ruth, and Ruth laughed and grinned with happiness. Bridget walked back to the kitchen to cut up the cake, wrap the pieces in napkins and put them into party bags.

*

"I'm going to go on holiday," Bridget said sharply, as she sat in Ruth's living room that evening.

219

Penny had opened all her many presents from her friends, been thoroughly overwhelmed by the sheer volume, variety and pinkness of all her gifts, eaten three pieces of birthday cake for her tea and gone to sleep in the middle of a sentence when tucked up in bed.

Ruth barely reacted. Bridget had been on lots of holidays by herself throughout the years. She was often planning little trips and trotting about the place. Ruth sipped her tea.

"Lovely," was all she said.

"No, I mean, I'm going to go away. For a long time, a few months, maybe."

Ruth gawped at Bridget and put her mug down. She looked confused.

"What do you mean, months? What about work? What about us? And *where*?" she asked, in a panicked voice.

Bridget stifled a huff. *What about you?* Ruth hadn't been terribly worried about where she was and what she was doing for a decade now. Suddenly, Bridget wasn't going to be there, and Ruth was all upset. *Good,* she thought. *About time.*

"I don't know 'when' yet. Work will give me a... sabbatical, of sorts. I have almost a year's worth of annual leave saved up." It was true; Bridget hadn't taken any holiday for a long time. She'd had no need. What would she do with it, anyway? "I was thinking of going around Europe, seeing the sights, Paris, Vienna, you know. Maybe America. I could see Liam." Bridget hadn't considered America and Liam until she said it out loud. She stirred with excitement at the idea. Liam's eight children had produced fourteen grandchildren – and counting. They'd moved from Philadelphia five years ago and lived on an enormous farm in Montana now – or 'ranch' as they called it over there. She

220

quite fancied that now she thought about it.

"Oh," was all Ruth said.

She never thought Bridget would disappear for months at a time like this. She didn't like the thought of Bridget's house empty. No Bridget to pick up the phone when she called. It reminded her of when her mother had died and Bridget was away at university, and then when she had lost her first baby. She had Donal and Mr Quinn but she had felt all alone. She didn't like this. At all.

"Oh," she said again, and looked at Donal for support. He was eating a plate of leftover party food and thoroughly enjoying himself in the process. "We'll miss you, won't we, Donal?"

Donal hadn't been listening properly. He nodded in agreement with Ruth. "Oh, yes, we will," he said enthusiastically. "We'll certainly miss you. And so will Penny."

*

Penny had cried hysterically at the airport when they dropped Bridget off with her cases. Three months seemed like an exponentially long time. She loved her Auntie Bridget so, so much; she was upset that she didn't see her that often even though she only lived next door, and now she was going to get on an aeroplane and go to some other countries and Penny wouldn't see her for weeks.

"Hey now, I'll bring home lots of presents for you," Bridget said, stroking Penny's masses of red hair as she clung to Bridget's middle and wailed. Ruth and Donal hovered awkwardly. "And for Mammy and Daddy as well," she said, eyeing them, and smiling. Bridget was relieved to be going, but she hadn't expected such an outpouring of grief from Penny. She was touched but deeply wounded to see what her going was causing.

"Come on, Penny. Auntie Bridget is going to miss her flight," Ruth said worriedly, looking up at the giant flashing screens in Dublin airport. Bridget had suitcases to check in and Ruth was an anxious flyer. Bridget only had three hours until her flight took off and she wasn't in the sort of hurry Ruth thought would be appropriate. "Anyway, we need to get you home; you have a school trip to look forward to, poppet!"

Penny stopped crying and reluctantly let go of Bridget. This was true. All the primary schools in Dublin sent the children on a week-long trip to the Aran Islands before they left; the other, now grown-up children in the family had all gone when they were young too – although in those days, it was two weeks. Ruth would never have allowed Penny to go if it was still two weeks. She wasn't all that thrilled about it now. Penny, on the other hand, had been ecstatic to go and be with Patrick and Mary all the time for a whole week; it was going to be so much fun.

Bridget looked at Ruth and felt guilty. She'd forgotten about the school trip. If she'd remembered she might have booked her own trip for later, so Ruth had company in case... Well, it was too late now. She had bags to check in. She was being met at the airport at the other end, but no one else knew that. She had to go.

Ruth kissed Bridget on the cheek and hugged her firmly. Bridget patted her shoulder with her fingertips.

"Be careful and send postcards," Ruth said sternly.

Bridget sipped on her gin and tonic the air hostess had brought her. She rather liked flying; she had done it many times. The hilariously brief forty-five-minute flight from Dublin to Liverpool was one of her favourites. The guilty feeling she'd had when she last looked at Ruth had not subsided. But, to be honest, she'd felt guilty for ten years.

Her and Maire exchanged letters every couple of months. Bridget had paid any expenses that had come up for Maire's university studies and made sure she had enough to live on until she was able to earn money herself. Maire assured her that her friend, with whom she was still sharing the flat, was working and settled and as happy as seemed reasonably possible. Bridget sent updates and photos of Penny, at Maire's request. She had that photograph of Maire in the kitchen that she'd taken before Maire had left, as well as several dozen letters from her, hidden away in her room. Maire had a photograph of Bridget; presumably she had kept it. They'd taken the forbidden photos on Ruth's camera. It was the ultimate betrayal.

And now this – was this a step too far? It was too late now if it was. Anyway, she was looking forward to it. Ruth didn't seem to care what Bridget was doing, how Bridget was feeling, how alone Bridget was. Ruth probably wouldn't even ask to see photos or hear stories from Bridget's trip; she'd be too full of telling her all about Penny's school trip and Penny's end of year results and the newest slight curl of Penny's hair. Not that she ever minded any of that as such. But Bridget was still a person.

She collected her bags off the carousel as quickly as she

could. They had taken an age to appear and she was desperate to get out of this part of the airport. She had never been to London Stansted before. In fact, she'd never been to London before. She dragged them briskly through 'Nothing to Declare' and was relieved that there was no passport control for Irish citizens at this airport; that would save her a few precious minutes. She practically ran down the concourse and emerged, out of breath, into the 'Arrivals' waiting area.

Bridget saw her immediately. Her bright red hair stuck out like a post box in a sea of murky brunettes. It was still curly. Bridget charged at the now thirty-year-old woman on the other side of the railings and hugged her as hard as she could. She found she was crying. Maire was crying. They laughed and cried and jumped up and down with excitement.

"It's you," Maire laughed through her tears. "Bridget, it's really you."

CHAPTER THIRTY-EIGHT

Ruth had dropped Penny off at school that morning as normal, except she wasn't wearing her prim little uniform and had a holdall with her instead of her book bag. She'd helped Penny to pack her things the night before, written her a little note and hidden it with her socks, and when they said the rosary together, they said a special prayer for nice weather and a good time.

Donal had asked hesitantly if he ought to take the morning away from the shop to be with Ruth. Ruth had said no; she would be all right.

She was home now, and she wandered the empty rooms of her house. Penny would be gone for six nights, and Ruth would pick her up again from the school on Sunday night. She could hardly wait. She missed her so much already. If she'd had any, or all, of the others, they'd have had to sell this house and move somewhere much bigger, with a lot more bedrooms. Mr Quinn's house had served them well in their twenty-five years of living there.

Ruth padded upstairs to her and Donal's room. She took off her clothes and put her pyjamas back on; they were still warm from when she'd taken them off this morning. It was a bit chilly today; she was pleased to be back in their warmth. They were a thick cotton and wool blend, yellow, a button-down long-sleeved top and long-sleeved pyjama pants. She put her fluffy socks back on. She climbed under the duvet. She was still there when Donal got home from work.

CHAPTER THIRTY-NINE

Maire and Bridget woke up with sore heads. Maire had booked them a hotel near central London so Bridget could see the sights. She was staying for three days – Maire had booked the week off work – and then she was going off on her travels around Europe. After the first couple of hours of excitement and amazement, a sadness settled on the pair of women, as they realised, after ten years apart, they'd be separated again in just seventy-two hours.

They'd gone to a pub near Liverpool Street station and got rip-roaring drunk. They remembered laughing hysterically, drinking whiskey, eating chips, and not much else. They'd poured over photographs and stories of Penny. Maire told Bridget all about her nursing training, her new hospital, and said she hoped Bridget looked on it as money well spent. Maire's friend had met a man and moved out; Maire had kept the flat for herself and was hoping to buy it from the council soon. Bridget moaned about Ruth and spoke about how she felt so left out of their family. Maire asked about Fionn.

"They had another baby," Bridget had slurred carelessly.

Maire had looked blankly at Bridget and tried not to react. "Oh," she said, and gulped her drink. "It's nice they worked things out," Maire said. "What did they have?"

"Another boy," Bridget admitted. "Sorry, I shouldn't have said anything."

"Oh, why not," Maire had said, shrugging. "It's not my business, is it."

It wasn't a question and Bridget didn't answer it.

Penny was still his only girl. Maire was proud of that.

They didn't talk about Fionn anymore after that; Maire had stopped asking about him in her letters as Bridget rarely told her anything.

On the first of the three days, Maire took Bridget to the Tower of London in the morning and the Houses of Parliament in the afternoon. Maire spoke at length to Bridget about all the facets of British history she'd learned in the past ten years, as they walked around the gloomy walls of the Tower and admired the ravens.

In the afternoon, Bridget lectured Maire on the abysmal treatment of the Irish people under British rule, the sort of thing her own ancestors had fought in the War of Independence against, as she looked around the very building in which a lot of those decisions, to their national detriment, were made. It was a remarkable building, she said, but it made her agitated. Maire was embarrassed and hastily scratched the British Museum off her mental list.

They went to a pub just off Waterloo Bridge after that and drank themselves silly on Guinness – which, they could both agree, just wasn't the same.

CHAPTER FORTY

Brenda's phone was ringing. She had dropped Mary and Patrick off this morning for their week-long school trip; they had been exceptionally excited, and Brenda was looking forward to some child-free time. She was about to pour a cold glass of white wine as the phone rang. She hoped to God it wasn't her youngest sister, who had a habit of phoning in the evenings and whining for hours about nothing in particular. She answered it with trepidation.

"Brenda, Brenda it's Donal," he said in a hurried voice.

Brenda was surprised; Donal never phoned. It was always Ruth, and anyway, the children were all gone. He sounded upset.

*

"I'm a dentist, not a psychiatrist," Brenda said, confused, as Donal took her coat and hung it up in their hallway. "Perhaps she needs to see someone like that."

Donal didn't like to say that her profession had nothing to do with it; she'd adopted a child, and he couldn't understand why that was tearing Ruth's life apart, and apparently not Brenda's.

"No, no, she won't talk to anyone that she doesn't know," Donal said hopelessly, shaking his head. He'd asked her, lots of times. "You're still a doctor. You must know what's wrong with her."

Brenda sighed. She was a dentist. But she and Pat did have a couple of psychiatrist friends who talked at length about their patients. One of them had recently finished a post in the US, working with the Vietnam vets and, as a result of his discovered horrors therein, was just starting to look into trauma and panic disorders which were woefully under-researched. Brenda didn't know what Ruth had to be panicking about particularly but, perhaps, if she asked carefully, she might tell her. She followed Donal upstairs.

"Ruth," she said delicately, opening the door to Ruth and Donal's bedroom. She felt so embarrassed to be in their private space. Other people's bedrooms were a secret, sacred place. "Ruth, it's me, Brenda."

Ruth lifted her head wearily from the pillow. Her face was red and puffy and the pillowcase was covered in mascara stains. She started whimpering at the sound of her own name. Brenda slipped in and Donal went to follow.

"No," Brenda said sharply. "No, let me," and she shut the door sharply before Donal could follow her.

CHAPTER FORTY-ONE

Bridget and Maire had to decide to stop drinking before they lost any more of their three days to headaches. After a tour of St Paul's Cathedral, a slightly windy picnic in St James' Park, an extensive gawp at Buckingham Palace, afternoon tea at an upmarket hotel in Kensington and a noisy but thoroughly enjoyable football match at West Ham, Bridget and Maire found themselves once again hugging and sobbing at an airport. Three days had flown by in a blur of giggles, pubs, television films in their hotel room in the evenings, and enormous old buildings. Bridget had quite liked London. There was also no doubt that she still fervently loved Maire, with all her heart. This visit had made her feel alive again. It made her feel young again. She was like a young thing in her twenties going on a jolly around the world – what the young ones now called a 'gap year'.

"We'll do this again, yes?" Bridget snivelled into Maire's shoulder.

"Oh, God yes," Maire agreed. "Enjoy your travels." Maire wiped her eyes, sharing a packet of tissues from her handbag with Bridget. "Where is it first?"

"Rome," sniffed Bridget. "Pizza and gelato await."

"And handsome Italian men," Maire teased.

Bridget shook her head hopelessly and kissed Maire on the cheek. She took her bags that Maire had stuffed with all the books that were still banned in Ireland and sadly mounted the escalator, looking back over her shoulder and keeping Maire in her sights for as long as she possibly could.

CHAPTER FORTY-TWO

"Donal," Brenda said.

Donal leapt up from his seat at the kitchen table where he was clearly worried sick.

"Donal, don't worry. She is all right."

"What's wrong with her?" he asked.

Brenda bade him sit down and she did likewise. "There's a term; the Americans use it. It's been used only for about the last ten years or so, mostly for war vets. It's called *post-traumatic stress disorder*. Have you ever heard of it?"

Donal shook his head. Of course he'd never heard of such things. He wasn't a doctor.

"It's not very well researched, I'm afraid, but I'd say that is what she's suffering from. The losses, Donal," Brenda said gently. "Ruth has lost almost everything she has ever cared for. She is frightened of being abandoned. It reminds her too much of everything – everyone – that she has lost. That's been her war, Donal."

Donal thought about Ruth's life. Her father had died when she was only two, but she claimed to have memories of it. Bridget was away in Galway when Mariah had died, when Ruth was only twenty-two, still not speaking to Ruth for having had the audacity to marry himself. Then John had moved away; they lost the first little one and then his own father had died. He had cherished Ruth, and she him. Then, the other four; the twins were particularly hard on Ruth. They'd lost poor Dermot. Bridget had now gone away for months, and Penny was spending the night somewhere that wasn't her own bedroom for the first time since the day she

231

was born. It made sense. She had lost so much. She was terrified that one day Penny would discover where she had come from and leave her too. The extent to which she clung to Penny wasn't healthy; he knew that.

Donal nodded to show Brenda that he understood.

"Also, her mother wasn't very nice," he added.

"She mentioned."

"What can I do for her?" Donal asked.

Brenda passed him a piece of paper. "That's a friend of Pat's; he's looking into this sort of thing," Brenda replied. "But she needs to talk to someone, someone qualified, Donal. Not me."

"Okay."

Brenda stood up to leave and Donal jumped out of his seat to get her coat.

"Thank you," he said. "Thank you for coming."

Brenda just nodded. "Call that man, so."

"I will."

*

Donal took the week off work and, by the Wednesday, he had coaxed Ruth out of bed, into the bath and then into some clothes. He and Ruth went out for walks and to lunch in nice pubs and hotels in the city. Ruth wouldn't walk at St Stephen's Green, though, not since... She talked to him about how she felt. He'd not liked to talk about it, years ago when it was all happening, Ruth reminded him. She'd bottled it up so that he wouldn't be upset, and she couldn't bottle it anymore. Donal said he was sorry. He'd listen intently now, he promised. He squashed down his own rising, inescapable grief, as he had done five times before. Ruth agreed to meet Brenda's man, just once, to see if she liked him and if he seemed to be the sort of person that she felt she could trust.

On Sunday night, they walked hand in hand to Penny's school, where they awaited the coach full of excited children and exhausted teachers. They met Pat and Brenda and stood with them, chatting politely. Ruth and Donal didn't know if Pat knew about Brenda's visit and they weren't going to ask now.

When the coach pulled up and she saw Penny's tiny face gleaming against the window glass, all the colours of the world flooded back to Ruth. She had done it. Penny was home.

Penny talked non-stop for four days about her trip. Ruth and Donal nodded and pretended to be listening after the first two, which Penny seemed to neither notice nor take offence to. The noise of her endless chatter filled the house and, for that, Ruth was glad. Ruth was happier, so Donal was glad. Ruth said if Penny could stop talking and take a breath for just five minutes, she had a surprise, and passed her a postcard from Auntie Bridget in Rome.

CHAPTER FORTY-THREE

Bridget felt miserable at the thought of the long, arduous journey ahead of her. Liam and his family lived in the furthest depths of Montana, on the most incredible ranch with the dearest horses Bridget had ever seen. In exchange for six weeks bed and board after having leisurely floated around Rome, Barcelona, Vienna and Paris for the preceding month, drinking coffee and eating croissants and gelato and kaiserschmarnn, Bridget had happily agreed to pitch in with the laborious farm work. In the evenings, she had contentedly sat around the fire with Liam and his jolly American wife, their two youngest children and their families who still lived in the ranch as well, listening to their stories of everything she had missed out on since Liam had emigrated in 1974.

In Rome, Bridget had cried every morning, pained at Maire's absence once again. She marvelled at the Colosseum and the Sistine chapel, weeping happy tears at Vatican City. She bought a new pink rosary for Penny from a market stall nearby and lived off pepperoni and mozzarella panini for days. She drank sangria in Barcelona in glorious sunshine. She went to the opera in Vienna and was propositioned by an Austrian violinist who she met in the bar afterwards. She had politely declined and gone back to her hotel alone, but she had been tempted. In Paris she did whistle-stop tours of the Louvre and the Eiffel Tower and spent the rest of the time eating, without a shred of guilt.

But Montana, that had truly been the highlight of the trip. If Ruth was Mariah's least favourite child, Liam had been a close second, and he'd never for the life of him been able to understand why. The second of her three boys, he wasn't tall and effortlessly intelligent like John. Nor was he cheekily handsome and funny like Dermot. He was just Liam, in the middle, with a strong affection for British punk bands and who earned disappointingly average school reports.

When their father Seamus died, John strode naturally and smoothly into the role of man of the house, bringing up the troublesome little sisters, who had arrived mysteriously in the boys' teenage years, and sorting all of Seamus' affairs. Dermot had fallen to bits and Mariah spent every waking moment supporting his every emotional need. Dermot, after all, had been the one who had found Seamus lifeless and crumpled on the kitchen floor. Ruth was only two and stopped saying 'Da Da' after a few weeks of noticing that he wasn't there anymore. Bridget was just a baby and didn't remember a thing. Liam had no role to step into and no one to care for his grief. He wanted nothing more than to grow up quickly, and then get away – the further the better. Which he did.

Liam's relentless joy and vigour for living life, despite all of that, made Bridget's heart sing. He'd left home at eighteen, worked on the ships, and sent Bridget toys and postcards from around the world. Liam hadn't been especially wounded to hear of Dermot's marrying a Protestant girl; he cared nothing at all for politics, or anything that might promote conflict of any kind. He hadn't made it to the wedding because he was at sea, and he avoided any news about Northern Ireland because it made him feel agitated and worried, but when he'd heard of the tragedy of Dermot and Leanne, he'd emptied his savings account for an arduous, multi-stop flight from Philadelphia to Belfast for the funerals.

The flight had been delayed, and they'd missed it; Liam was sorry for Bridget's being alone there. They were easily the most alike of the five siblings. They looked the most alike, too, even now.

Six weeks with him had flown by. Bridget uncomplainingly mucked out horses with Liam's grandsons and helped to fix a couple of fences at least once a week that routinely refused to stay standing in even the slightest glimmer of poor weather. Liam's wife, Marianne, had Bridget help her and her youngest daughter break in the new horse. Bridget had been terrified, but that was soon forgotten when four weeks later she was riding around the ranch on Mosey, feeling extraordinarily at peace, as though she had done it every day of her life.

Evenings round the fireside had been Bridget's favourite. Some of the other ranch hands who lived in little cabins dotted around joined them. They had the most wonderful rapport with the children, whom they had seen grow up, for the most part. The little ones said they couldn't understand Bridget. The teenagers made fun of her Irish accent and she made fun of theirs, and all their Americanisms. The workers called her ma'am. It was the most extraordinary thing.

She hadn't seen Dublin in over three months, and all that stood between her and the fair city now was a forty-minute drive in Liam's truck, a two-hour bus journey, a seven-hour flight to New York via Denver airport, a three-hour wait, and another seven-hour flight to Dublin. So far, she'd got as far as the bus. She sighed. She may well not see Liam again in the flesh in her lifetime; it was one of those things that one just knew, after passing certain milestones in one's life. She already missed the children and the horses and the extraordinary, beautiful mountains. This journey was going to be unpleasant.

CHAPTER FORTY-FOUR

"Can you see her yet, Penny?" Donal asked his extraordinarily overexcited daughter at Dublin airport. She was carrying a huge banner she had made herself that said: 'Welcome Home, Auntie Bridget!'

Ruth had put on make-up for the first time since her 'episode', as she'd taken to calling it. They were all excited. Bridget had diligently sent postcards from all her European locations, as well as letters and photographs from Montana. Penny had read them all over and over again and took them into school to show her friends; she cried sometimes at night because she missed Bridget so much.

"There she is! There she is!" Penny was screaming as Bridget appeared through Dublin's sliding doors. The banner was quickly thrown on the floor as Penny ducked under the barrier and ran straight into Bridget's weary arms.

*

Penny was surrounded by her gifts on the floor. She was delighted with them. Ruth and Donal were just as happy with their bottle of champagne and photos of Liam's enormous family. Penny had a plastic Eiffel Tower, a pink t-shirt that said '*J'aime Paris*', a children's book about the Cathedral of the Holy Cross and Saint Eulalia that Bridget had found in their gift shop, her new pink rosary from Rome, and several lifetimes' worth of Austrian chocolate. Penny beamed at the hoard – the chocolate especially. Bridget was exhausted and being propped up by the strength of Ruth's coffee and not much else.

"Bridget, I need to ask you something," Ruth said quietly.

Bridget murmured sleepily in response; she'd rather hoped she'd have a bit longer to adjust to being home before having to do favours for Ruth.

"I need to go on Fridays for these... appointments, you know," she said.

Bridget sat up, looking concerned. "Appointments for what?" she asked.

"Oh just, nothing to worry about, just appointments," she said nervously. "But, look... Penny has missed you; she did wonderfully away on her school trip before and I-I-I wondered if you might like to... have her, on Fridays, at yours."

Bridget was speechless. She'd never had Penny in her house on her own before. "Really?"

"Yes, would you like to maybe... take... take her after school, give her tea; she could stay overnight and perhaps you could take her to dancing in the morning? Oh yes, she does Irish dancing now," Ruth said proudly.

Penny nodded in agreement, distracted by her book.

Bridget beamed.

"She's very good. And then we'll have her back after that, if you could bring her home?"

"Yes. Yes, I mean, of course," Bridget said. "Of course."

"You can drop the day at the hospital?"

"Anything," said Bridget.

Ruth looked agitated and nervous as she spoke, but she was smiling at Bridget, and nodding at her as she spoke to show she consented to her own words.

It was a huge moment for Ruth, Bridget realised. She

wondered what had changed in her absence. Had Penny really had missed her that much? Or maybe it was Ruth who had missed her the most? Bridget leaned in and hugged Ruth with more vigour than she had in years.

"Thank you."

CHAPTER FORTY-FIVE

Bridget peered into her spare room which had, quite recently, taken on a new title – 'Penny's Other Room'. As she spent every Friday night in there it seemed fitting enough; it had taken Bridget a few years to finally stop thinking of it as Maire's room. She hadn't been ready to go back to it just being the 'spare room' after that, an ownerless pile of textiles and wood, a rudderless ship in which the light was almost never on. Bridget had bought a new pink frilly bedspread for it – God knows, Penny loved anything pink and frilly these days – but kept the dark maroon curtains. They did an excellent job of keeping all the light out.

Penny was sound asleep and snoring gently. She was totally thrilled about being picked up from school by Auntie Bridget, even though Bridget had done it every Friday for a couple of months now; she wasn't yet over the novelty. She'd come to Bridget's and they'd played cards, watched television and Bridget had made lamb stew and apple tart for dinner and dessert. Penny completed her Irish homework flawlessly – according to herself – to the amazement of Bridget. Penny did her maths homework to even more amazement from Bridget. Penny had checked her bag for the morning to ensure that she had her Irish dancing shoes and had merrily gone to bed when Bridget had asked her to. It had been the most perfect afternoon and evening.

Penny was such a good little girl. Bridget marvelled at her from the doorway and had no desire to be anywhere else, doing anything else. Penny was now almost eleven years old; it just didn't seem possible. When Fionn had come to them all that time ago, Ruth and Donal had kept their opinions mostly to themselves about the affair between Maire and Fionn and put all their concerns into the matter of the baby. Their behaviour, his affair, was none of their business. Of course, for Bridget, the conversation had been quite different, and she'd told him exactly what she'd thought of him, as Bridget tended to do. All her concerns were for the sweet thing he'd netted with his lies, who found herself unexpectedly resident in Bridget's home.

*

She had been surprised, she remembered, to see Fionn's car on her and Ruth's shared driveway that day when she had returned home from work. It had been a difficult shift, she remembered, one of those ones where they were overrun with patients and were running out of everything useful; the autumn showers hadn't stopped, a 'when it rains, it pours' type of day, in every sense. All she had wanted to do was come home, pour herself a gin and enjoy some silence. It wasn't like Fionn to visit out of the blue so her first instinct was to panic that something had happened to the children.

"You've done *what*?" she had yelled when he had mumbled out his explanation.

Fionn had recovered slightly from the shock of not getting the eye-watering scolding from Ruth and Donal that he was certain he'd receive, but he was now getting it from Bridget instead. He probably should've expected that. That was on him.

"I... I do love her, though."

"And what good will that do her, now?" Bridget shouted

at him. "For God's sake, Fionn. How could you *do this to her*?"

Fionn was confused. He wasn't sure which 'her' that referred to: Clodagh or Maire. Either way, the sentiment stood – how could he, indeed?

"I just… I didn't mean to hurt—"

"Oh, well, at least you didn't mean to," Bridget said, shaking her head. "God save us, Fionn. So, what, you were waiting here all day to tell me this and hope I'd be sympathetic?"

"No… actually, I was hoping you'd… help."

He explained to a stunned Bridget that he'd asked Ruth and Donal to adopt the baby, and they had agreed. He asked Bridget if she'd consider taking the girl in as a lodger, of sorts, and keeping an eye on her throughout the duration; then, Ruth and Donal would collect the baby once he or she was born. He had it all worked out; he was going to make the transport arrangements tomorrow. All he needed was Bridget's agreement. It never appeared in any papers or on the television, but they both knew what happened to unmarried pregnant girls who had nowhere to go, didn't they? Bridget wouldn't want that for her great-niece or great-nephew, now, would she?

"No," she had admitted. "No, I would not. You're an idiot, Fionn."

"I know."

"You explain yourself the second she arrives. Tell her who you really are and what you've really done."

"I will."

Bridget sucked her teeth to avoid saying anything else she might regret. She knew her mother would be turning in her

243

grave to hear her speak to a family member the way she had just spoken to Fionn. But Mariah wasn't here now.

"Please don't say 'I told you so'," Fionn said sadly.

Bridget pitied him a little then. "I'll never say that to you, Fionn."

"But you did tell me so."

"Yes, I did."

Bridget put the kettle on and uncovered a cake she'd made the day before. She cut off an extra big slice for Fionn and put three sugars in his tea. She stroked the hair on the back of his head the way she had done when he was a little boy, when she had babysat him, and he was having trouble falling asleep. She didn't say anything else.

*

Bridget still wasn't that interested in getting married; it wasn't a regret and she didn't feel lonely with no husband at home. But, as she'd said to Maire so very long ago now, she might have enjoyed the mothering side of it all. That part of it she'd missed out on felt like a bit of a shame, now. Bridget gently shut the door on sleeping Penny and tiptoed into her own bedroom. It was quite early still, but she thought she'd get herself off to bed as well. She felt tired all of a sudden.

The next morning, Bridget left Penny getting dressed in her own room as Bridget went off to shower. She didn't have long; they'd both slept in a bit late and by the time Bridget had hurriedly made a bowl of cereal for Penny and herself, they hadn't much time to get to Penny's dance class that started at ten o'clock. The water ran lukewarm, and Bridget decided that would do. She lathered up her hair, quickly, and

244

scrubbed harshly with a loofah at her arms and legs. She rinsed herself in the lukewarm water, wrapped a towel around her, put on her dressing gown and opened the bathroom door.

She flew across the landing like a mad woman.

"What on EARTH are you doing?" she screamed at Penny, as she saw her little legs bouncing off the edge of the bed. She was sitting on the edge and had Bridget's bedside drawer open. She had something in her hand.

Penny stopped dead.

"What on EARTH have you done?"

Penny didn't know what she'd done. She'd had a nosebleed come on all of a sudden and she wanted a tissue, but she couldn't go in the bathroom to get toilet paper because Aunt Bridget was in the shower. She didn't want to go downstairs to the kitchen in case she bled on the carpet, which was cream coloured. Bridget kept a packet of tissues in her bedside drawer as a matter of principle and Penny knew this. As far as she was concerned, she'd done everything right – or at least hadn't done anything particularly wrong.

Bridget snatched the thing out of Penny's hand just at the point that her eyes filled up with shocked tears. Bridget realised that what she was holding was a packet of tissues. Blood was dripping from Penny's nose onto her clothes. She had a look on her face that Bridget had never seen before, and Bridget was horrified to see that Penny was afraid.

"I'm-I'm sorry. I just-I just…"

Bridget shut the drawer quickly but gave the packet of tissues back to Penny. She wiped the blood off Penny's face very carefully and dabbed at her clothes; it was unlikely they'd get all the blood out of those. At least they were dark colours and it didn't look too bad for now.

"Please, Penny, I am very sorry for shouting at you. I shouldn't have done that," Bridget said gently.

Penny was eager to agree and accept. Bridget had never, ever told her off before and she wasn't about to make it worse. She shouldn't have been in Auntie Bridget's bedroom. It was like going to Patrick and Mary's house and going into their mammy's room; you just didn't do it. It was private; it was very rude. All she'd wanted was the tissues; she hadn't seen anything else.

Bridget ushered Penny out so she could get dressed and told her to wait downstairs with her things; she could put the television on if she wanted to.

Penny smiled but left in silence; she'd hardly said a word since Bridget had leapt at her from the bathroom. Bridget dressed quickly and blasted her hair with a hairdryer, not before emptying a shoebox and retrieving all of Maire's letters and the photograph of her from the drawer, stuffing them into the box and burying it at the back of the wardrobe.

Bridget found Penny sitting downstairs in silence with her coat and shoes on already. She tried to be jovial and normal with Penny as she drove her to her dancing school. Penny did respond to her, but in a much shorter and less friendly way than normal. In previous weeks, Penny had talked Bridget's ear off the whole drive to the school. Today she was virtually silent. Bridget turned up the car radio as the quiet was making her uneasy.

Penny hopped out the car with a short, "Thank you!" and didn't look round at Bridget again.

Bridget drove around the back of the school and parked her car in amongst the others. A lot of the mams went into the class and watched or stood in the corridors, chatting and gossiping. She didn't want to put Penny off her dancing, and Ruth had asked if she could possibly avoid the other parents, as she didn't want Bridget to have to answer questions about where Ruth was and why she wasn't doing the dancing run herself.

Bridget stared angrily at the grey clouds in the grey sky and the empty grey concrete of the car park. She was angry with herself, of course; she would have had no cause to shout at Penny and scare her like that if she herself was not hoarding secret letters and photos against Penny's mother's express wishes. Of course this was her fault, but she did rather wonder if, eleven years on, it was really worth working this hard to keep all these secrets after all.

But, as ever, it wasn't her decision.

CHAPTER FORTY-SIX

"Imelda?" Ruth suggested.

"No."

"Theresa?" said Bridget.

Penny scoffed. "After Theresa Murphy in my English class? No thank you."

"Frances?" said Donal.

"Boring," Penny yawned. "What were all yours?"

"Margaret," said Ruth.

"Constance," said Bridget.

"Daddy? Just out of interest?" Penny asked.

"Er... Hubert."

Penny and Bridget sniggered.

"Hey now!" said Donal. "That was a great name in my youth, I'll have you know."

"Things have moved on since the Middle Ages, Daddy," Penny giggled. "Anyway, I suppose I am meant to choose my own confirmation name by myself and everything. Father Kelly said it was 'part of the responsibility'." Penny rolled her eyes. "But there's just so *many*," she complained. "And none of them sound like me."

Bridget thought back to when she and Ruth were around Penny's age, about fourteen, approaching their confirmations. John had chosen their confirmation names for them, with Mariah's approval. Bridget liked hers, but Ruth hadn't been too thrilled with Margaret, at the time – she already had a Mary in her name, and it was too close to that, she felt. Also, to that end, to Mariah as well.

248

Penny was sitting at the kitchen table in her nightgown still, while the others sat or stood around, drinking tea and eating the scones that Bridget had brought round. Ruth never pressed Penny to get dressed before lunch at weekends, but Bridget didn't like to see her lounging around in her nightclothes at the table. Her red hair fell long past her shoulders now. She wore long stripy hockey socks with her nightdress. Penny didn't come to Bridget's on Friday nights anymore; Ruth had stopped having appointments and Penny was often out with friends now, at the cinema and the parks and other girls' houses. Penny yawned.

"How about... Ailbe?" said Bridget. She looked quickly at Ruth and Donal to see if they'd react. To see if Maire had ever told them and, if she had, whether they had remembered. Bridget was sure she hadn't – it rather looked like she hadn't. "I'm sure there was a Saint Ailbe."

"Ailbe," Penny said slowly. "I quite like that."

"Wasn't Saint Ailbe a man?" asked Donal. "That's a man's name, isn't it?"

"Well, yes, originally, but there's been lots of girls called Ailbe in the last hundred years or so," pressed Bridget. She didn't know if that was true. She'd only heard of the one, after all.

"I've never met a girl called Ailbe," Ruth said, searching her memories. "Although, I've never met a man called it, either."

"Me either."

"Or me." Penny bit her thumbnail. She often did that while she was thinking.

Bridget's heart raced. Was this just a pinch disrespectful? Probably. But if Penny liked the name, then Penny liked the name. She wasn't forcing the girl.

"Oh, no, I think I met an Ailbhe once," Donal said. "She ordered a whole house full of floor tiles, and they were hideous. Spelled A-I-L-B-H-E, is that right?"

Bridget didn't like to say that wasn't how Maire spelled it. She'd seen it, dozens of times, on the letters she'd written.

"Yes," Bridget conceded. "I think that's right."

"Ailbhe," Penny said again. "Thanks, Auntie Bridget. I like that one."

"Grand," Bridget said. "I'll boil the kettle. Who's for another tea?"

The family murmured in agreement. Penny wrote *Ailbhe* down on a sheet of paper underneath *Catherine* and *Monica*. Bridget smiled to herself. There was a one in three chance – it was the least she could do.

PART THREE
2002–2003

CHAPTER FORTY-SEVEN

Maire blinked, rubbed her eyes and blinked again at the name on the chart. It was written above the woman's head as well, on a whiteboard in marker pen, as clear as day. It was a common enough name in Ireland, but not here. She put her glasses on to be sure. She stared at the woman. If it wasn't her... well. Doppelgängers certainly did exist. She *had* been real all along.

"Nurse," the woman croaked. "Nurse."

"Mrs Mulligan, I'm here. What do you need?"

"I'm not a Mrs, and I need a drink." She spoke in a hoarse voice, like she'd been smoking for decades.

Maire glanced at the chart. Decades indeed. She looked at the patient's water jug. It was empty and so was her cup, so she scuttled to the nearest sink and filled it as quickly as she could manage, still staring at the woman over her shoulder as best as she could. She put the jug down on the table quickly, sloshing it a little over the sides, and held the cup up to the patient's hands who took it gingerly.

"Alma... Alma Mulligan," Maire said, stunned.

Alma looked at her and narrowed her eyes, as if in great thought. Then she saw what Maire was seeing. Her eyes flashed to Maire's staff name badge and widened with shock and disbelief.

"Maire?" she said in a low voice. "No, no it can't... just *can't* be..."

"It is me, Alma! From school... from... Ireland."

Alma gulped her water, handed the cup back to Maire and wiped her mouth with the corner of her hand.

"Maire, I can't..." Alma shook her head and chuckled. "Why are you here? Don't tell me you married some dreadful Englishman."

Maire laughed. She was shocked but somehow elated. England had given her a vastness of anonymity she could never have had in Ireland, and she had rejoiced in it. But now, her past had come back to her – and she found, to her surprise, that she was delighted. She clasped Alma's hand as she sat beside her in the visitor's chair. She hadn't seen anyone from her past since... well. Since she'd left it. She was glad to see Alma. It was such a blessing. What an almighty coincidence that she should be here, of all the places in the world.

"God save us, I haven't seen you since—"

"Since I was a fallen woman and made to disappear? Yes, that's about the size of it."

Maire didn't know what to say. Clearly, Alma was used to that. She sounded like a Londoner now, with not much trace of her Irishness left – not like Maire, who still sounded as though she'd got off the ferry just yesterday.

"Heard about it all, I suppose, did you?"

Maire nodded awkwardly, guiltily, and said nothing.

"I got one of those... domestic placement things," Alma explained. "They sent me here, the services, the council, whatever they're called. I nannied for a family until I dropped. Then they took the baby and went to America. I think, anyway. Nice couple actually. That's what you want, isn't it?"

Maire was stunned at her candour. She wondered how many times Alma had told that story, so quickly and so offhandedly. She hadn't heard of a 'domestic placement thing', but then, she hadn't initially heard of Bessborough either. Apparently, no one had. They all appeared to exist in secret, on an entirely 'need to know' basis. It seemed like the well-meaning, Mass-going, law-abiding general Irish public did not fall into the bracket of people that needed to know what went on behind the gates of these places. She couldn't believe that it had been almost twenty-five years for Alma – probably twenty-six years since she last saw her at school. A little over twenty for Maire, and her little lucky Penny. Bridget had written last week to say Penny was going to graduate this coming Friday with First Class Honours. Alma's child could be married, walking around an American *boulevard* talking about *elevators* and *apartments* and drinking coffee instead of tea. Alma had only been sixteen when she had become a mother. Maire wondered if she herself, too, would be considered to have had what one might call a 'domestic placement thing'.

"What did you have?" Maire enquired. She wasn't sure it was a polite question, but then, Alma hadn't been the politest person, and probably wouldn't mind.

"Boy," Alma said, not minding at all. "Cute thing he was. Little blue eyes."

"Ah, like you."

"Like his rotten da." Alma coughed roughly and then chewed the side of her mouth. She'd let a bit of Irish out and was trying to reel it back it. She was a Londoner now; all that was long gone. She must be more careful.

Alma had oceans of sadness in her eyes; anyone could see that. Maire smiled pityingly.

"So, you're a nurse now," Alma said.

Maire grinned proudly and plucked at her uniform. "Evidently."

255

"Ah, that explains it, then." Alma noisily drank more water.

"What do you mean?" asked Maire.

"Well, your mother told my mother that you'd finally gone away to study. Quite right too, given what a brain box you always were. It would have been just criminal if you hadn't. Stuck in that bloody pub. She never said what it was you were studying though."

"Oh."

"I see it was nursing. Not a bad choice I suppose. God, she was upset though, wasn't she?" Alma continued. "Obviously missed the heart out of you."

Her mother had not been wrong, in fact, to tell people she'd gone away to study. She just didn't mention the brief interlude in between when she'd been in Dublin, living in someone else's house and giving birth to someone else's child. For herself, Maire had always wondered what her mother had said. She hadn't dared make contact in almost two decades because she was certain, absolutely certain, that they would have written her straight out of their lives in disgust. But Mary Mulligan had also done that to Alma, all those years ago, and now it seemed like…

"So you… you still hear from your mother, after everything?" Maire asked.

Alma nodded. "Yeah, yeah. I know she told everyone I was dead to her or whatever, but she couldn't help herself in the end," Alma said, smiling. "It took a few years but…" she shrugged. "All I had to do was write a letter. You never stop being a mum once you are one."

Maire smiled. She knew Alma was right. She'd felt like a mother every day since Penny was born, she just hadn't been able to actually… do any mothering. Not to her, anyway. Maire mothered her patients something chronic.

"So, you must have got married?" Alma said.

Must I? Maire wondered. "No," she said simply. "No, I'm… not very interested in all that."

Alma shrugged. "Shame," she said. "I could see you married. I was married, for a bit." Alma scowled and looked at her grubby, yellowing fingernails.

Maire didn't like to ask any follow-up questions as she had already been told, in no uncertain terms, that Alma wasn't a Mrs. Alma didn't offer any further information on the subject.

"Oh, do you remember that girl you used to run about with, Ailbe?" Alma asked.

Maire's blood went cold at the sound of Ailbe's name. She didn't know what to think, what to say – what her face might be betraying almost immediately. She wasn't about to tell Ailbe's horrific story to someone whose family had been particularly unkind to Ailbe, even though they weren't all that different. Alma was looking at her expectantly and she wasn't speaking. Should she say no, and protect Ailbe's anonymity? She couldn't do that. Oh God. She hoped Alma wouldn't ask lots of questions; she really didn't feel like answering them. Her skin prickled. Her heart was in her throat.

"Mm-hmm," Maire croaked. She coughed. "Yes, yes of course I… remember her. Why?"

"I heard her da finally went to prison for the lifetime."

"Really."

"Murdered someone. The nephew, I think? Or the brother, Ma wasn't sure."

"Oh."

There was no brother; Ailbe was the only child. Ailbe's father had murdered Ailbe's cousin – the father of her child - and was serving a life sentence for it; some justice, sort of, for the family's endless crimes against Ailbe and the village at large. Maire didn't say anything else.

Alma seemed quite pleased with her slice of juicy gossip and was disappointed with Maire's apparently lacklustre reaction to it.

Alma had over-exerted herself speaking and started coughing again. Maire affixed the oxygen mask to her face and patted her lightly on the back of the head.

"You know you're supposed to wear this more often," Maire said in her stern nurse's voice.

Alma nodded obediently at her, wheezing deeply.

"I'll come back a bit later," Maire assured her, before turning and hurrying off down the ward, no longer able to hold back her grief.

CHAPTER FORTY-EIGHT

Penny was graduating. It was, as with everything to do with Penny that Ruth was involved in, a huge to-do. The university would perform the ceremony of course, and take group photographs of all their graduates, and then there was a cocktail reception in a large marquee on the lawn behind the campanile in the square. Ruth bought a new outfit, for the most money she had ever spent on clothes in her life. Donal was wearing his best suit. Bridget wore smart top and trousers from her existing wardrobe but bought a new pair of court shoes for the occasion. Ruth and Donal were beaming. Bridget, less so.

A little over four years ago, when Penny had been in the midst of trying to decide with which of the many exceptional universities in the UK and Ireland she would share her talents, Bridget's Sunday morning routine of coffee and reading the Sunday papers was interrupted by a key in her own front door, a terrific banging and hysterical tears.

"She-she she won't let me go," Penny had sobbed. "She-she's ruining it all!"

Bridget made Penny tea and toast. How an argument with her mother had managed to occur before breakfast on a Sunday, Bridget would never know. She listened to Penny explain that Ruth was more than happy for her to go to university to study Economics, as was her chosen subject, but as long as she stayed in Dublin and lived at home.

Bridget was almost as downcast as Penny. She had seriously hoped they were past all this with Ruth. Bridget herself had only gone to Galway for her own study, and that was in the '60s of course; but university had changed so much since then. The adventure it would provide for Penny now would be extraordinary. The chance to live in another country – not necessarily England, Scotland maybe, Wales – would be an amazing opportunity for her, at her age. Ruth wouldn't even entertain Penny going to Galway and certainly not to Queen's in Belfast, not after Dermot. Penny had assured her that was all over now, but Ruth was not convinced. She never had been – not since the Agreement, and not now. It was Trinity College, or University College, or not at all.

Penny then said the one she had her heart set on was the London School of Economics. She wanted to change the world – she'd start with Ireland, naturally – and the very best degree available in Economics was what she had wanted. She had the grades. She had the references. All she didn't have was her mother's blessing – and of course, Donal went along with whatever Ruth said and wouldn't challenge her at all.

Bridget frowned as she realised the root of Ruth's concern. Had it been the Liverpool School of Economics, Ruth may well have let her go. The slightest mention of London and Ruth would of course have clammed up and then refused to let her go anywhere. She should never have said, eighteen years ago, that's where Maire was going. Of course, she didn't say anything about the money or what Maire was going to do – that was too obviously linked with herself – but, if she could persuade Ruth that Maire wasn't in London anymore (which Bridget knew full well she still was) Ruth might let Penny go. But there was no way to do that without revealing she was still in touch with Maire eighteen years after Ruth had forbidden it. There was nothing to be done. Bridget stroked Penny's hair and stayed silent.

260

Penny had stayed in Bridget's kitchen for about an hour, sobbing and snuffling and verbally bashing her mother. Bridget did her best to vouch for Ruth, but she found it hard. She wanted Penny to have whatever it was that Penny wanted; Bridget wanted her to have an adventure. Mary was going to St Andrews in Scotland to study History and Caoimhe was going to a music conservatoire in Birmingham – but Patrick was going to University College and living at home. They wouldn't have to break up. Penny sniffed. She didn't want to break up with Patrick and have long sad phone calls between London and Dublin until the inevitably grizzly end to their young love.

Penny had sloped home to apologise to Ruth and agree to go to Trinity College. After all, their Economics degree was excellent, and it fed straight into a graduate programme at the Bank of Ireland that Penny was sure to be a terrific candidate for, once she graduated with the Honours she was definitely going to get. She'd never have to leave Dublin at all if she followed that particular path. Ruth was thrilled.

Bridget seethed quietly at Ruth from her kitchen table. Penny had always had the best of everything, all her life; Ruth had seen to that. Except for this, the only thing that really mattered, the only thing Penny had ever actually asked for. What was Ruth expecting – that Penny and Maire would bump into each other in exactly the same pub at exactly the same time, marvel at their similarities, and disappear off into the sunset together without a moment's thought for anyone else? Penny wouldn't abandon her parents. They would probably never even be in the same street. What on earth would be the odds of that, anyway? She hardly thought the secret was worth keeping anymore, especially now that

261

Penny was eighteen but, as ever, it was Ruth's decision, and Ruth had decided to keep the secret alive. Who were Bridget and Donal to argue with her?

For Donal's part, he too was partial to a Sunday newspaper before playing his favourite eighteen holes at Killiney. Retirement was suiting him splendidly. He could hear the girls arguing in the kitchen and, as always, he left them to it. He didn't like to get involved or take sides or generally be included in any of their numerous disagreements. Personally, he couldn't see anything wrong with Penny going anywhere she wanted to go for university, especially seeing as Ruth and Penny seemed to have absolute daggers for each other all the time lately. Perhaps some space would do them good. But it wasn't really his business. Ruth had said that before.

Donal had continued to read the paper while Ruth and Penny bickered in the kitchen. There was a small article that said the convent rest home for unmarried mothers, overseen by the Congregation of the Sisters of the Sacred Hearts of Jesus and Mary in the outskirts of Cork city, had delivered its last baby and finally shut its doors after seventy-two years of faithful service to the community, 1922–1998. There was a photograph of a group of kindly looking nuns in white habits outside a Georgian-looking manor house. Donal was surprised. He had no idea that such a place had ever existed. He scanned the article, then turned the page.

*

"There she is! Here she comes, look!" Ruth was shouting loudly.

262

Penny and a group of her friends were slowly making their way through the crowd of graduates on Trinity College's main square in their robes and boards, taking photographs on digital cameras and hugging and kissing. Some of the girls were crying. Patrick was with them; he'd graduated from UCD last week and so had come along to witness Penny's ceremony.

"They're going to be so happy, aren't they?" Ruth said cryptically, stealing a look at Donal.

Donal grinned.

"What do you mean?" Bridget asked.

"Patrick came to see us last night while Penny was out having her hair done," Ruth gushed excitedly. "He's going to propose! Tomorrow, I think; they're having a lunch somewhere with his parents and he's going to ask her then." Ruth and Donal looked beside themselves with glee.

Bridget was stunned, not at all happy. "She's only twenty-one," was all she said. She didn't smile.

"So was I!" Ruth said happily. "Mammy was only nineteen."

"Yes, and wasn't she miserable," Bridget said sharply.

Ruth glared at her.

Donal looked uncomfortable. To be fair to Bridget, from what he'd seen from his years on the other side of the garden fence, Mariah had certainly seemed miserable with her lot – every part of it, in every sense. But that was hardly his business. Hardly his place to say.

"For God's sake, Bridget," Ruth snapped. "Can't you just *try* and be happy for us, just this once?"

Bridget smarted. It was all she had ever done. The bare-faced cheek of... "Well, I'm just saying, if she was my daughter, I—"

"Yes, but she's not your daughter, is she, Bridget?" Ruth barked. "She's mine. *Mine*, not yours." She turned away from Bridget and put on a sweet smile as Penny ran to Ruth. "There she is!" she cried. "There's my clever, clever girl!"

CHAPTER FORTY-NINE

Three days later, Alma Mulligan's words were still on Maire's mind. More to the point, Alma Mulligan's person was also still on Maire's ward. After the initial shock and delight of seeing her, Maire found that Alma's presence was making her feel increasingly uneasy. Alma still was, as she had always been, a profoundly indiscreet woman. But, Maire reminded herself, Alma didn't know anything. She hadn't let on about herself, or Ailbe for that matter. Alma couldn't possibly know what had really led Maire here, and whether Ailbe was involved or not. Or, indeed, where Ailbe was now.

Alma was wearing her oxygen mask like Maire had told her to and was peering into her purse with some intent. Maire was immediately concerned something had gone missing. She approached Alma's bed with caution.

"Everything all right there, Alma?" she asked gently.

Alma looked up and nodded. When she breathed and spoke through her oxygen mask, she sounded like a super villain.

"Ah, yeah, come and look," she said to Maire.

Maire peered into Alma's purse with her. She was looking at a black-and-white photograph.

"There he is, my boy."

From what Maire remembered about her schoolfriends and the villages they had all grown up in, the Mulligans had very distinctive faces. They had very square jaws, all three of the girls, the same as their father, and a small button nose. This photograph was of Alma as Maire remembered her, when she was barely sixteen, holding a small boy that was

the absolute image of her. The shape of his face, the nose –
there was no doubt about it. He was a Mulligan all right.

"Alan," Alma said. "They called him Alan. They wanted
to choose as he was going to be their wain and all, and they
chose that because it sounded like Alma, which was nice of
them." Alma's speech was starting to sound like she was
becoming short of breath. "They took this the week before
they left and let me keep it."

"Where is he now?" Maire asked.

Alma shrugged. "I don't know," she said. "We didn't keep
in touch like, that wasn't part of the deal. America. That's all
I know. They didn't say where."

"He'll have... he'll be having an extraordinary life,"
Maire said encouragingly.

Alma smiled and nodded enthusiastically. "Ah yeah, he
will," she said. "That was all that made it bearable. I've
watched all the American TV shows and that, in case he
became famous. Shame he was born here, though, he can't
ever be the president."

Maire laughed. A Mulligan president – now that'd be a
sight.

"No, of course, that is a shame."

Maire sat down in the chair next to the bed and Alma
talked more about her son. She'd only been with him for two
months before the family had taken him on the ship to
America. They'd had to go on a ship, because they had so
much furniture and so many possessions. They had three
children already, all girls, that Alma had nannied for six
months before giving birth to Alan. She'd enjoyed her job
immensely; she'd just appreciated an income and a roof over
her head to start with, and the children had become obsessed

with her growing belly that they understood to be a sibling for them. When they were told they were boarding a ship and Alma wasn't going to be on it, they had been inconsolable.

"I don't work with children anymore, though," Alma said.

Maire nodded.

"Too hard, y'know."

Alma had got a job as a typist in the council offices and was a lodger with another family until she met her husband. She lived alone now, in a council flat in Bethnal Green. She put her purse away and lay her head back on her pillows.

"I think I'll… have a little sleep now, Maire," she said sadly. "I might be going home tomorrow."

Maire looked at the figures. Alma wasn't going anywhere for a while yet.

"Press your button if you need anything," Maire reminded her.

Alma already had her eyes closed and didn't respond.

Maire walked away towards the nurse's station and wondered if it wasn't high time that she wrote to her own mother. As Alma said, it might have taken some years, but you never stopped being a mother once you were one. She wondered if – no, she hoped that – her mother was still her mammy. Maybe all she had to do was write the letter.

CHAPTER FIFTY

"Clodagh!" Fionn was calling from the other room.

Clodagh smoothed Luke's hair over his sleeping face and slipped out quietly, shutting the door. Luke looked ever so much like their Little John; he was definitely her favourite grandchild.

"Oh, sorry," Fionn whispered, "are they all asleep?"

"Yes, they are," grumbled Clodagh, "no thanks to you. What's the matter?"

Fionn was holding a crumpled note in his hand and he gestured it towards her.

"The holiday you booked to Spain," he said. "It sounds lovely, Clodagh, really, thank you for sorting it, but—" He stopped abruptly, expecting her to anticipate his concern. She did not; instead, she stared at him blankly.

"What?"

"Well, you probably didn't realise, but we'll miss Penelope's wedding. It's the day after we would have left."

Clodagh started down the stairs, and didn't look back at him as she said, "No, actually, I did realise." She was already in her armchair, poised and ready, for when Fionn marched into the living room and shut the door behind him.

"How could you, Clodagh? She'll be so upset that we're not there. We knew the date of the wedding weeks ago; she'll know we booked the holiday after and it looks deliberate."

"It is deliberate."

"Not for me! For the love of God, Clodagh, why are you always so unkind to her?"

"Unkind?" Clodagh smarted. She stared at Fionn like he

268

was a stranger and felt the rage build up inside her. Rage from twenty-five years ago, and every day since. It bubbled at the surface, ready to overspill. "Unkind," she repeated, shaking her head.

"If you weren't ever going to forgive me," Fionn said quietly, shifting his gaze from his shoes to his fingernails and back again, "you should have said back then. You didn't have to be a part of this."

Clodagh's eyes filled with tears as she stared at Fionn, her husband who had been more like a mortgage-paying, bed-warming housemate these last two decades since Michael was born. Did she hate him? She wasn't sure.

"I can't believe…" she stuttered, determined not to let him see her tears, "… that after all this time, you still don't understand."

"Clodagh, I'm *sorry*," Fionn wept, kneeling on the floor in front of her. "I was unfaithful and—"

"Jesus, Fionn, this isn't about that," Clodagh said coldly, though she let him hold her hands as he cried.

He cried more than any man she'd ever met. She didn't think men were supposed to cry, but he cried all the bastard time. What he'd had to cry about compared to her these past twenty or so years, she wasn't sure. He sniffled, like the boys used to when she told them off.

"Well, what then?"

Clodagh felt mildly sorry for him in that moment, for his ignorance. He was lucky he'd never had to raise that daughter after all. He'd never have understood a damn thing she ever felt.

"When that girl told you she was having your baby, the first person you told was your da," she said firmly. "Then you high-tailed over to Ruth and Donal. And then you roped in Bridget. And when did your loving wife find out about all this? *Once you'd already moved her to Dublin*."

Fionn knelt in silence as he looked up at her.

Clodagh continued. "It was humiliating. Everyone knew before me. Everyone comes before me. Ruth and Donal got the baby and I didn't."

There. She'd said it now. Fionn's mouth fell open slightly and he stopped crying with a sudden, shocked hiccup.

"I-I didn't... I didn't think—"

"No," Clodagh said calmly. "And you never do. Every time I see her, Ruth and Donal's little angel, it reminds me that not only could you be unfaithful, but that you don't think about me. Ever. If you had just *asked* me, Fionn," Clodagh was crying too now. "We couldn't divorce. We were going to have to stay together no matter what and we could have raised her here, as ours, and I could have learned to love her as ours. Instead, I have to watch her be theirs, and a bit yours, but not at all mine. And Bridget loved that girl, the mother, far more than she's ever loved me."

"Clodagh, Bridget loves—"

"*Don't!*" Clodagh wailed. "She does not, and she will not. They hate me. They've always hated me. Do you even know what that feels like, not to have everyone charmed by your mere existence, *all the time*? You should have stayed here and been a normal doctor like I asked you to. But no, you had to leave us, go miles away every month and administer to the poor and sick like some kind of priest with a bag of pills. Like the last good Samaritan on the earth. It was a *nightmare* here!"

She almost screamed the last part. It was she, after all,

who had sat up all night and all day with colicky babies and naughty toddlers that sucked every joyous impulse out of her, while Fionn was in bed with some teenager in the country. She'd had no help. She'd had no family. Fionn's family wouldn't come near the house.

"You want to fix everyone else's problems and be a hero in this family," she continued. "But you forget... you forget..." she sobbed. "You forget the only person you're supposed to be a hero to is *me*."

They sat quietly for a while as Clodagh wept and Fionn rested his head against her knees. He'd pretended not to hear Clodagh crying lots of times, and he wanted to block it out now, but he couldn't. This was all his fault. He thought about the drive home to their house from Ruth's when he first told them the news, twenty-five years ago. He was sick with fear and disgust with himself. Every time he thought about it, the waves of those emotions crashed over him again, and he felt afraid. He had wanted to tell her. But he didn't. He couldn't. He was a coward; he knew that.

"I know I was unkind but I couldn't let myself love her," Clodagh said.

Fionn said he understood. At last, he understood.

"I'm sorry. And we shouldn't have done it," Clodagh continued quietly. "We shouldn't have got married. We were too young and we all would have been happier."

"But... but the boys..."

"I just couldn't stay with my parents any longer, you know that; it was just too awful."

"I-I know, and I don't regret—"

"It's okay, Fionn, I know what life has been like for you, because of me," Clodagh said. She'd stopped crying and now seemed quietly defiant, as though the weight of the world had been lifted from her. For the first time in a long time – ever, maybe, she thought – she felt peaceful. There was a stillness in her heart that she couldn't explain. "And I know you can't see it yet, but I did it for you, love."

Fionn lifted his head to look at her. "What?"

"The holiday. I know you wanted to go to the wedding but I kind of thought… well…" She stroked the side of his head where his hair was greying. "I really thought you might not want to watch another man give your only baby girl away."

CHAPTER FIFTY-ONE

Mary was busily painting a clear topcoat of varnish on Penny's nails. The sun was shining through the window; that was good. It would make for some lovely photos outside the church. Ruth and Bridget were upstairs, re-doing their make-up before the photographer arrived, because they couldn't stop blubbing. The flowers had been delivered ten minutes ago – a bit late, but that was all right. She'd wanted yellow roses, daisies and big white peonies. When Penny's nails dried, she could put her dress on and, once she had her dress on, she could let Donal in.

Donal was hiding from the women in Penny's room. He was very proud of the way Penny and Patrick had decided to wait to live together until after they were married – and, he assumed, wait for other things as well – and so, for today and today only, this was still Penny's room. After today, this would officially become 'Penny's old room'. It would go back to being the empty spare bedroom it had been for almost two decades until she had been born. When he had painted yellow elephants on the wall for her and assembled her wooden crib.

Donal tied his tie in the mirror. Goodness gracious, he looked old. He remembered the first time he had ever seen Penny, at the foot of Bridget's stairs. Wrapped in Bridget's tea towel. He had worried, even then, about this day. As soon as Ruth had said they had a girl, he pictured this. When Penny came down the stairs, proud as punch, in her white communion dress at seven years old, the bottom had fallen out of his stomach – and never really gone back, it seemed.

He was happy for her. Patrick was a glorious young one. The Gavins were a terrific family. He couldn't have wished for better for his little girl – his only little girl. But he felt sad. Today he would do the walk he had dreaded for the whole of Penny's life.

The only thing stopping Ruth from having another breakdown was the promise of grandchildren once Penny and Patrick were married. He feared, desperately, for her mental health after this day. She had gone to her appointments for a couple of years, and seemed better, but Penny wanting to go to university had undone it all. He daren't ask what she wanted to do with this room once Penny was gone. After today, he knew, after Ruth had smiled for the photographs and thrown her confetti and Penny and Patrick were away in their car, she would fall apart all over again. He feared it greatly.

*

Fionn tied his tie in the mirror. Good grief, he felt old these days. He'd done this twice now; once for Little John, once for Colm. Not for Michael, of course – but there'd be other ceremonies for Michael. Other milestones to be immensely proud of, and he was. It was a terrific undertaking, what Michael was doing.

On those occasions, as the father of the grooms, he'd walked up the aisle after handing out Orders of Service at the church door with one of the boys, to endless handshakes and congratulations, and then sat at the front of the church, holding Clodagh's gloved hand. This time, he wasn't going to do the walk to the front of the church. He would sit at the back in a pew on his own, like he had done at Penny's baptism, and Penny's first Holy Communion. The church had been so packed that day, no one from the family had seen him there.

Clodagh had gone to Spain with a friend. It turned out the room Clodagh had booked had twin beds anyway. He had come to enormously appreciate Clodagh's gesture on his behalf, to protect him from this day and what it meant. But she had said: '*watch someone else give your only baby girl away*'. He had thought long and hard about this. As much as he had wanted her to be, Penny wasn't his baby girl. She was Ruth and Donal's baby girl. They had raised her; they had loved her; they were all she knew. And that, after all, was what he had wanted, wasn't it? Twenty-five years ago, when he had hurriedly written back to Maire, to get her in that black car and give their baby to the sad, constantly bereaved couple that longed for a child. He hadn't wanted to face the music of his own composition. She was someone else's child now, by his own arrangement. She also wasn't a little girl anymore either. She was all grown up now.

*

"Mr Quinn!" Mary called, as she ran up the stairs to Penny's bedroom. She was wearing a lilac bridesmaid dress and had her hair neatly coiled into a bun.

Donal thought she looked beautiful. She was a lovely young one as well, that Mary.

"Mr Quinn, she's ready."

Donal followed Mary down the stairs, and he realised this was the first thing he was ever going to do with Penny before

Ruth. Ruth had done all her other firsts. She'd changed the first nappy, given the first bottle; she was always the first to see Penny's reports and certificates at school because he was at work. She had even spotted her first, in her cap and gown, as she walked over in a group of her college friends on the day of her graduation. But this – this he had insisted on and, somewhat miraculously, he'd got his way. Ruth had seen the dress already, of course; she'd gone to the bridal boutique with her and had been there when she bought it.

"Ready?" Mary asked.

No, of course he wasn't ready. What father was ever ready for this? Mary opened the door to their living room. In a way, this was the room in which he had first become Penny's da. The day they said yes to the possibility of her. His heart stopped at the sight of her standing there, in the middle of the room. His heart was breaking and exploding, all at once. There she was, his little six-year-old girl invariably sporting an alarmingly high ponytail that Ruth insisted was 'the fashion', in a wedding dress and Ruth's veil. He hadn't seen that veil in forty-one years. Her red hair was curled and sat prettily on her shoulders.

"All right?" Penny asked. She had make-up on. Her nails were painted. She smiled so widely that the corners of her mouth almost reached her eyes.

"Yes," Donal said, pulling out a hanky and wiping a single tear from his left eye. "Yes, I am all right."

CHAPTER FIFTY-TWO

Maire smiled as the officiant made her legal welcome and told them about the fire exits. Maire was there in her capacity as witness to the bride, and she couldn't have been happier, or prouder. The groom's brother, Simon, sat on the other side of the aisle in the tiny registry office, as the second witness. They were the couple's only guests. Maire had met him briefly outside and he seemed like a nice man. Clearly, it ran in the family, she thought happily.

God, she was proud. Here was a bride who didn't give a hoot for tradition. This bride had plumped for a bright pink outfit from a department store they rarely went in, because they couldn't usually afford it. But Maire had insisted – 'It's your wedding day', she had said. 'Just this once, treat yourself'. And she had. Maire had bought her the hat, as her something new. She'd said she didn't want flowers but changed her mind at the last minute, so Maire had run to Tesco and bought her two bouquets of daffodils from a bucket at the front of the shop. Maire tied them up with some ribbon she had in a drawer.

But there was sadness about this day too. Shortly after today's festivities – which consisted entirely of this brief ceremony and, if Maire knew her friend, a colossal drink up and buckets of chips at their favourite pub in the East End – the newlyweds would be off to their new lives in America. Steve worked for Ford – Maire had listened multiple times to stories of his work and colleagues and still, after five years, had no idea what it was he did – and he was being transferred to work at the Ford headquarters in America. It was partly the reason why they had decided to marry, after years of cohabitation and being terribly modern 'partners' – the economic climate in America was much more forgiving to married couples, although for the life of her, Maire couldn't work out why that was.

They would stay in touch, of course, but it was the end of an era. A very significant era; goodness knows how many years, decades now, of Maire's life. Maire's heart broke a little at the sight of her dear friend's happiness, and what their happiness as a couple now meant for herself. But, at the same time, their happiness was all that really mattered. It had been their only goal when they'd arrived on the ferry to England from Ireland twenty-two years ago. To find happiness, and to keep it. She was so proud of how far they'd come – of course, they'd both needed a bit of propping up every now and again, especially at the beginning. They'd had each other for that. They'd both wanted the radio on in the flat constantly for the first five years because the silence made them sad.

But looking at this couple now, they were so, so happy. Any idiot could see that; it was a joy to behold. Maire glanced over at Simon, who was looking at her with concern. Perhaps her face betrayed her feelings. Her selfish feelings, Maire reminded herself. She smiled. He smiled too.

CHAPTER FIFTY-THREE

"Ah now, there's a beautiful bride," said Father Kelly.

Donal was helping Penny out of the car, and Mary and Caoimhe fluffed the train of Penny's dress. The car had been unnecessary, really, as they lived so close to the church, but Donal had insisted. This, Penny thought, was exactly the point of a family priest, and a family church. Father Kelly had been there for everything. He'd baptised her as a baby; he'd administered her first Holy Communion; he'd confirmed her. Now, he was marrying her. She hoped he'd still be alive to christen her children too, although that was unlikely.

Father Kelly disappeared back inside the church. She hoped Patrick was all right. He usually leaned on Mary in times of stress – there had been quite a debate over whether Penny would be allowed to have Mary as her chief bridesmaid, as Patrick had high hopes of having her as his 'best woman'. In the end, Penny had won, and Patrick settled for his college friend Callum, whose idea of a stag weekend had made Patrick fear for his life on several occasions.

Penny and Donal heard the organ burst into life. Caoimhe went first, gliding elegantly in her high heels. Mary followed after, tottering awkwardly on hers. She wasn't used to heels at all but had insisted on giving them a go for Penny and Patrick's big day – *'anything for you, Pen'* she had said. Penny slipped her arm through Donal's and he held her hand with his other. The time had at last come, the moment he'd been dreading since he'd first seen Penny's tiny face through a bundle of tea towel. She was all grown up. And by God, she was perfect.

They stepped together into the cool darkness of the church. They turned a corner at the font, and they walked slowly together up the aisle of adoring faces towards Patrick and Callum at the front. Callum stole a glance over his shoulder and grinned. Bridget and Ruth were holding hands and weeping through huge smiles. Patrick received a clap on the back from Callum and he turned. His face broke into an enormous smile, and Penny beamed back at him. Patrick's eyes filled up with tears.

Father Kelly looked on and admired the happy congregation, lit up gloriously by the sunshine through the stained-glass windows that had kept him company for the majority of his own, very elongated adult life.

Donal wanted the walk to last forever. He didn't want to let go of her hand, and when she wriggled her arm free of his he was still holding it.

"Daddy," she whispered. "You can let go now."

He pulled her hand to his mouth and kissed it. He smiled at Patrick. Patrick mouthed 'thank you' through his own spilling emotions. Donal stood back from the couple and waited for his line.

"Who presents this woman in Holy Matrimony?" croaked Father Kelly. He was spectacularly elderly. And to think, thought Donal, that he himself had felt old this morning.

"Me," he said. *Oh, no, that wasn't right.* "I-I do," Donal stammered. He didn't move. He stared hopelessly at Father Kelly, who smiled politely and nodded towards the pew with the empty seat next to Ruth where Donal was supposed to sit. He shuffled there sadly and sat down. Penny's train was so vast, it almost touched his feet. He thought back to her

280

childhood. She was so, so clever, he just couldn't get over it. She was already working for the Bank of Ireland in some graduate capacity and doing exceptionally well. She looked immensely happy, and that was all he had wanted. They had done their job. They'd done it well.

"Do you, Penelope Mary Quinn, take this man, Patrick Cillian Gavin to be your husband?"

Donal looked at Ruth. She was holding up better than he'd thought she would. He chastised himself for thinking so little of her, that she wouldn't rise to the occasion like this. Ruth beamed back at him and squeezed his hand.

"I do."

*

The hotel popped another bottle of champagne for the guests' glasses as Penny's friends buzzed around her. They admired her ring; they admired her dress; she was the first one of all of them to get married. They teased her about the night ahead and she blushed uncomfortably; she was the first to be married, but the last to do that. Ruth and Donal were standing with their own friends, drinking and laughing and being thanked profusely for the grandest day. It had been a beautiful service. It was going to be a beautiful day yet.

Fionn squeezed his way through the merriment and approached Penny.

"I'm so sorry, girls," he said, "may I steal the bride just for a second?"

The girls giggled and bashfully shrunk away to the bar; they had hoped Penny's handsome doctor uncle – or cousin, or some such relative – would be here.

Penny gaped in surprise and gave him a big hug. "I didn't think you'd be here!" she exclaimed. "I thought you and Clodagh were in Spain!"

Fionn marvelled at her. It was the closest he'd ever be to seeing Maire in a wedding dress. They looked so alike, it hurt.

"Oh, I'm afraid I was booked to speak at a conference on Monday, so I wasn't able to go," he said. "Clodagh has taken a friend. They'll have a lovely time. She's sorry to miss your big day, though, of course," he added quickly.

Penny smirked. That wasn't true. "Well... thank you so much for coming," she said. "There's plenty of food, so. Help yourself."

"Thank you." He paused. "You look beautiful, Penelope."

"Ah, thanks," she said, blushing and swishing her dress. "I should hope so, it all cost an absolute fortune!"

Fionn laughed. He'd assumed as much. He'd bought them a sandwich toaster and hidden it behind several other large boxes of presents that he assumed were kitchen appliances of some description. He'd wrapped it carefully himself last night, after Clodagh had left for the airport, in expensive wrapping paper. He hadn't written a card or tag to go with it but had stuck a large ivory bow on the top after a few minutes' deliberation.

"You should get back to your guests, Penelope," Fionn said. "It's not fair of me to monopolise the bride."

Penny nodded and gave him a quick kiss on the cheek. "Thank you for being here," she said. "I hope it goes well."

"What goes well?"

"The conference?"

"Oh." Fionn took a swig of his champagne. "Of course.

282

Yes. Thanks." He watched Penny swish away in her beautiful lace dress, back to her friends. The photographer called for a photo of the bride's family. Fionn gulped the last of his glass and went quickly to the bar for a top up.

CHAPTER FIFTY-FOUR

"Good grief, you're only married," Maire said, incredulously.

Steve's new Irish wife swallowed the last of her glass of whiskey and lemonade and called to the barman for another. Simon had insisted on buying a bottle of champagne for the four of them to share, but the bride was – literally – having none of it. She was a whiskey drinker. She was, after all, fiercely Irish, and a mere twenty-five years in London and the rest of her life in the States wasn't going to change that. Steve, Simon and Maire had instead enjoyed the bottle between them.

Maire marvelled at them as a couple. Steve knew all his new wife's secrets: all her pain, all her losses, all her history. Maire had admired her insistence on being upfront.

"There's no good in lies, Maire," she had said. "If he's going to love me, he's got to love it all."

And he did love it all. He'd phoned Maire the day after he'd been told all about it, the horrific story of how she had come to be an Irish girl living in London, a childless mother, with emotional scars that he couldn't even begin to imagine. He'd wept and been angry – not at her, but at the system and the family that had so gravely let her down. It could have been so different. A *family* member! And the cruelty of Bessborough. He couldn't stand it. He thanked Maire for rescuing her from that terrible place, and for bringing her here, so that he had the privilege to meet her and give her the life she had always deserved. Now, he had topped it all off by making her his wife. Maire wanted to cry with happiness.

The gift of life, just like Bridget had said.

"So, what about you?" Simon was asking Maire. He looked drunk. His lovely eyes gleamed with emotion. "How is it possible that a young lady like you is not married?"

Maire sighed. She didn't like it when drunk men in pubs asked her this. She didn't really care for drunk men in pubs at all anymore, truth be told.

"This young lady is forty-three, thank you," she said. "And to be honest, I'm not really interested in all that."

"Oh, I'm sorry, are you divorced?" he asked.

"No."

"It's okay if you are. Steve is divorced."

"I'm not divorced."

"Okay. So, I can't interest you in something a bit more than... chips?" He gestured to their several empty baskets on the bar, greaseproof paper at the bottom stained with ketchup. "Come on, it's almost six, and these two are about ready for bed I think."

Maire grinned and blushed. They were, very much, kissing like teenagers up against the bar. "All right," she said. "I'll grab them a taxi. Do you know anywhere nice?"

PART FOUR
2012

CHAPTER FIFTY-FIVE

Bridget had started trying to get out of bed, and the combined strength of Ruth and Donal was barely enough to keep her from doing it. Penny had called the doctor a week ago, who said an ordinary water infection often presented as 'disorientation' in the elderly and told them to make sure she drank plenty of fluids, before scurrying off to her other patients. Penny had smarted; she supposed at seventy-two Bridget could just about be considered 'elderly', but that didn't mean she liked to hear it. A nursing strike at the hospital meant none of Bridget's former colleagues could come and administer any help either; Ruth didn't want to call Fionn.

Ruth blamed herself. She should have realised something was amiss when she came round last week to find Bridget frantically emptying her CDs out of the unit and piling them all into cupboards instead, changing the order of her fridge magnets with a manic urgency, saying the state they were in was 'really upsetting' her. Ruth had been puzzled but made Bridget a coffee and suggested she might like to have a lie down, which she did. After that she'd been all right, as far as Ruth knew. Until today, that is.

Bridget had never really been ill. She had always said it was because she was a nurse; she was around illness so much that she'd never catch anything now. She had a cold every November and that was about it. She'd never broken a bone or had to have her appendix out; aside from some medicinal assistance with the change, she'd never so much as peeked into a pharmacy for most of her natural life. Ruth looked at her now and was baffled. She hardly recognised her.

It wasn't that she even seemed... *ill,* as such. She was just so confused. She was manic with bewilderment that had no obvious source, and no clear end. She requested the oddest things at the oddest times – *my red suitcase, you know the one, from when I went to London last year.* Ruth didn't want to point out that Bridget had never been to London in her life and, what's more, she was quite sure that Bridget had never owned a suitcase that wasn't a murky brown one that she'd bought cheap from the market off O'Connell Street. She wanted lamb for breakfast, whiskey before noon. She asked to smoke, which she'd given up more than half a century ago.

After Donal had found the smashed up remains of Bridget's treasured Compton & Woodhouse ladies in her washing machine, he had finally called Penny, despite Ruth's insistence that it would be no good upsetting her. Bridget had started weeping inconsolably and asking for 'her sweet girl'. Ruth had insisted, but Donal made the call.

"Where is she?" Bridget was sobbing. She kept her eyes on the door. "Where is my sweet girl? Why hasn't she come home?"

"She's on her way, Bridget," Donal said gently, taking his place back in his chair at Bridget's side.

Ruth reached for his hand and held Bridget's with her other. The doctor had said she might have 'episodes' and then it'd probably clear up on its own, or with some antibiotics if they absolutely insisted; they waited and waited, but the episodes didn't seem to stop.

"She is?"

"Yes, she is. She's on her way; you just watch the door Bridget, and you'll see her."

Bridget stared at the door and fidgeted with urgency. Her eyes danced around the doorframe; she tried extending her neck to see the top of the staircase.

"Auntie Bridget!" they heard from downstairs, after a door slam and hurried feet running up the stairs. "Auntie Bridget, I'm here," Penny cried, as she threw herself into the room still dressed in workout clothes. She started to cry as soon as she saw Bridget, greatly altered from how she knew her. Penny sat at the foot of the bed and reached out, and realised Bridget was still looking at the door. She hadn't reacted to Penny coming in at all. She'd not even remotely acknowledged her.

"Bridget, Auntie Bridget, I'm here," Penny pleaded, and Ruth tried to coax Bridget's increasingly distressed gaze to Penny. But Bridget continued to stare at the door and cry.

"Oh, where is she?" Bridget wailed. She strained to see past Donal's shoulder and look anxiously at the landing. "She was all I had. She was *all I've ever had.*"

"Auntie Bridget," Penny implored, "Bridget, look, I'm—"

"That's it," said Donal, loosening his hand from Ruth. "I'm sorry, girls, but I'm calling an ambulance. Now."

CHAPTER FIFTY-SIX

The sight of Bridget's things was enough to make Penny want to wail. They hadn't moved, of course they hadn't – there was no one here to move them. Yet, somehow, she was surprised to find everything exactly as it was after the wake. She hadn't been in since then; she couldn't bear it – Bridget's coffin in the living room, kissing her cold, waxy forehead, her rosary shackling her hands together for all eternity. She couldn't go in there. Suddenly she had a torrent of visions that made her feel queasy – boxes, a skip on the driveway, bags of clothes for the charity shop. People barging in here for viewings, estate agents wearing blue suits with brown shoes telling these intruders that the rooms full of Bridget's hideous patterned carpets have 'so much potential'. New families wandering around Bridget's living room, thinking about replacing Bridget's gas fire with something more modern and – side glance to one another – 'much safer'.

Patrick had offered to accompany her, but she wanted to be alone. Anyway, someone had to be at home with the girls and put them to bed. She hoped someone in the family, one of their literally dozens of relatives, would buy the house and move in. It had been Conghaile house since it was first built. That couldn't just... *end,* now.

The air was stale but still smelled like Bridget, just about. The harp was gathering dust. The only thing missing from any normal day – apart from Bridget herself, of course – was from the kitchen, no smell of baking apple tart or Irish stew. That was how you always knew if Bridget was away – the kitchen wasn't being used. And now she'd never use it again.

Penny sniffed. Thank God she'd never had any siblings so that she would never be in the state her mother was in right now.

Who dies from a UTI? That had been Penny's first reaction when she'd been told. She hadn't cried or thrown herself into the arms of her husband, like Ruth had done. She'd just coldly asked the question – who dies from a UTI? This is ridiculous. You're being ridiculous, she had said. I want to speak to a different doctor. But a different doctor said exactly the same thing; it wasn't just that – infection led to infection led to unpreventable, inexorable liver failure and uncontrollable sepsis and eventually Bridget's body had just stopped. It was rare, but it happened. Penny couldn't believe it. Penny wouldn't believe it.

Penny padded lightly upstairs to the bedroom. Making too much noise felt like sacrilege; she didn't want to disturb... well, nothing. No one.

Spare room.

Spare room first, not Bridget's.

She creaked open the door and thought of all the sleepovers she'd had in here. It was such a shame that Bridget had never had children of her own, a little red-headed rascal to draw on her walls and eat the mud in the garden. To sleep in this room, with Dublin GAA wallpaper and matching bed sheets and curtains. Penny smiled; God, how Bridget would have loved the sight of that. Or maybe a little girl, like Penny had been once, crying until she passed out cold because her soiled teddy bear was still in the washing machine and she couldn't have it in bed with her for the first time in living memory. In fact, her own childhood bedroom had been just on the other side of this wall.

Penny had always liked this room, but she wasn't sure why. It was nothing special – very old wardrobes on very old carpet and a very old-fashioned frilly bedspread. That, at twenty years old, was the newest thing in here. There was a clutter of equally old, worn paperbacks on a very old bookcase that was clearly being held together by the power of prayer and nothing else. An old chair with extra blankets slung over it. Dark mulberry curtains that shut out the whole world. The most uncomfortable pillows of all time. Bridget hadn't changed anything in here for decades; and yet, it moved her still, in some way that she couldn't identify. She ran her hand softly over the bedsheets.

The spare room took less time to empty than she had expected, mostly due to the fact that very little in it was really Bridget's. The old photo albums and boxes could go back to Mam and Daddy, that was fine; her second-best coat and old scarves were mostly Christmas presents bought by the cousins who had hardly known her and were never worn. So, no love lost there, thought Penny, as she bundled them into black bags labelled, 'Oxfam'. To her horror and amusement, she found a box full of VHS tapes at the back of the wardrobe, unlabelled. The orphans had suffered enough, she thought, as she stuffed the dreadful pillows and old bedding into bags intended straight for the bin. Penny hummed to herself while she worked, this little tune and that, that Bridget had played on her harp on Sunday evenings. Penny used to listen through the wall when she was small and, later, sat with a tea in hand in Bridget's living room, just listening. How she'd miss that.

She couldn't put it off any longer, she knew; Ruth would ask when she went back how much she had managed, and she couldn't let her down. She creaked the door open, peered in, and covered her mouth with her hand to muffle the sound. She was only here to escape the sound of her mother's non-stop sobbing and she certainly couldn't stand the sound of her own. Her shoulders heaved. She gave herself a shake. Bridget would hate this – *stop it, Penelope. Stop it right now.*

Penny had never really been in Bridget's room much before she got sick; she'd been very private about her space and her things, and even as a little girl Penny had learned not to go snooping around in here. That's just what she felt like now – a big, overgrown naughty child, a snooper. She sat down on the edge of Bridget's bed and breathed in. Her smell – it was still here. The black-and-white photograph of Penny's grandparents who she'd never met was gathering dust on the bedside table. She buried her face in Bridget's pink dressing gown hanging on the back of the door and sobbed.

She heard the bells of St Katherine's after a period of time, she didn't know how long exactly, but with each clang of the bell she realised it must be far later than she had thought. She was wasting time. She forced herself to shuffle up, pull out the bedside drawer and then empty it carelessly all over the bed. A Bible, to be expected, with the corner turned down to – yes, of course – John 16:33. A small statue of Our Lady. An unopened packet of tissues. A photograph of Penny's parents in the Aran Islands, with a scribble of Bridget's handwriting on the back. Another dreadful, battered romantic novel.

Next, she went to the wardrobe and started heaping armfuls of Bridget's clothes onto the floor. Jumpers in plain pastels and beige tailored trousers that seemed to go on forever. Sixteen identical boxes of what certainly appeared to Penny to be sixteen pairs of identical black orthopaedic shoes. Wait, fifteen – one of the boxes was different. Bigger, but lighter, and it rattled. She opened it.

CHAPTER FIFTY-SEVEN

Ruth felt utterly empty. Two dead siblings, two dead parents, five dead children and her eldest, favourite brother John was now over ninety. Surely, it wouldn't be long before it was just her and Liam left; Liam would also be ninety this year. She didn't know how they'd managed it; their father Seamus had died in his early fifties and there they were, his eldest two sons, both making it to ninety. The odds of that must be astronomical. She'd seen some of her other friends develop an age-induced depression over the years, and with an apparent genetic lenience towards centenarian-hood on her side, she hadn't worried about it too much before now, but now that it was here, she hadn't realised it would be like this. A lot of her friends from when Penny was little were a good deal younger than her, anyway; they had no idea yet what was coming to them in a decade or so. And what's more, Bridget was Ruth's *younger* sister. Her younger sister had beaten her to the grave. Bridget had officially beaten her at everything, Ruth thought bitterly.

She had floated through the funeral and sat in silence in an armchair at the wake. She didn't want to speak to anyone, and no one dared speak to her. They didn't know what to say. Some tried to say how sorry they were, but Ruth just looked blankly at them, as if they were crazy. They'd seen widows in better shape than Ruth. She barely slept and refused to eat; she lost a stone in weight in a little over a fortnight. Of course, she still had Donal, but apart from practical things like remembering to put a wash in the machine and cut the grass, he hadn't been much help. As he had always said, he didn't like to talk about it. Ruth didn't bother to talk to him.

Donal had no siblings. Penny had no siblings. Between them they could not comprehend the depth of Ruth's misery and woe, and she had told them so, the day after Bridget had died. Her body had been brought over from the hospital morgue and was laid in the coffin on her own dining table in her own lounge, ready for visitors. Ruth had bound Bridget's hands with the rosary herself. She prayed, frantically, obsessively, mournfully for the repose of Bridget's soul, for hours every day. Her Bridget, who alone had stood between their mother and Ruth on Mariah's most spiteful days to defend her. Bridget, who had carefully and safely delivered Ruth's only daughter into the world. Bridget, who had answered the telephone every single time Ruth had ever, ever phoned her, in seventy-two years.

And now, she was gone.

CHAPTER FIFTY-EIGHT

Penny was mystified by the contents of the box.

21.08.1980

Dear Bridget,

We're settled into the hotel for the time being; it's very nice. Thank you so much for making the arrangements for us. The lady that owns it makes shortbread. It's not as good as yours. I have a couple of weeks before I have to go and register at the college and we start doing basic things in surgeries and the local hospital right away. I'm very excited, but also very nervous. I don't suppose anyone will leave me alone long enough that I might accidentally kill someone on my first day, will they? Hopefully it'll just be blood pressures and leaflets to read. I want to be good at this, Bridget, I really do. I want to make you proud!

I took the underground into the centre of the city today and had a look at the Houses of Parliament. There were lots of people there but to be honest, I think the post office is better. I know it's only a post office, but don't you think it just has something so special about it? I miss you so much, and the house, and your apple tart. How is Penny? Is it okay to ask? Maybe it isn't. I hope Ruth and Donal are happy too; I'm sure they are. I don't suppose Fionn has asked about me, has he?

You know I can never thank you enough for everything you've done.

All my love, Maire.

20.10.1980

Dear Bridget,

Guess what? I took blood today and I didn't faint. Perfect Jemima did. I don't want to sound unchristian, but it really was one of the greatest moments of my life. How's Penny? What's happening with Fionn, anything?

Penny thought this was all rather odd. Bridget had never mentioned having a friend in England. Especially one that, evidently, knew the family, and knew her. And yet these letters went on. For pages, and for years.

14.05.1987

Dear Bridget,

Well, that's the last time I take your stupid advice. Went for coffee with Handsome Jack. Absolutely dreadful time, never again. Men are horrid.

Today Jemima delivered a stillbirth. I don't think I've ever seen such devastated people in my whole life. She was supposed to be the supportive one, to the family, you know? And she completely fell apart. Everyone did, all the nurses. I sat with her in the staff room for three hours and she just wouldn't calm down. It was horrible, Bridget. It made me think about Penny and what would have happened if something had happened to her, right at the last minute like that. Remember when we used to sit in the kitchen and watch her wriggling around, kicking me in the ribs every five minutes? And Ruth was beside herself with joy even then. I wondered if getting into this would be too hard because of her and I do still think about her every day, every single day Bridget, but it's not hard at all, because I'll never forget

Ruth's face. She was a mammy, she always was – a mammy with no baby to love – and what if something had happened to Penny like something happened to the Miller baby today and she'd never had her chance? It just broke my heart, really Bridget.

How is Penny getting on at school? I think an all-Irish school is a great idea. She can be so much better at it all than we were. Is she still doing well with her maths?

Penny's whole body felt cold. She felt her stomach drop through to her legs and the ends of her fingers and her toes started to fizz. She wanted to grip the letter but it slipped through her hands, which had started to shake. She read it again. To make sure. She was upset, after all – recently and very significantly bereaved, no less. It's easy to misunderstand things when one is upset.

But no.

There it was.

A mammy with no baby.

She had to read more. It was so obviously a massive mistake and she had misinterpreted something because she hadn't read everything. She didn't have a complete picture. It was a mistake. Her hands moved independently of her mind and picked up another one.

15.04.1998

Dear Bridget,

I've heard about the Agreement; thank God for that. I know it was all in the North but I've never forgotten that day with Dermot and I just always really thought that something would happen to you and the family. Thank God. The reports from the BBC are always so bleak and terrifying and I don't really think they understand what's happening there any more than anyone else does.

Anyway, I have news that I know will make you happy. Horrible Maureen is finally retiring at the grand age of four thousand years old and they've opened her position for Ward Manager. I'm applying. I just wish you were here to help me! I wouldn't even be here at all if it wasn't for you, Bridget. Don't ever think I don't remember that.

Penny rummaged and started looking at the dates – October 1989: *Thank you for Penny's school photo. She is so beautiful.* December 1999, to usher in the new millennium: *I can't believe Penny's gone to university! I'm so proud of her. She'll end world poverty or something; I can't wait to watch.* May 2003: *Our little girl is married, Bridget, I can't believe it. What a dress! It must have cost a fortune. What's Patrick like?* July 2008: *Well, I can't believe it. I'm a granny, as I live and breathe. What a beautiful wee thing.*

There was a photograph that had been taken in Bridget's kitchen, as it had looked about thirty years ago with the dark wood cabinets and the beaded curtain over the back door. It was of a woman who, if Penny didn't know better, could have very easily been her. The letters were a few years old. There had to be a more recent one. She wanted the most recent one; did this woman even know that Bridget had died? There was no one untoward, or unrecognisable, at the funeral. Someone would have to tell her. Maybe it would be herself. Penny was furious with Bridget for having died, and not being here to answer her questions, to explain herself and all this. Penny frantically tossed the various letters aside until she found it.

It was at the bottom so Bridget must have buried it on purpose. January 2010. The most recent one. The ink was smudged.

Dear Bridget,
  I don't want you to be upset, but I got the results...
  Stage Four... aggressive...
  They've done their best...
  Give my baby a squeeze. Please don't be sad for me.

Underneath it was an Order of Service for someone called Maire Connelly. The woman in the photograph on the front – the same woman as in the other photograph she'd found, Penny realised quickly – looked even more horrifyingly, frighteningly similar to herself. It was like looking at a programme for her own funeral, with someone else's name on it.

Penny didn't move. She felt like her racing heart was pumping ice around her body. She felt weak and nauseous. She'd read dozens of letters and watched a life she never knew existed built up, and then brought down again – not completely unlike her own, she realised. An hour ago, she hadn't known this. Just one hour ago, she'd been the miracle, mythical born-in-middle-age child of Ruth and Donal Quinn. Now – what? Now, she was the shame-ridden issue of a dead birth mother she couldn't even meet. How was that fair? How was that right?

The world outside had got dark; St Katherine's chimed nine times. Penny didn't want to think about the outside world. It had continued to move on, without Bridget. People wandered the streets as if nothing had happened. How dare they, she had thought then, how dare they just get on with their lives. *Bridget Is Dead,* she wanted to scream. *And so is this lady.* She felt the same now. How dare they. How dare all of them.

Something was niggling at her; what was it? Something she'd seen, but she hadn't been looking. It was here in the room; she'd seen it not so long ago this evening. She shuffled herself to the bed where she'd upended the drawer and first read it. But not really *read* it. *Ruth and Donal, Aran Islands, February 1980* Bridget had written on the back. They stood smiling against the coastline, the wind blasting their hair away from their heads, while a German backpacker took their photograph on Donal's second-hand camera. And finally, she saw it – her mother, six weeks before Penny was born, looking as slim as a pole.

*

The sound of the shutting front door seemed to rouse Ruth.

"Oh, sweetheart," she said faintly, as she saw Penny walk through the living room door. "You're so late! How did you get on?"

Penny looked around at where Ruth had been sitting almost constantly for the past week. There were tissues in heaps all around her feet, and several mugs on coasters on the end table. The liquid in them had stained the edges and gathered little pools of curdling milk on the top like lily pads on ponds. Her eyes were puffy and swollen. Her fingernails were bitten almost to the cuticle. She fiddled with the blanket Donal had spread across her knees in the darkness. She looked exhausted.

"It was…" Penny began, fingering the photo in her pocket. Ruth blinked. "It was difficult but it's all right," she said, perching on the edge of the sofa next to her. "I didn't get around to her bedroom. I'm sorry. I'll come back tomorrow and do it, okay?"

"Okay," said Ruth. She looked like she was going to cry again.

Penny looked at the woman she had always thought was her mother. She didn't know what to think. She didn't know what to feel. Two hours ago, she had been someone. Now, she was someone else. What she wouldn't give, now, to go back two hours and be who she used to be. All her life, the whole time… She could have inherited diseases that no one knew about. She could have a genetic heart disorder and fatal allergies and a predisposition towards life-shattering cancers and no one would know. They'd celebrated all her birthdays with big, expensive parties. Ruth had answered questions about Penny's birth and said *I, we, your da and I.* She was a liar. Bridget, too, had been a liar.

"I'll clean up all this and get going," Penny said, picking up mascara-stained tissues and collecting three mugs in one hand.

Ruth sniffed. "Thank you, love," she said. "I think I'll go on up to bed now and see your da."

See my da, thought Penny. Now there's an idea.

CHAPTER FIFTY-NINE

It did occur to Penny fleetingly that she wasn't one hundred percent sure he was the right one. It didn't make a huge amount of sense, but this lady, Maire... she'd asked about him by name. Asked if he'd asked about her, like she was a lovesick teenager at secondary school. And Clodagh. Clodagh detested Penny. It had to be him and, if it wasn't, surely he'd be just as shocked as she was to find out and maybe could help her uncover the truth. Because that was all that really mattered now – the truth.

After an utterly sleepless night and an argument with Patrick that morning about her sniping attitude, Penny drove to the home and parked her car; she walked in through the automatic glass doors and gave her name to a pretty nurse behind a desk. She didn't want to give herself time to think about it or give herself an opportunity to talk herself out of it. She walked through to a pink armchair-ridden day room with enormous windows, scanned the space, and finally looked into the blank eyes of the woman in the wheelchair, the woman who had always hated her. At least, now, she could understand why.

She couldn't imagine the pain of a cheating husband, thank God, and so the thought of Clodagh experiencing such agony, and then having to see the resulting child every year to boot, and act like she didn't know otherwise, was sad. It was awful, in fact; Penny could see that. Clodagh's life had been a tragedy; much more so than hers. Perhaps it was a good thing now that she couldn't even remember the day before yesterday.

Fionn was sitting next to her, with his heart full of secrets. He wasn't the only one. Ruth and Donal and Bridget had all known. Clodagh had known. Uncle John had probably known, and God only knows who else at this point. The whole street could have known, and no one told her. The only person, it seemed, that the world had kept the secret from was her.

Father. "Fionn." It was all she could say. Her heart was beating in her throat.

"Penelope!"

Penny rolled her eyes as he stood up with vigour.

"What a nice surprise! It's so good of you to come and see us. To see Clodagh."

He hugged her awkwardly; she patted his shoulder with her fingertips and leaned away. He released Penny and turned back to look at Clodagh, who was peering at them with mild interest.

"I'm glad you've come. We don't get a huge amount of family visiting."

Penny nodded; she couldn't take her eyes off Clodagh. She had lost so much weight, and her eyes that used to sparkle so much looked empty now. Penny thought of how beautiful she'd been for so many years. Mean and cold, but undeniably beautiful. Clodagh coughed onto her hands and looked at them in bewilderment.

"I don't understand," Penny said quietly. "She's so young still. Don't only like... old people get this?"

Fionn shrugged defeatedly. "It's rare," he said. "Very rare, at her age. But it does happen. She's one in a million is Clodagh."

His mouth smiled kindly at Penny, but his eyes didn't

follow suit.

"So does she, um..." Penny stumbled, "understand anything? Like, what we're saying?"

"Understand?" Fionn rubbed his chin. "Yeah, I'd say she understands that she's safe, that the food is all right, and she can eat it, but she doesn't remember anything. Everything is brand new. She thinks I'm a doctor most of the time. I mean, I am of course." His voice cracked a little. He swallowed and shook his shoulders. "Just not her doctor. It's almost unheard of, to be this advanced at her age, like I said ... the boys won't come here."

The boys. Of course. Little John – who now stood at a neck-breaking six feet, five inches tall with three lanky sons of his own and who had been pleading with the family for the last fifteen years for everyone to stop calling him 'Little'; Colm and his wife and their twin daughters, and Michael, who five years ago had taken holy orders and become a fully-fledged Catholic priest. Penny's... brothers. Penny's brothers, and nieces and nephews. She hadn't even thought about them, and whether they knew. They were nice young men; she liked them a lot. Michael, especially; she'd always loved Michael from the first day they had met. Penny continued to stare at Clodagh, whose face broke into the most beautiful smile, innocent like a child. Clodagh had never, ever smiled at Penny before now. Penny smiled back.

"Beautiful girl," she said suddenly. Her voice was dull, like she was speaking through a voice changer. "My favourite granddaughter."

That was good enough for Penny.

"Fionn... how could you get my mother pregnant and just hand her over to Bridget like she was nothing and lie to me my entire life. You and everyone."

Fionn looked at her. For a second, he wondered if he had misheard, but knew, really, that he hadn't. Colour drained from his face, but his expression didn't change; he just looked at her, for moments and moments that seemed like years for both of them. Penny knew then that he was the one. Her blood rushed cold all over again. She wondered if she looked like him. She hated him because Donal wasn't her father, not really, and this was all Fionn's fault. It was so unfair.

Fionn had known, somewhere, that this moment was coming. He wasn't naïve like Ruth and Donal. He knew Bridget would've fallen in love with that girl over three decades ago – it was so easy to fall in love with Maire. They would've kept in touch. There'd be something, a scrap of evidence – or maybe it had been Ruth, cracking under the strain of her grief who had finally broken and told Penny the truth. Secrets didn't stay buried forever. They couldn't. He had so hoped, for all their sakes, they'd always get away with it. But they hadn't. He hadn't.

This moment had been inevitable, and now it was here.

He looked over at Clodagh, who looked back at him as though she had never seen him before and started chewing her thumbnail. He needed to open his mouth and say something. Penelope was staring expectantly. He wondered if she was going to shout at him like her mother did, the last time he ever saw her.

"Penelope, I…"

Then silence.

"Yes?"

He didn't say anything else. He looked like he was going

309

to cry, but he didn't. He just kept looking at her. He searched his brain for words. It was empty.

"How could you, Fionn? How could you do it to..." Penny bit back on herself. "To poor Clodagh!"

"I'm sorry."

"You're sorry."

"Yes, darling, I am, I'm sorry, I'm sorry," he said, and then he started to shake. "I'm so sorry. I was married and I was so worried; I'd worked so hard to build up everything, my career and my family, and everyone would have been so embarrassed. Father was so ashamed. I was ashamed!" Penny looked like her mother and it made him want to die on the spot. "But your mother was... I wanted you to be looked after, and stay in the family, and Ruth so badly wanted a child and I..." He tailed off, realising what he'd begun to say.

"And you didn't," Penny completed. "You didn't want me."

"That's not what I said."

"It's what you meant. Did my mother want me? Did she want to go to England and have me taken care of?"

Fionn felt crushed at her words; sending Maire for a termination had never, ever entered his head. He wouldn't kill any part of Maire, not on his life. He wouldn't. And he didn't!

"Oh my Lord," she said. Penny had misread his guilty face entirely. "That's what you told her to do, isn't it?"

Fionn paled. He was starting to feel sick. She was so much like Maire; his heart felt like it was breaking. He opened his mouth to apologise, to tell her she was very, very wrong, but the wrong sounds came out.

"Can... Can you please not raise your voice in front of

Clodagh. You know how much you upset her."

Penny felt like she'd been punched. She was speechless. Clodagh had never mattered to him; she wouldn't be here if that wasn't the case. Obviously, her mother – her 'real' mother – hadn't mattered either. He was beyond reason. She didn't even know why she'd tried. He'd watched silently and done nothing as Clodagh had bullied her all her life, and now?

It didn't feel possible that she could share DNA with this man. She wished this was all a terrible mistake.

Penny exhaled, shook her head in disgust and looked away from Fionn. She marched straight over to Clodagh. She knelt at her feet and kissed both her hands, whispered some words that Fionn couldn't make out, and then walked away without looking back at either of them. The nurse who had checked Penny in not five minutes ago watched her walk out with confusion and mild concern.

Penny felt in her soul that it was the last time she'd ever see them. She never wanted to see that dreadful man again. Her world had ended. Her life was a lie. And it was all his fault. Fionn slumped down into the armchair beside Clodagh and put his head in his hands. Why – *why* – did he have to have such problems getting the right words out, when it mattered most? Penelope was gone now, thinking he'd wanted her syphoned out of her mother's body and into medical waste before her heart had even beat for the first time – and it wasn't true. It just wasn't true. Penelope was all he had to prove that, once, a glorious and beautiful and kind girl like Maire had ever loved him. They were both gone forever. He tried to hold Clodagh's hand, but she was confused, and pulled it away.

311

"Beautiful girl," Clodagh repeated confidently. She watched Penny out of the window, storming to her car, wrenching open the door and slamming it shut, leaning her head on the steering wheel and bursting into tears. Clodagh sniffed. She looked at Fionn coldly. "You're a bastard, whoever you are," she said.

CHAPTER SIXTY

Penny felt nauseous as she pulled her car into the driveway. She'd kept this new information to herself for a couple of weeks, and now that Ruth had stopped crying every day about Bridget, Penny supposed it was as good a time as any. She didn't know what she was going to say. She remembered what Patrick had said to her the best part of twenty years ago – *they're still my mammy and daddy*. She didn't know if Ruth would tell her the truth or try to perpetuate the lie. Maybe she'd get angry with Penny. There'd probably be crying. Penny hated crying.

Ruth was in the kitchen, loading the dishwasher. She threw her arms around Penny as she always did, as though she hadn't seen her for months.

"Daddy's out," Ruth said.

Just as well, thought Penny.

"Mammy, come and sit here for a minute," Penny said, pulling out a chair at the kitchen table. Ruth looked confused but merrily obliged. "I need to show you something."

Ruth felt her heart leap; she was elated. Another one! God, how she loved being a grandmother. This was how Penny had told her about the girls. To think she would have *three* little grandchildren in just a few…

"This," Penny was saying. She was handing her a photograph.

Ruth was ready to explode and weep with happiness at the sonographer's picture, with Penny's name in the corner and the shadowy shapes in the middle. But that wasn't what it was. It wasn't black and white. It was green, and blue, and grey.

"I found this when I was clearing out Bridget's room," Penny explained calmly. "It's a lovely photo, Mammy. Do you remember it?"

Ruth was confused. She did remember it, vaguely; it was her and Donal in the Aran Islands, what, thirty years ago? Maybe more? She didn't understand what this had to do with anything. It had to be the second time they went because they didn't have the camera the first time. The Germans! Oh, yes. Now she remembered. She smiled.

"It was taken before I was born, Mammy; look at Bridget's writing on the back," Penny said gently, sliding the photo out of Ruth's fingers and turning it over.

Ruth read Bridget's handwriting and frowned at Penny. She was tired. She wasn't following.

"Mammy, look," Penny said again. "It was taken a couple of months before I was born. But you don't... you don't look pregnant. You weren't pregnant then, were you Mammy?"

Penny's heart broke as she saw the colour drain instantly from Ruth's face. The photograph went limp in her hand and she started to crumple, like her head was too heavy for her neck to support.

"Bridget... wrote the wrong date," Ruth said. She forced a smile and nodded at Penny, willing her to agree. "Silly Bridget, making you all worried like this."

"She didn't though, did she, Mammy?"

"You know what Bridget was like, she was such a scatterbrain."

"Mammy."

"She just... made a mistake. Look, I'll make some tea—"

"Ruth, just admit it!"

314

The outburst shocked both women. Penny was stunned at herself and opened her mouth to apologise. Ruth recoiled from her and put the photograph down on the table, writing side down.

"Oh, God, Mammy, I'm so sorry..."

Penny tailed off as she watched Ruth intently for signs of what would happen next. Suddenly she felt afraid – of what, she wasn't sure.

Ruth didn't speak for a long time. She searched her brain for remaining excuses, explanations, mistakes that Bridget had made. But Bridget didn't make mistakes. There was nothing more to be done, nothing further to hide.

Ruth picked up the photograph and looked at it again. Yes, she remembered that day, how she'd searched the sky for Dermot and Leanne. How she'd cursed the Lord for denying her the one happiness she so deserved, so craved, and how she held the fragile belief that when they came home, all of that was about to change.

She turned it over again. There was her name and Donal's, and the date, and the place, all present and correct in Bridget's familiar handwriting. Bless her, she'd kept the photograph all these years.

Damn her.

She'd kept the photograph all these years.

And look what it had led to now.

"You're still our daughter, Penelope," Ruth said, her voice shaking. "I hope... I hope you'll always be our daughter. But I wasn't pregnant with you, no. That part... that part didn't happen. I'm sorry."

Ruth had always believed that once Penny's childhood was over, she would never have to worry about this again.

Especially now that poor Clodagh was wasting away in some nursing home; all the pieces of the puzzle had gradually drifted away from them. Anyone who had known their secret had moved on or passed away. She felt cold. Her body was covered in goosebumps. She could hear her heart in her ears.

"Can you please tell me what happened?" Penny asked. She reached out for Ruth's hands and held them firmly. "I love you, Mammy. Nothing will change that. Just... please tell me the truth."

Ruth cried and sniffed too much to speak at first, and spluttered between sentences as she told Penny that her and Donal had lost five children who had never been born.

Penny was shocked – this had never been mentioned to her before.

There was a young girl from the country who was in trouble and needed a nice couple to adopt her baby. They'd been put in touch with her; Bridget had looked after her during her pregnancy because she was a nurse and Maire was a nice girl, a very nice girl, despite... well, it was more common than Penny probably realised. But it wasn't that Penny wasn't wanted – it wasn't that at all. Ruth pleaded with her to understand that she was so wanted and so loved and that was why she was here.

Penny was crying too but she smiled at Ruth. She kissed Ruth's hands. Ruth wiped Penny's tears off her face.

"Fionn is my biological father, isn't he?" she said gently.

Ruth looked shocked. "How could you... how could you possibly know—"

"A country girl just appeared, did she?" Penny sighed. She didn't want to tell Ruth about the letters; she couldn't be the reason Ruth held a grudge against Bridget after the poor woman had died – the photo was damning enough. "I'm guessing a *travelling locum doctor* put you in touch, y'know, a doctor with a wife who *hates* me."

Ruth simply nodded and blew her nose noisily. Penny was so clever, after all; she'd made a good guess there. She had sometimes wondered how this conversation would go if the worst had ever happened; Penny was a lot calmer than she had ever imagined her to be. She didn't seem to be angry with Ruth at all. That had been her worst fear. That, and...

"I'm sorry, darling," Ruth said. She looked into Penny's eyes that were so unlike her own. "Oh God, you hate us... you hate us... you're going to leave us!" Ruth started to wail loudly and put her head in her hands on the table.

"Oh God, Mammy, no!" Penny cried, jumping up out of her chair and embracing Ruth. She sobbed too, loudly, into Ruth's shoulder. "You... you treated me like..." She couldn't speak. Her shoulders were shaking uncontrollably.

Ruth had done nothing but cry for weeks and she had just started to feel better and now Penny had come in and steamrolled her life with this. Perhaps she shouldn't have said anything and let sleeping dogs sleep on. She felt terrible.

"You treated me like a princess, Mammy," Penny cried, and she meant it. She couldn't fault a second of her life. She couldn't if she tried.

Ruth held on to her and whimpered.

"I couldn't have had a better time. A better life. I couldn't have. I couldn't have. I'm so glad you're my... I'm so glad I have you. I'll never leave you. I promise. I promise. I'll never, ever leave you."

*

An hour later, Donal arrived home. He dropped his golf clubs in the hallway and whistled as he came through to the kitchen. Ruth and Penny were sitting at the kitchen table, eating slices of cake with mugs of hot tea. They both smiled at him.

"There's my girls," he said happily, stooping to kiss Penny first, and then Ruth. "Oh, dear, been crying again I see," he said, and stroked both their heads. "Bridget wouldn't have this, you know. Let's go to the pub for tea."

He snapped off a banana from the bunch in the fruit bowl and whistled again as he walked away to the living room. They heard the floorboards creak under his feet, the armchair sigh as he settled into it, and the buzz from the television as he turned it on.

Ruth nodded morosely as she passed the photograph back across the table to Penny. Penny tore it into four pieces and dropped them silently into the chasm of the kitchen bin.

CHAPTER SIXTY-ONE

Penny shut her own front door gently behind her. She searched each room quietly for Patrick, who was poring over books at the kitchen table. He had decided eighteen months ago to abandon his horrible job in finance with his horrifying boss and pursue a PhD; Bridget had encouraged him to do so.

"Aw, hey," he said, catching sight of Penny. "You feeling better?"

She didn't want to respond to that. He'd been very supportive since Bridget had died, taking care of the house and Bridget's affairs that Penny didn't feel up to dealing with herself. After cleaning out Bridget's house, she hadn't wanted to talk to him for a couple of days. He kissed her every morning but didn't press her for what was wrong. He wasn't an idiot.

"Where are the girls?" she asked.

"Asleep," he said proudly. He was good at bath time and bedtime and story time. It was, by far and away, his favourite part of parenthood.

"Patrick, do you remember when we were children," she said slowly, "and I told you if I ever had a secret, I'd tell you about it?"

"Not especially, no."

"Remember, when you got your new goldfish? We were, what, eight?"

"Ah, Fleck and Bubbles!" Patrick said happily. "Yeah, I remember. Go on."

"My parents adopted me from a teenager in the countryside who had fallen in love with Fionn. He cheated on Clodagh, I don't know for how long. He got this girl pregnant and then he left her."

Patrick's mouth fell open and his book slowly folded itself shut. He raised his eyebrows. Penny pursed her lips. Nobody spoke for a while; the kitchen tap dripped ominously in the background.

"You're joking," he said eventually.

"Nope."

"*Fionn?*"

"Yep."

Penny told the whole story to a stunned and silent Patrick. How she had found the letters in Bridget's bedroom. How she had confronted Fionn and he'd confirmed the suspicion. How she had told Ruth that she knew, and they had decided not to tell Donal, or the rest of the family. How her birth mother, Maire, had died of breast cancer in London two years ago.

"Oh, I am sorry," he said at last. "So you can't even meet her now."

Penny shook her head. She wasn't sure if she would have wanted to meet her, but perhaps it would have been nice to have had the choice.

"Everyone is... everyone is dying," she said hopelessly.

Patrick reached out for her hand. "No, they're not," he said gently. "I'm so sorry about your... about Maire, and Auntie Bridget, of course. But we're all still here. We're all still your family."

Penny closed her eyes. She wished Bridget was here. Bridget was really the only one she wanted to talk to about any of this. Bridget had taken care of her mother as though she had been Bridget's own child; Ruth had admitted to that

320

much, and the letters she'd read and kept in the boot of her car for two weeks certainly painted a clear enough picture of that.

"I need you to tell me…" Penny said. "I need you to tell me how to deal with this. How to deal with them. How did you do it?"

Patrick poured them both glasses of wine and put his books away.

"It's different," he said. "I always knew. And I was always okay with it. Mary is still my sister, even though she's the one that looks like them. She also got Dad's eczema. *I* have no such privilege," he said grinning.

Penny didn't smile back. She didn't feel like joking.

"This is a shock, Penny, and it's the shock that is making this so hard," he said, "but eventually you'll realise that it doesn't actually… *matter*. They're the ones who raised you. They're the ones who have always loved you. It doesn't matter where you came from. All that matters is who you are."

Penny knew he was right, but Patrick didn't have any idea who his biological parents were. He'd had no interest in it and made no effort to find out. Like he had always said, they were still his mammy and daddy. Maire, her letters… she had always asked about Penny. She had clearly always cared about Penny. The 'P' necklace that Bridget had given her for her confirmation twenty-three years ago had been from Maire, not from Bridget. Penny had worn it every day until she was married.

Ruth and Donal weren't the only ones who had always loved her.

"But they lied to me," she said. "My whole life."

321

"I know. That's… hard. It is, and you can be upset about that for a little while if you insist. But, honestly, what else did you expect them to do?" he asked.

Penny didn't know how to answer that. Yes, actually, she did insist on being upset. There had been so much love, but so much dishonesty. It was hard for her to imagine, with all of Ireland's changes in her lifetime, how Maire and the women that came before her had lived – the decisions and the sacrifices they had been forced to make. They had no alternatives. They had very few choices.

"You could have a ma out there somewhere, Patrick."

"I already do," he said, sternly.

He was getting agitated; Penny didn't like it when he got like this.

"She's called Brenda and she's a retired dentist and she lives with my da in Beaumont. Yeah, there's another woman out there somewhere, Penny, but I don't know what's going on in her life. I don't know what challenges she faces and what secrets she has to keep."

Penny was quiet.

"She might have got married, had a bunch of wains and moved on. Even if I did want to know, which I *don't*, imagine the trauma, the trauma for *her*, of me interrupting her life now and saying, 'Aw hey, remember me?'. It's not all about us, Penny. We have to think of them too."

Penny felt suitably chastised, which she didn't think was altogether fair. Patrick had been told the truth early on in life, which Penny had not. He'd also had a sibling; she didn't. He had no idea how she was feeling as their experiences were nowhere near the same. She had just had the shock of her life, and he wasn't even trying to be sympathetic.

322

Penny stood up, poured her wine down the sink and went to bed.

*

By midnight, Patrick hadn't come up to join her, so Penny assumed after their argument that he'd made himself up a bed on the sofa. That was usually what he did when they quarrelled. *Had* they had an argument? She wasn't really sure. In any case, she felt like having some time and space to herself. 'If she insisted'. Yes, she did insist, thank you *very* much.

She thought about her and Patrick's daughters. They were four and two. If she was right – and her maths was *always* right – that was the age Little John and Colm were when she was born. She thought about her daughters' births, an excited rush to the hospital with Emily, a long, arduous labour with all the pain relief that the hospital would give her, and Patrick by her side, cheering her on, wiping her forehead, patiently being told to shut up because he had no idea what true pain really felt like. With Andrea – Andy, they called her – it had been so quick they'd barely made it to the hospital; Penny almost gave birth in the maternity ward corridor. Emily had peered from Patrick's lap into the transparent cot that Andy slept in, wrapped up in a hospital blanket and wearing a pink hat.

Emily had said, "Oooh," and prodded her gently with her finger.

If someone had marched in, picked up her sleeping baby from her hospital cot on the very day of her birth and stomped out again, there was nothing in the world that would have stopped Penny throwing herself out of bed, eight stitches and all, and chasing them down the hospital corridor until she had Andy safely back in her arms. If someone crept into the house now, stole Emily from her bed as she slept in her pink unicorn pyjamas, Penny wouldn't stop until she had killed the perpetrator herself.

But someone had done that to her mother. Her mother, Ruth, had done that to her mother, Maire. Sure, it was all arranged. Maire knew that was what was going to happen. Maybe Maire didn't even want Penny. That was possible. In which case, Ruth was her rescuer. But the letters, they just didn't sound like someone who didn't want their baby. Of course, she couldn't have raised Penny herself even if she had wanted to. Which it sounded like she did. And Ruth, poor Ruth, she couldn't have a baby herself, from her own body. In the end, the whole family had fit together like puzzle pieces. She hoped Maire had seen it that way.

Her life, as she had said to Ruth earlier that day, had been glorious. She'd been spoilt, utterly; she'd had an excellent education which had led to a very fruitful career. She had wonderful friends still from early childhood; Ruth had nurtured those friendships faithfully, as they couldn't give Penny a sibling. Donal was a fun-loving, did-all-the-voices, gentle, wonderful man. If Maire had been forced to raise Penny alone, she wouldn't have had a da. She wouldn't have had Donal. He was, truly, the very first love of her life.

If someone had taken her girls, she would have wanted to know, every single day of their lives, that they were well. Maire had wanted to know, and Bridget had told her. It comforted her to know that Maire had clearly been sent photographs and updates on her wellbeing, and all the big milestones of her life. She had *wanted* them. Maire had seen Penny in her confirmation dress. In her school uniform. In her graduation robes, and in her wedding dress. Penny wanted to cry.

Bridget had loved both Penny and her two mothers. She'd done her best by them both, as far as Penny could see. Ruth and Donal had received a miracle and they'd certainly treated her like one. Fionn had always been kind, as much as possible. And Maire had made a sacrifice so that Penny could live, and Ruth and Donal could be happy. By the sounds of it, she had been a busy woman, saving all sorts of people from all sorts of things in her job as a very senior nurse. She'd probably not have been able to do that if she'd had Penny.

Penny crept out of bed and visited each of her daughters in their bedrooms. Andy was in a 'big girl bed' now, as she called it, and Penny wondered if perhaps they might have another baby. When she'd settled down a little from the shock. Andy was glorious and red-headed, like herself. She went to Emily's room and stroked her soft, dark hair that she had inherited from Patrick. Two lovely girls, so different, but so perfect.

Patrick had pulled out the sofa bed and made himself comfortable on that. There was only junk and a sofa bed in this room. Perhaps they had space for another baby, in here; they could live without the sofa bed. Penny snuggled up behind Patrick and leaned her head on his back. He sleepily took her hand and held it against his chest.

"All right?" he whispered.

"Yeah," Penny whispered back, and she meant it. "I'm all right now."

CHAPTER SIXTY-TWO

It had been mercifully easy to track Maire down, once Penny had found the strength to make the phone calls. She knew Maire's last address, of course, from all her letters, and the hospital where she had worked was the same one where she had died. Penny wondered what that must have been like for the staff: Maire's colleagues and friends, suddenly treating her as a patient in the place where she had cared for thousands of others, for decades. For Maire, too, being on the other side of things all of a sudden – in the bed on the ward, instead of beside it. Her cancer had been very advanced when it had been discovered, and she'd had a sudden, unstoppable cardiac arrest and had gone very quickly in the middle of the night. That's what Penny had been told.

Ruth had been shocked and very sad to learn from Penny that Maire had died. She had given Penny her blessing to seek out Maire if she could, with Ruth's love and good wishes to the brave woman who had so selflessly made her a mother. She remembered her as a curly-haired, bonny nineteen-year-old, and, somehow, she'd never stopped seeing that whenever she thought of her, even though Penny was now far older than Maire had been when she'd given birth to her. Ruth had really liked Maire, and she'd hoped Maire had liked her. She'd always believed that a girl like that would battle on and have a happy life. She'd had enough of hearing the news that people had died.

There had been a funeral, of course – very well attended by all accounts, by Maire's many subordinate nurses, the doctors, the surgeons. She had been immensely well liked.

326

Her friends from church also, neighbours, and her bridge team. Penny had smiled at that – what was more English than a bridge team? If she'd stayed in Ireland, it would have been a reading club or a rosary group. She couldn't imagine her Irish countryside ma turning into a right – what did they call it? – a right 'East-ender'. Maire's neighbour Susan had been very obliging, offering to meet Penny and escort her where she needed to be once she'd arrived. Penny brought along the programme from Maire's funeral in her pocket. The nurse's choir from her hospital had sung 'Just a Closer Walk with Thee'; the family had played that for Bridget as well. What a coincidence.

It was cold in England, but not as cold as Ireland. It was expensive in London too, but not as expensive as Dublin. She'd bought herself lunch in a pub and expected some change from a £20 note, but there wasn't much. London people were quiet, and nearly always alone. She wondered if Maire had really been happy here, or if, after a time, she'd really missed the boisterous Irish pubs, the ceilidh bands and the GAA. She spoke about a friend in her letters who had come over with her, so at least she hadn't been alone. London had been Maire's home for so long – more than half her life – but she wondered if perhaps, after a while, she had found she'd preferred her old home.

The cemetery was in Newham, which Penny had never heard of. She flew into a small regional airport in Essex and took the train into Stratford. Everything was grey, and busy, and noisy. Penny had bitten the bullet and written to Fionn at the last minute – she didn't phone, she couldn't face hearing his voice still, not yet – and told him where she was going. He hadn't responded. That was okay, she had decided, after the initial feelings of disappointment. It might be nice to have some time to herself. With her mother. Ruth would always be her mammy, but this lady – well. This lady was Ma. Mother.

Penny had taken the bus from the station at Stratford to Newham and Susan had met her at the bus stop. She'd shaken Penny's hand formally, said how sorry she was about 'the whole business' and walked with her quietly to where Maire was now. She didn't know how much Susan knew about their story and she didn't feel like asking; Susan seemed to have more sense than to let on, and she didn't chat on the way. She was sorry, though, that Maire's flat had been emptied when she'd died, then let on to others, and nothing had really been kept. She'd left everything in her will to charity and hadn't had all that many possessions. Books, though, hundreds of them. The Book Trust had thought Christmas had come early.

Penny smiled weakly. Bridget, also, had been partial to a good book.

It was a simple headstone, and Penny learned so much about her ma in those first few moments. A birthday. Middle names. The familiar, but Anglicised, surname Maire had chosen for herself.

Maire Roisin Teresa Connelly
01.11.1960–28.02.2010

She had died within weeks of her final letter.

"It was lovely to have met your Aunt Bridget," Susan said. Penny smarted at the sound of her name.

"You met her?"

"Well, yes, your Aunt Bridget, she was at the funeral,"

Susan said. "Maire left instructions that she was to be invited over for the... oh," she continued, regretfully, "should I not have said—?"

"No!" Penny exclaimed, and she smiled broadly at her ma's friend. "No, I'm... I'm really pleased Bridget came. It's just that... Bridget passed away herself a few weeks ago."

Susan looked crestfallen. She said how sorry she was.

"And for you to lose such a close friend of your aunt's as well," she said, gesturing towards Maire's headstone. "I am sorry."

"Thanks." So Susan didn't know who Penny really was. That made things easier, she decided.

"Of course. Oh, also, there were these," Susan said, reaching into her pocket and pulling out a small bundle of letters.

The handwriting didn't seem to be Bridget's, and the stamps were Irish and quite recent. Within the last five years or so, she guessed.

"I didn't like to pry into it all too much. I hope you don't mind. I had a little look to see if they were important." Susan looked uneasy, "but it looks like they're from a couple of women she knew in the village she was in, before..." Susan tailed off awkwardly. "I kept them but there's been nobody else to give them to – until now. There were a couple of Irish women at the funeral; I guess it was them. In any case, I think she might have had sisters."

Sisters. Penny felt her heart give a little leap as she stifled a laugh. More troublesome aunts.

"I'll go now, and give you some peace," she said. "It was so nice to meet you."

They shook hands again as Penny thanked her, and she

329

watched Susan walk away across the frosted pathway. As she followed Susan into the distance with her eyes, she noticed for the first time how immense the cemetery was, the thousands of people that had wound up here. It wasn't the busy streets that betrayed how massive London was – it was the magnitude of the cemeteries. She'd strolled right past them all on her way here without a second glance. She wondered what terrible secrets they'd died with.

She turned back to Maire's headstone and looked at the black letters etched into it. Her picture on a canvas, Penny thought. After a quick calculation, she realised Maire had been twenty years old when she had given birth to Penny. Penny was that age twelve years ago. She had been in her penultimate year of university. She and Patrick hadn't even... well. Their lives, and so many other things, had been so very different – and Penny knew it was all because of this woman's extraordinary sacrifice, when she was so very young still.

Penny wondered how things would have been different if Maire had lived. Would she have wanted to meet her? Would that have been harder? She wasn't sure. They might've met up in a park, or a coffee shop, somewhere quiet, like on the reality programmes on television. They'd look at each other and Maire would cry and Penny might cry and they'd embrace and marvel at how alike they looked. Penny wondered if she ought to be crying now and felt a twinge of guilt that she wasn't. She would have wanted to thank her in person, though. Thank her for her own life, and for her parents and family that she had enjoyed for thirty-two extremely happy years.

"Hi, Ma," she whispered. She felt a tingle of emotion she

couldn't identify. This was still only a stranger, she reminded herself. Just a stranger and a stone. "It's... er... nice to finally meet you."

She stood quietly for a while and then found herself chatting – 'I work in a bank; my husband's name is Patrick, and guess what? He was adopted too. He took it better than I did. I'm really good with numbers; do I get that from you? Fionn's wife hated me to death. Now she has Alzheimer's and no idea who I am, or you. I have red hair. But you probably know that.'

"Sorry to interrupt, Penelope."

Penny spun on the spot. Fionn was wrapped up for the cold in a thick winter coat, wool scarf and a hat. He was walking with a cane now; that was new. She stared at him like he was an apparition.

"I came to London once before," he said, removing his hat and ruffling his grey hair. "I knew what to expect. Weather-wise."

Penny didn't smile or speak. She looked back at the stone and the flowers. Fionn crossed himself and held his hat over his heart. They stood side by side, quiet for a long time.

"I'm very sorry for my behaviour the last time we met, Penelope," Fionn said, in a quiet voice. "Only I'm not terribly good at having confrontations with women that I've wronged. I wish you could ask... well. She'd tell you."

Penny tried to hide her smile. She hoped Maire had given him hell at the time, and Clodagh too. She didn't hate Fionn. But she didn't know anything more at the moment, apart from that.

"I want you to know," he continued, "that I never, ever considered a termination for your mother. Not ever."

331

He looked very sincere. Penny didn't really know how to respond to that.

"Do you think I look like her?" Penny asked at last.

Fionn coughed. "Yes," he said softly. "Very much so. Although when you were young, I'm afraid to say, you rather looked like me."

"Mammy said I looked like Uncle John."

"Exactly."

Penny didn't ask but she had always wanted to know, and so she was grateful as Fionn began just to speak, with no expectation of response. He spoke about meeting Maire in the queue for the post office and treading on her foot, listening to the band at Brannigan's – he'd always remembered the name of the pub – and thinking that she was the most beautiful girl he'd ever seen in his life, until Penny herself. Penny smiled at that, nudging him gently with her elbow, and called him a name. He told her what he'd done to Maire by not telling her the truth, and what he'd done to Clodagh too, how he hadn't said anything until after all the arrangements were made. It was his fault, he insisted, not Maire's. Her mother was innocent in all things.

Bridget had told Fionn that Maire was dying when Maire had written her that final letter. He'd known that she'd passed but he didn't think she'd want him at her funeral, after how he'd treated her, so he'd refused to accompany Bridget and she had come alone. He had grieved, in private, for two very long years.

He said again how sorry he was. Penny didn't say it was all right, but she decided he might as well be forgiven. After all, he'd come a long way.

"Everyone wanted you, you know," he said. "You

could've very easily had six parents."

Penny sighed. From Penny's point of view, she'd had at least five all along, anyway. She'd read up a lot about adopted children and abandonment issues and identity crises on the internet since finding out she, too, fell into a secret statistic. But she had been loved, as so many adopted children are; there was no doubt about that. That alone gave her comfort.

"It doesn't look like she got married ever," Penny said. The space underneath her name and dates of birth and death, where many of the graves around her had said *Loving wife, cherished daughter, greatly missed mother* were filled with the words of John 16:33 – the same as Bridget's.

"No, evidently not," Fionn responded quietly. She had said, after all, that she never would. "She took the family name though. Kind of. That's... that's nice." Fionn thought about the last time they had been together – not the time she had shouted at him in Bridget's spare room. The last time they were happy. He had kissed her and promised himself that he would remember that kiss for the rest of his life. So far, so good.

"Do you feel like a drink?" Penny asked sharply. "The pubs here aren't Irish but they're not all bad."

"Hmm," he chuckled. "The Guinness in England is terrible."

"It is," Penny laughed. "Absolutely awful. But the whiskey holds up quite well." She reached out her hand and patted Maire's headstone. "Bye, Ma," she whispered. "Thanks for... thanks for having me." To her surprise, Fionn reached out too.

"Bye now, Maire," he said.

He let his hand linger on the stone longer than Penny

333

thought he would. He straightened up and put on his hat and sniffed heavily. His eyes were streaming, probably from the cold.

"Will you tell me more about her on the way?" Penny asked. The walk to the pub was a bit of a long one.

"I'd love to."

He offered Penny his arm.

She took it.

PART FIVE
1980

EPILOGUE

Maire had finally made it down Bessborough's increasingly dreary path to another wall with a small iron gate. The roses at the start were clearly just for show. Beyond that, she could see a concrete, three-storey house, with a glass parlour attached, and other buildings beyond it. It was a huge, sprawling estate. At one time, she assumed, it must have been the seat of considerable wealth. She pressed the buzzer at the side of a gate and a small woman appeared after just a few moments. She spoke in a quiet, lonely voice, assumed Maire was a new patient, and hurried with her to the great oak doors at the front of the house. The girl then left, around the back of the house, as silently as she had appeared. Maire took a deep breath and stepped into the building.

The sight of what was inside made her draw a sudden breath. It was so cold; clearly none of the summer heat from outside had penetrated the walls. Dark too, she realised as she looked around at all the closed shutters and curtains. At one time this would have been someone's home, she thought; the lady of the house would've been greeting people here at this door, kissing cheeks, taking coats, or perhaps a maid doing that while her ladyship waited in a 'drawing room' for her visitors. She'd read books like that; she always thought it had sounded quite nice.

The thought of Ailbe walking in here, alone and vilified, without even her own name, made Maire's throat clench. In the far corner there was a young girl mopping the floor. Maire took a few steps forward and realised, yes, she was pregnant. Very heavily pregnant. She looked exhausted.

"You've got some nerve, coming here alone and in the daylight. Name?"

Maire jumped out of her skin. There was a nun in a doorway she hadn't noticed as she'd come in, looking at her over a pair of glasses. She didn't look much older than Maire, and she didn't look particularly well either. It wasn't the same one that had prised Ailbe away from her last year; she'd remember that woman's face forever.

"Name?" she said again, looking impatient and agitated.

"Oh, um," Maire stuttered. The nun sighed. "Maire" – she searched her brain – "Conghaile."

Sister just sighed. "No," was all she said.

Maire blinked. "No?"

"No," she repeated. "We're not expecting you today. Or at all. When was your last bleed?"

Maire was taken aback, and then she realised. "Oh no, I'm not... I've actually, already—"

A loud crash made Maire jump again and look to the back of the hall. The girl with the mop had collapsed and upended her bucket all over the floor.

"Oh God," said Maire, looking at the nun, "shouldn't we—?"

"No," she replied, in the same tone as before and without looking up. "Someone will get her."

Maire couldn't regain focus as she watched the girl on the floor, lying like a rag doll, perfectly motionless.

"So, what do you want?" the nun asked Maire sharply. "We're very busy here you know."

"Yes, yes," stammered Maire. "I'm so sorry. I'm here to collect someone. My friend."

Sister pushed her glasses up her nose and didn't look back

338

at Maire. "You are supposed to call ahead for collection."

"I'm sorry. I did write."

· Maire looked back at the mopping girl, still on the floor. Another nun had appeared on the stairway and stepped over her body without even looking down at her. Maire was shocked. Was Ailbe treated like that? She must have been. Maire seethed. This place, it was a hellhole. *But that's why I'm here,* she reminded herself. To be brave, like Ailbe, and get her out of here.

The nun disappeared into a room with a tiny plaque on the door that said 'Office' and resurfaced with a huge leather-bound book, the sort Donal had recorded his sales and expenses in. She opened it towards the back.

"Fine," she snapped at Maire. "Name, date of arrival."

"Ailbe Donnelly," replied Maire, pulling herself up to her full height. "I don't remember the date. November sort of time. The nun who brought her in told her to call herself Ciara."

The nun glanced up at Maire at the sound of her assumed name and, for a brief moment, looked something other than monstrous. Then she avoided Maire's eye, tidying things away.

"Oh, her," she said casually. "Yes, she was here. Troublemaker. The baby was adopted a couple of months ago. She's not here now."

Maire felt her heart fall through her stomach. The thought of coming to get Ailbe was all that had kept her going these past few weeks. She couldn't now leave without her, that was unthinkable. And if she was not here, then where on earth...? She wouldn't have gone back home; her parents would never have had her back in the village, let alone the house. She swallowed hard. She'd told Ailbe she'd come back for her. Why didn't she wait?

"The baby?"

"Well, yes, obviously there was a baby," the nun said, rolling her eyes. She glanced down rapidly at the page of the book and back up at Maire. "Male child. Sister Thomas named him Patrick, born on the seventeenth of March."

She looked at Maire, who had started to cry silently at the thought of Ailbe going through the same pains, the same agonies, but without a Ruth and a Bridget. Without a family. A wee boy, pink and wriggling, like her wee girl.

"Some dentists from Kerry had him, if you must know. She was a tiny little thing, wasn't she?" the nun said. "No strength. Didn't last long I'm afraid."

Maire's sob caught in her throat. "What-what do you—"

"Out there," she interrupted, pointing to a door behind Maire with a brass knob and a frosted glass window. "If you *must* stay. Now, I have to get back to work Mrs Conghaile. As I said, we're very busy here with *all you girls*." She slammed the book shut and strode back into the office. She didn't come back out.

"Sister, what's out—"

"God bless you, Mrs Conghaile," she called through the half-closed door.

*

The sunshine beat down on Maire's neck as she knelt on the floor and covered her mouth with her hand. If she could, she would scream and wail and throw herself fully on the ground and beat it with her hands. She wanted to beat every inch of

340

this place with fists and battering rams made of her own rage, as she sat here in a garden full of nuns' graves where Ailbe had been all these months. All this time, while Maire sat with Bridget eating lamb stew and learning how to embroider. While Maire sat with Bridget and learned to play the harp. While she lay in her warm bed reading Sean O'Casey plays, feeling her very healthy baby wriggle around happily in her belly. All the letters she had written to Bessborough that had all gone unanswered. Undelivered, she guessed, just like Fionn had said.

All that time, Ailbe had been here, mopping until she collapsed and then lying dead in the ground, with just one, plain concrete cross overlooking them all. There was nothing here with Ailbe's name on it. This was a small cemetery for the nuns that had died in service, so, she must be here too. Where else was there? Maire thought of Ailbe's son. Little Patrick, at least he'd made it out. She hoped he'd be loved.

"Maire. You must be Maire."

The sound of her own name stunned Maire. She looked up into the sun and saw the outline of a thin woman with dark hair in the doorway. Maire stared at her. Was she supposed to recognise her? She didn't.

"Ciara said you'd come," the woman said. "She said I'd know you by your hair."

Maire wiped her eyes but didn't stand up. The woman stepped out into the garden and shut the door quietly behind her. She wasn't a nun. That was something.

"Hi?" was all Maire could say.

"I'm Vida."

"Hi Vida."

Vida got down on the floor alongside Maire.

"I don't think she's actually buried here," Vida said quietly.

Maire looked confused.

"They pretend it's here but look at the ground. None of it's been dug up for years."

"Where is she, then?"

"We don't know," Vida said, shaking her head sadly. "They wouldn't tell us."

"What happened?" Maire asked, incredulously. Fionn had promised her Ailbe would be all right. Ailbe had promised that, wherever she was going, she would survive.

"Infection," Vida said simply. "They think maybe there was a bit of the... what's it called... 'placenta' left behind, whatever that means? I don't know how that happens. She went downhill really quickly. Couple of weeks, I think it was. Ten days maybe. She did well to hang on that long to be honest."

Maire looked at the ground. She didn't know what to say. It happened, she knew; sometimes women died. Sometimes babies died. But so rarely. Why Ailbe? Why did it have to be Ailbe? Why was no one looking after her? Why didn't she have any medicine?

"I'm so sorry about Ciara," Vida said.

"Her name was Ailbe, not Ciara," Maire said defeatedly.

Vida smiled with interest. "Really? She'd never tell us her real name. We're not supposed to... share, here."

"Oh."

"My grandma was called Ailbe."

Maire tried to smile. She was glad that Ailbe seemed to have had a friend here. In fact, she was surprised. Her last new friend had been Maire herself.

"Did you have a baby too?" Maire asked.

Vida nodded. "Yeah. She's still here. I thought I'd hang on and work for a bit, you know, before… going back home."

Maire didn't know her but she could see the fear in Vida's grave eyes when she spoke about going home. Maire didn't like that. She thought of the sort of home Ailbe would have been going back to if she'd had to. Maybe it was the same for Vida. She didn't like the thought of that at all. For Ailbe, or Vida, or anyone.

"Is Vida your real name?"

"No. But I quite like it though. I might keep it."

"Good for you," said Maire. "Did you know 'Vida' means 'life'? It's Latin." She smiled at Vida as Vida shook her head but looked pleasantly surprised. Maire studied her face properly for the first time and saw nothing but emaciation and pain. Bridget had said, the gift of life. She could do that.

"You don't want to go home?" Maire asked.

"Not especially, no." She paused, looking down at the patch of earth again. "Ailbe was great, wasn't she?"

Maire didn't realise she wasn't ready to hear Ailbe talked about in the past tense until Vida had done it. She didn't want to cry anymore. Ailbe wouldn't have stood for it. She would've told her to stop being an eejit and pull her damned self together.

"Vida…" Maire began. *The gift of life.* "I have two ferry tickets to Fishguard. And a hotel room in London with two beds in it. If you don't want to go home…"

Vida's eyes widened. Some colour ran to her cheeks.

"… you can come with me."

Vida stared at her. Maire stared defiantly back at her. She tried to smile, to show she wasn't crazy.

"Oh no, I couldn't," Vida said finally.

"Why not?"

"Well," said Vida, and then she didn't say anything else.

She was thinking. Her daughter Felicity was due to be adopted any day now; she didn't want to have to do the walk a second time. She could tell – she was Felicity's mother, after all – that there was something very, very wrong with Felicity. She might not live all that long. Vida didn't suppose the adoptive parents would be told that; that's why she was being adopted so early. Vida hated it here; she hated every single day of it. She could only anticipate that next year, maybe the year after if she was lucky, she'd be back here again. Twice she'd been told by the Sisters that she was 'free to leave at any time'. Was there a good reason, really?

"I don't even know you."

"You knew Ailbe. That's enough for me."

"I have a great aunt who lives in Brighton," Vida said. "Is that near London?"

"I don't know," Maire said. "Want to come and find out?"

*

Maire stayed with Ailbe – wherever she was – for as long as she could. She'd never, ever come back here as long as she lived. So, this was it, this had to be it. Maire whispered to her everything she had wanted to tell her for months: the content of her fruitless letters. She told her at length about Fionn and the family, about London and nursing, and Ruth and Donal who were going to raise her Penny. Her little lucky Penny, who she'd thought about every moment and had so desperately wanted to name Ailbe instead but, as they'd said, it wasn't her choice. Didn't that horrible sister in there say someone called 'Sister Thomas' named Ailbe's baby Patrick? Yes, she was sure that was right. So Ailbe didn't get to choose either. That was one thing they'd had in common after all this time, at least.

Vida had gone to get her things and say goodbye. Maire couldn't quite imagine the agony of the next few minutes of Vida's life – Maire's own baby had disappeared into another's arms after just a few minutes of life. She hadn't raised her at all. But she had some idea of what saying goodbye meant. She had loved Ailbe with her whole soul, every day, for fifteen years. That wasn't going to stop now, just because she wasn't here anymore.

Maire didn't wait to be thrown out; she wanted to leave this damned place of her own accord. One of them deserved that privilege. She kissed her hand, touched the unnamed cross and she didn't look back when she left. She didn't look at anyone. She closed the front door gently behind her – she wanted to slam it but didn't want to wake up the babies. For a place supposedly filled with mothers and babies, you actually couldn't hear many babies. She thought of them, all asleep upstairs.

She walked back down the driveway; the walk that Ailbe never got to make. Her and Vida agreed to meet at the gates in case there was a scene with the Sisters – although, Vida said, that probably wasn't likely. Maire had given Vida the cash for her 'release fee' in case she was asked for one; Vida had kissed Maire with gratitude and promised to pay her back once she got a job in London. Maire saw the gates in the distance coming clearer into view as the sun shone down on her, glinting off the iron and the loosened padlock. The gates were still open.

Tomorrow, she was going to England, and she was taking Vida with her. Vida didn't have to go home to whatever it was that awaited her there – and she, Maire, was going to be a nurse. And she was going to be the greatest, best nurse that there had ever, ever been. She was going to save lives. She was going to save babies. Maybe one day, she would come back to Ireland and save lives and babies here too. She was going to do it. Absolutely, she was going to do it. For Ailbe, for the mopping girl, and for them all.

ACKNOWLEDGMENTS

My enormous and heartfelt thanks to everyone at Cranthorpe Millner Publishers for believing in this book enough to bring it out into the world – particularly Kirsty, who first contacted me with an offer of publication; Shannon for her marketing expertise, and Sharon and Victoria for their fine editing work to make this book the best it could be.

This story simply wouldn't exist without the expert journalism of Deirdre Finnerty, who wrote the article 'The girls of Bessborough' for the BBC that initially captured my attention (and who has since published a further non-fiction work on her findings) and inspired Ailbe's part of the story. I am also truly indebted to my former Irish landlady in Dublin, the wonderful Evelyn Galvin, who spoke so candidly about her knowledge of secret adoptions in Ireland, from which the inspiration for Maire's story came. I am so thankful for the motherly love she gave so fully while I lived there. Thank you, Evelyn, with all my heart.

June Goulding, a Bessborough midwife in the 1950s, published her memoirs *The Light in the Window* in 2005 to tell the true stories of the horrors she witnessed there. This memoir formed a huge part of my research when writing *The Walk*, and I thank her both for her bravery all those years later and for doing what she could back then.

I am so grateful also to Emma, Natasha and my mum for reading early drafts of the book and encouraging me to continue with it; with special thanks also to my Great Aunt Lilian who, in her nineties, so passionately advocated for the story that she offered to write a letter to 'the people' I was sending the manuscript to and demand it be published immediately. That is the sort of support that every writer should have, and I am blessed that I have her. And don't worry, Lil! 'The people' did publish it after all. Enjoy the book.

Last but not least, thank you to my husband Bradley, who supports me in everything I do, and to our daughter Melody, for teaching us everything about love that we thought we already knew. Her existence and the fact she has made me a mother adds more to this book than anything else could ever have done. Mumma loves you, little one. Thank you for everything.